35·27

P9-BXY-777

35923004172526

BLOOD WILL TELL

Recent Titles by Jeanne M. Dams

*The Dorothy Martin Mysteries
from Jeanne M. Dams*

THE BODY IN THE TRANSEPT
TROUBLE IN THE TOWN HALL
HOLY TERROR IN THE HEBRIDES
MALICE IN MINIATURE
THE VICTIM IN VICTORIA STATION
KILLING CASSIDY
TO PERISH IN PENZANCE
SINS OUT OF SCHOOL
WINTER OF DISCONTENT
A DARK AND STORMY NIGHT *
THE EVIL THAT MEN DO *
THE CORPSE OF ST JAMES'S *
MURDER AT THE CASTLE *
SHADOWS OF DEATH *
DAY OF VENGEANCE *
THE GENTLE ART OF MURDER*
BLOOD WILL TELL *

* *available from Severn House*

BLOOD WILL TELL

A Dorothy Martin Mystery

Jeanne M. Dams

Severn House Large Print
London & New York

Newmarket Public Library

This first large print edition published 2016
in Great Britain and the USA by
SEVERN HOUSE PUBLISHERS LTD of
19 Cedar Road, Sutton, Surrey, England, SM2 5DA.
First world regular print edition published 2015 by
Severn House Publishers Ltd.

Copyright © 2015 by Jeanne M. Dams.

All rights reserved.
The moral right of the author has been asserted.

British Library Cataloguing in Publication Data
A CIP catalogue record for this title is available from the British Library.

ISBN-13: 9780727894601

Except where actual historical events and characters are being described
for the storyline of this novel, all situations in this publication are
fictitious and any resemblance to living persons is purely coincidental.

Severn House Publishers support the Forest Stewardship Council™
[FSC™], the leading international forest certification organisation. All
our titles that are printed on FSC certified paper carry the FSC logo.

Typeset by Palimpsest Book Production Ltd.,
Falkirk, Stirlingshire, Scotland.
Printed and bound in Great Britain by
T J International, Padstow, Cornwall.

MAR 2 2 2017

Acknowledgements

As usual, I owe a great deal to many people who helped me with this book, but I must especially thank Terence Faherty, another Hoosier, the author of excellent crime fiction, and all-around nice guy, for allowing me to give his name to one of my characters. You're a gentleman and a scholar, Terry! And my very sincere gratitude goes to Mark Zubro, author and friend, who read the manuscript and made invaluable suggestions. Mark, this is a much better book because of your insights, and I thank you sincerely.

Note

For those readers unfamiliar with the 'college' system at Oxford and Cambridge, I recommend an excellent essay by Derek G. W. Ingram to be found on the Collegiate Way website: http://collegiateway.org/colleges/ingram-1999. The subject is fairly complicated, and quite unlike the way other universities are organized, and I feel far less qualified to explain it than Dr Ingram. Readers will note that I have modified procedures in my fictitious college of St Stephen's to suit my own purposes.

One

'But this is beautiful! Clean and modern and comfortable, and our very own bathroom!'

Alan laughed at the surprise in my voice. The only other time I'd stayed in an English university was years ago at a Dorothy L. Sayers Society convention. My first husband and I were living in England for an exchange year, and he was busy lecturing somewhere, so I went alone to Somerville College at Oxford. Somerville was Sayers's college, and I was full of romantic ideas about the City of Dreaming Spires.

Oxford turned out to be a busy, crowded city with a perpetual traffic jam. Some of the colleges were beautiful and some were ugly. Somerville was very attractive, and very much like Sayers's fictional Shrewsbury College in the book *Gaudy Night*. We had our meals 'in hall', and that part was all I had expected. The lectures and presentations themselves were great, and I made a number of fast friends.

The accommodations, however, were what one might charitably call basic. I had a small single room with a narrow bed and, as I recall, no closet or even wardrobe for my clothes, only a drawer or two and an exposed rod. No hangers.

But the worst part was that the bathrooms, and toilets, were down one flight of stairs. I was a lot younger, of course, but even then I usually had to get up in the middle of the night to use the toilet, and padding downstairs barefoot in an unfamiliar place at three in the morning isn't my idea of fun. So I hadn't been overly enthusiastic when Alan asked if I wanted to go with him to a conference at Cambridge.

I had been wrong, and I now admitted it handsomely. 'I'm so glad you invited me along, love. This is great!'

'St Stephen's is one of the newer colleges. The earliest buildings went up in Victoria's time, but, as you see, they're all built in the Georgian style. And this block of guest accommodations was renovated quite recently – hence all the modern amenities, including en-suite facilities.'

'These rooms are only for guests, then?'

'Yes, which is why the college can host conferences year-round. I believe students used to live here, but when the new student wing was built, the college officials worked out that they could turn quite a nice profit by housing guests in and out of term. So here we are.'

I hadn't, when I agreed to come with Alan, figured out what I'd do while he was busy at the conference. It was a five-day symposium on law enforcement, concentrating on the interaction of the police with the community, and he'd been invited to speak about some of his experiences during his many years as chief constable of Belleshire. I find it hard to remember that Alan is still a Very Important Person in the world of policing, and his opinions and expertise were sought not only all over Britain but in other parts of the world as well. I was very proud of him,

2

but I couldn't imagine that the sessions would have any particular interest for me, though I'd been courteously told I'd be welcome.

However, Cambridge is a beautiful place that I've visited far too seldom. I decided I'd spend most of my days just roaming. I could wander along the Backs (the backs of the colleges), bordering on the river Cam. Maybe I'd take a ride down the river in a punt. I'd certainly go to Evensong at King's College and at St John's. There would be plays and art exhibits and concerts at the various colleges, and I could shop to my heart's content in the wonderful outdoor market in the city centre.

The only part I hadn't looked forward to was living for several days in college rooms, and now that worry had vanished.

'OK, now we're here. Do you need to be some-place immediately?'

Alan looked at his watch. 'I should go over and register. The first session isn't for nearly an hour, but there'll be people to greet, people I haven't seen for some time – you know how these things go.'

'I do. Do you know where you're going?'

'More or less. And I can follow the crowd.'

'Then leave me your map, and I'll unpack and follow in a bit to do the "wife-of-dignitary" routine.'

He grinned and gave me a peck on the cheek, and sailed out the door.

I soon stowed our belongings conveniently in the generous drawers and wardrobe (with plenty of hangers). Picking up my purse, the college map and the keys to our room and the staircase door, I sallied forth.

I was immediately lost. Unlike the ancient colleges, built around a quadrangle, St Stephen's looks more like an American college campus, with buildings here and there, now in long rows, now at right angles, with additions jutting out oddly.

And they're all built of the same pale stone in the same Georgian style, so they all look alike.

Alan's conference was assembling, I thought, in Newton Hall. I peered at the map. It was a photocopy of a photocopy. The tiny letters identifying the buildings were blurred, and the explanatory legend not much better. I searched for NH. Was this it, here in the corner? No, surely that was HH.

On a mid-afternoon in late April, there would surely be some student around that I could ask. I looked up and saw not a living soul.

We had come in past the porters' lodge. That had to be here, right by the main entrance gate. It was in the opposite direction from where I thought all the main college buildings were, but I didn't have too many options. I trudged off, only to find a notice on the door: *Back at 3.30.*

It was now twenty past three. Drat! I looked again at the map and decided that really was Newton Hall, right there. So that long building with all the separate entrances to the various staircases leading to rooms – the building where we were housed – was this one here, and if I walked down this long pathway and then took a sharp left past this oddly shaped building

4

apparently labelled PQW (surely not!) and then right again, that should get me to the conference site.

When I found what I thought was the right building, it too had several entrances. Each door had a letter incised in the stone lintel: A, B, C, and so on. I hesitated. The building that was to be our home for five days had similar markings, though ours were numbers. This couldn't be the right place; it must be a block of students' rooms.

I was looking for someone who could direct me. I would just go in and ask.

I couldn't go in. I'd forgotten that the staircase doors were locked.

This was ridiculous! I was beginning to panic, which was even more ridiculous. I was lost, not in a place far removed from civilization, not in a wild wood, or a sinister desert, but in college grounds, a college belonging to one of the oldest and most revered universities in the world, a place where the very word civilization might have been invented. There would be someone, somewhere, whom I could ask. Or, if not, I'd simply enter every building in turn until I found the right one. There weren't more than a dozen or so of them.

I turned around slowly, looking in every direction. That building was certainly the chapel. I could eliminate that one. And there were the two residence blocks. Very well, then. That building over there looked promising. I marched down a path and tried the first door I came to.

It opened. That was a start. I went in and found myself in a back hallway. No lights were on, and the only window was the small one in the door, so I couldn't see much. I edged along, feeling my way, and found another door, which opened into a well-lit passage. I could hear no voices anywhere, so apparently this wasn't the meeting place.

I could go on in hopes of finding someone to ask, or I could go back and try another building. Reluctant to face that dark, claustrophobic hallway again, I went through the passage to the door at the other end.

I saw that this was a building dedicated, at least in part, to the sciences. I had walked into a gleaming laboratory, a temple of spotless steel tables, microscopes and other equipment I didn't recognize, a bank of computers along one wall, all brilliantly lit by overhead fluorescents.

The cold, sterile atmosphere made the pool of red on the floor that much more shocking.

As my eyes took it in, and I gasped, I heard a slight noise and looked up to see the tail of a white coat disappearing through a closing door at the other end of the room.

I suddenly had no desire to speak to anyone, at least not to a person who had just left a room with a pool of blood on the floor.

Maybe it wasn't blood. There was certainly no person or animal bleeding in the room. There was, now, no one but me, and I was very much alive, as my rapid breathing and pounding pulse testified. But that faintly sweet, faintly metallic smell . . .

I heard a sound as of rubber shoes on a lino-leum floor. I turned and fled the room before my

6

brain made the decision, and I charged through that dark hallway with senses heightened by fear. It must have been that fear instinct, too, that led me straight to Newton Hall and a convivial group of people just about to get themselves organized for their first lecture.

I stopped for a moment to slow my breathing and compose my face, and then walked straight across the room to Alan and touched his hand.

He turned and smiled at me, and then took a closer look. 'Excuse me a moment, won't you, Halsey?'

He led me to a corner. 'What's wrong?'

My face must not have been as composed as I'd intended. 'Alan, can you leave for a minute?'

'Yes. Let's go outside.'

When we had achieved the needed privacy, I told him. 'I walked into the wrong building – that one over there. There's a fancy lab, with a big puddle of blood on the floor. And someone left the room just as I came in, someone in what looked like a lab coat.'

'What did you do?'

'Got out of there with indecent haste and came straight to you.'

'Good. Did the person in the lab coat see you?'

'I don't know. I didn't see him, or her. Only the tail of the coat as the door closed.'

'Are you all right?'

'I am now.' I smiled at him.

'Good,' he said again. 'In that case, I can leave you for a bit. I want you to come inside. I'll introduce you to one or two people, so you can mingle while I round up a couple of friends to look into this. Which building did you say?'

I pointed. 'I went in a back door on the other side. Then it's through to a passage, and the first door you come to. It's obviously a science building; maybe someone will know a better way to get to the ground-floor lab.'

I went in as Alan had directed. I mingled. I waited for Alan to return and raise a general outcry.

The conference attendees had nearly all gone upstairs where the sessions were to be held before Alan came back with his minions. He clapped his friends on their backs as they turned to the stairs, and came over to me. 'You're quite sure it was that building?' he said in an undertone. 'It's easy to get confused around here.'

I frowned. 'Quite sure. Why? What happened?'

'Most of the rooms in that building are kept locked. We were told by a student that they are off limits to anyone except those working there, because some of the experiments going on are sensitive to interference, and some involve pathogens. We were able to see the laboratories where classes were being taught, or other work was going on, including a large one on the ground floor that I take to be the one you were talking about. There was no blood or other untoward substance on any floor we saw, nor any sign of foul play. As for someone in a white lab coat . . .' He paused.

I waited.

'Every single person we saw in that building was wearing one. There was no way to tell which one you might have seen.'

Two

I stayed with Alan for the first session, after all. Somehow I didn't want to leave his side. I don't remember a word of what the lecturer said. I was back in that lab, seeing what I had unmistakably seen.

We strolled back to our room after the lecture was over. The schedule had left time for attendees to browse the literature tables and chat before changing for dinner. We chose to spend the time mulling over the puzzle – in low tones, since the large window in our room was open wide to the spring evening and to the path just outside.

To give him credit, Alan didn't hint that I was delusional. 'I'm sure you saw a puddle of something, love. The lights in those labs would do credit to a Hollywood sound stage, and the floors are white. You couldn't possibly have mistaken a shadow for a pool of red. I'm suggesting that it could have been some quite innocent substance, and that the white-coated person you saw simply came back, mopped it up, locked up the lab and went home.'

'Some quite innocent substance. Like what?'

'Wine?'

I shook my head. 'Wine is translucent and dark red. Burgundy-coloured, in fact. This stuff was thick and the bright red of arterial blood. Anyway,

9

what would anyone be doing with wine in a laboratory?'

'Drinking it? But I take your point. Some chemical, then, used in whatever work they're doing in there. I'm not an expert in such things, but there are people here who are. I can ask.'

'Alan, it smelled like blood!'

He frowned. 'But that would mean that it was very fresh, Dorothy. Are you quite sure about that?'

'Quite sure. I wish now I had taken a closer look, but I got scared when I heard that person coming back, or thought I heard him. I didn't want him to catch me in there.'

'That was sensible. But think, Dorothy! If that was blood, where was the wounded person or animal? Were there any further splatters or tracks to indicate something had been dragged or carried away?'

'No sign of dragging, or not that I saw. I could have missed that, I suppose, in the shock of the moment. But the puddle was smooth, with maybe two or three small splashes around the edges.'

'Hmm. I was going to posit a nosebleed, but that would create lots of splashes.'

'And no one's nose bleeds that copiously. I'm not good at estimating amounts, but that pool had to be almost a foot wide at the widest part.'

Alan gave it up. 'I'll make some enquiries tomorrow. Meanwhile, do you want to shower first, or shall I?'

On our way across the college grounds to our dinner, I asked Alan, 'Are there any Cambridge police here?'

10

'Of course, my dear. Several, in fact, from both Cambridgeshire and the City of Cambridge. Why?'

'I thought I'd like to meet them. Just in case,' I added hurriedly. 'Do we have assigned seats for dinner, or may we sit where we like?'

'I've no idea, but there's sherry before we sit down. I can introduce you then. But Dorothy—'

'I know. I'll be discreet. I just want them to know who I am, so if I need to talk to them about anything . . .'

He grinned at me. 'You're incorrigible, you know. You can no more keep away from a puzzle than a cat from cream. Even if it turns out to be something quite ordinary.'

'I have a lot in common with cats, and with the elephant's child. But this isn't going to be anything ordinary. I saw what I saw, Alan.'

It took a visible effort, but he nobly refrained from saying, 'Yes, dear.'

I was pleased to note that there were several people I knew in the anteroom where the conferees were gathered for pre-prandial libations – senior police officers I had met when Alan headed a training course, years ago. I waved to them, but stuck close to Alan as he led me in the direction of a small group of people I didn't know at all.

'Dorothy, I'd like you to meet Superintendent Barker and DCI Smith of the Cambridge City police, and Chief Constable Andrews. My wife, Dorothy Martin.'

I'm used to some slight reaction when I'm introduced, as my last name is not the same as my husband's – he's Alan Nesbitt.

11

Ultra-conservatives will frown slightly; liberals will smile and be a little extra-friendly. I wasn't prepared for the broad grin from Superintendent Barker.

'Oh, we've all heard of the celebrated Dorothy Martin,' she said. 'The American super-sleuth, the Miss Marple of the twenty-first century. Delighted to meet you!'

She shook my hand heartily. She was an attractive woman of fifty or so, stocky, her hair showing streaks of grey here and there. She wore no make-up, and no one could have called her beautiful, but hers was a face one would not easily forget. Her air of supreme competence had probably put her feet on the first rungs of the climb to her high rank, but I was willing to bet that her unexpected sense of humour had helped with the last few steps. The humourless have little insight into the way other people's minds work, and that's surely a necessity when dealing with the devious criminal mind.

The other two officers, men who looked exactly what they were, murmured the correct things. DCI Smith brought us all sherry, and we chatted for a few minutes about the state of crime in and around Cambridge.

'It ought to be such a peaceful place,' I commented. 'An ancient seat of learning, a place of culture and beauty . . .'

'And a modern city with a rather large proportion of foreign nationals,' said Ms Barker. 'That makes for a welcome diversity of cultural experiences, but it can also be a source of trouble. Other cultures have different mores, not always compatible with English ideas. And of course there are always language problems. Not among the students so much – they often speak far more correct English than I do – but there are so many others, often in the service sector, and they can be a challenge.'

The chief constable was frowning. 'I don't want you to give . . . er . . . this lady the wrong impression, Elaine. There is a tendency to blame foreigners for the rise in crime, but we must always be aware—'

'Of the necessity to be impartial. Not to mention politically correct. I believe Mrs Martin is quite intelligent enough to understand that I was analyzing a problem, not assigning responsibility.' She put the slightest stress on my name, to underline Andrews's awkwardness, and the dazzling smile she aimed his way was as effective as a glare in stopping his little sermon.

Rippling chimes called us in to dinner, and just in time, too. The coolness in the atmosphere would have made further conversation a bit chancy. But I had found my go-to person in the local constabulary. Elaine Barker and I were on the same wavelength. She'd help me if – when – help became necessary.

We were seated at the head table, as befitted Alan's VIP status, but far enough away from the chief constable that we didn't have to make conversation with him. We were, thank goodness, subjected to no speeches with our excellent meal, but the master of St Stephen's rose to welcome us with a few brief and witty remarks. I was pleased to recognize in him another kindred spirit, free of pomposity and posturing, and possessed of a formidable intellect. A second string to my bow.

We did not speak of the afternoon's 'incident', as Alan would have called it. I was inclined to 'calamity' as the appropriate word, myself. But whatever one called it, it was not a subject for idle conversation among people I didn't know. Alan was, I thought, still half convinced that it had been far less ominous than I believed. And as I knew perfectly well what I'd seen – and smelled – I also knew that someone nearby, maybe even someone at this conference, at this very table, had something to hide.

The less I said about it at this juncture the more likely I might be able to find out who that someone was.

'What are your plans for tomorrow, love?' Alan yawned, shed his bathrobe and pulled back his duvet. We had twin beds, not our preferred arrangement, but they looked comfortable, which was the main thing, after all.

'When's breakfast?'

'Seven thirty, I'm afraid. We're off to an early start.'

'Yipe! Not on my vacation, thank you very much. I'll make myself some tea and then find something in the town later.'

'And after that?'

It would be overstating it to say that he sounded apprehensive, but there was a certain uneasiness in his tone.

'I thought I'd wander around the college and

14

get myself oriented. I don't want to get lost again. And no, my very dearest husband, I am not going to dive into a den of murderers and get myself stabbed in the back.'

'Your metaphors need sorting.'

I ignored that. 'And then, since you won't be around to cast a jaundiced eye, I intend to go shopping.' I sat on the edge of my bed and kicked off my slippers.

He leaned across to kiss me. 'Let me know when you've dragged me into bankruptcy. Night, darling.'

I turned out the light and went to sleep, visions not of sugarplums but of bloody floors dancing in my head.

I didn't even hear Alan leave the room the next day. It was after nine when I finally rolled out and chased away the sleepies with a cup of strong tea. Then I headed straight for the porters' lodge in search of a better map.

The porter kindly gave me two. The college map was a generation or two newer than the one I'd seen before, and the markings were much clearer. He also handed me a map of Cambridge. It was one of those pictorial things meant as much for decoration as information, but it did show me how to get to the Market Square and the principal colleges, and also indicated two shopping arcades new since my last visit to the city.

'Mind how you go, love,' he said in a fatherly way. (He was a good ten years younger than I.) 'These cyclists are maniacs, riding up on the pavements like as not, and the pavements that

15

narrow you can get turfed off into the street before you know where you are. At least it's a fine day for you. The pavements get slippy when it's wet.'

I thanked him and promised to be careful, and set out to find the building that I was already thinking of as the 'scene of the crime'.

This time there were students around – lots of them. The practice of wearing academic gowns has long since been abandoned by Oxbridge, but students here, as all over the world, are instantly recognizable by their generally scruffy appearance and their ubiquitous backpacks. St Stephen's was evidently co-educational; the sexes seemed about equally divided. At least, so far as one could differentiate them. I was reminded of the old question about turtles. Presumably other turtles could tell which were girls and which were boys, but it was difficult for the rest of us.

I approached one young person whose long ponytail, smooth chin, and granny glasses led me to guess it was female. 'I'm sorry, but I can't seem to find this building.' I pointed to the map. 'I think it's where the science lectures are held.'

The person bent over the map, then straightened and pointed. 'Over there,' it said in a warm bass-baritone. 'Just by the plane tree.' He pointed to a large tree with maple-like leaves and a mottled grey trunk.

'Oh, so that's a plane tree. I've always wondered what one was. Back home, I'd call it a sycamore.'

'You're American, are you?'

I admitted it with a nod and a smile.

'You're quite right, you know. Same genus.

16

Ours are hybrids of yours and the Spanish variety.'

'You're a botanist?'

'Budding.' He looked at me over his glasses to see if I got it.

I groaned my appreciation. 'So is that one of the buildings you frequent?'

'For the lectures on occasion. But this is only my first year, and I'm not doing much lab work yet. That's most of what they do there.' His mobile pinged and he glanced at it. 'Sorry, but I'm late for a tutorial.'

'Off with you, then. And thank you very much.'

Now I knew for certain how to find my way back to the building any time I wanted. The question was did I want, just now?

I stood irresolute. I could go in and talk to someone. But about what? And suppose the person I happened across was the white-lab-coated phantom of the day before?

No, I needed to know more before I ventured back into that building. Firmly telling myself it was *not* cowardice that informed my decision, I turned my back on the plane tree and saw that I was facing the chapel.

I like churches, especially the lovely old ones in England. It isn't only that I'm a churchgoer. It's also that I like the feeling I find in spaces where men and women have worshipped for centuries. A spirit of peace and quietude dwells there, even – or perhaps particularly – when the place is still and empty.

I walked over to the chapel and opened the door. And nearly ran smack into someone coming out.

Mutual apologies ensued, and then we recognized each other. 'Ms Barker! Or should I say Superintendent Barker?'

'I'd prefer Elaine, if you'll allow me to call you Dorothy. We're two of a kind, I think. I've heard so much about you, I feel I've known you for years. Would you like a coffee? I was just going in search of one.'

'I'm panting for coffee. And a bun or croissant or something. I skipped breakfast. But shouldn't you be in one of the sessions?'

'I'm playing truant. It's Andrews holding forth, and I don't care for him any more than he does for me.'

I laughed. 'Understood. Where shall we go?'

We made our way towards the market, which is one of the highlights of Cambridge. On this beautiful spring day, it was crowded and noisy and exactly what a market should be. Resisting temptation for the moment, we passed the stalls with T-shirts and watches and cheeses and fish and imported strawberries and plush toys and mobile phones, and walked over towards King's College. On a side street there was a coffee shop exuding irresistible aromas.

I firmly ignored my dietary scruples and ordered a large almond croissant *and* a small chocolate one, and coffee. Elaine stuck to coffee, but made it a large café au lait.

When our orders came, she looked me straight in the eye and said, 'All right. What are you up to?'

Three

I had just taken a large bite of crumbly croissant. My quick intake of breath brought on a coughing fit, which was quite real, but also gave me some time to think. I swallowed finally, gulped some coffee to wash down the rest of the crumbs, and said, 'What do you mean, *up to*?'

'You know quite well. I saw what happened yesterday. You came into the room looking like a rag doll left out in the rain. You spoke to your husband, who quickly assembled a cohort and left the room. He was some time coming back, and when he did, what he told you left you unsatisfied. I repeat: what are you up to?'

I drank some more coffee. 'I should have known. I could see, last night, that you're an intelligent woman with an understanding of what makes people tick. No wonder you're a senior policeman. Policewoman?'

'Police officer. And you're being evasive.'

'Yes, well. You see, Alan doesn't believe me. And I don't suppose you will either. But I'll tell you.'

She said nothing after I'd finished. She emptied her cup and gestured to the waitress for another. I had another coffee as well.

'What are you going to do about it?'

'You believe me?'

'Provisionally. I've lived in Cambridge a long

19

time. Unbelievable things happen here as a matter of routine. And your story is too bizarre for you to have made it up.'

I breathed a long sigh. 'I do have some powers of invention. I can come up with a sound lie when there's good reason to do so. But no, I don't think I could have invented this. I didn't, anyway. As for what I'm going to do . . .' I took a long pull at my coffee. 'I don't really quite know. For a start, I suppose I should poke around in that building, but I chickened out this morning. I was just going to, but I changed my mind and went to the chapel instead. And I'm glad I did, or I might not have had the chance to talk to you.'

'Oh, I'd have made the chance. Not only did I want an opportunity to know you, but I could see that something had happened at the college, and I try to keep my finger on the pulse of Cambridge. It's more than just my job.'

An American might have said, 'It's my life.' In her more restrained English fashion, Elaine Barker was saying much the same thing.

'So you – that is, the Cambridge City police – have responsibility for policing the colleges?'

'Yes and no. University security services cover routine complaints, usually petty theft. They maintain and monitor the CCTV cameras in the colleges. There's actually very little crime on university property, compared with the rest of Cambridge. But in the event of anything serious, they call us in.'

'Wait! You're saying there are TV cameras all over the place?'

'I wouldn't put it quite like that. There isn't the budget to have them in, for example, every lecture room, every corridor, every assembly hall. They are in the locations most likely to be attractive to thieves or sex offenders. And before you ask, no, that probably does not include all the laboratories in the Hutchins Building.'

'That's what the science building is called?'

Elaine nodded. 'Then there's the Hutchins Garden, the Hutchins Theatre, the Hutchins Library . . . Need I go on?'

'Who was said Hutchins?'

'Stephen Hutchins, wealthy manufacturer. He made a great deal of money at his factory in Cambridgeshire towards the end of the nineteenth century, and donated piles of it to this college, perhaps because his name was Stephen.'

'Did he manufacture something the college bought in quantity?'

'Not directly, but I'm sure the students and professors bought them. After all, everyone gets bunions. And corns and ingrown toenails. His firm produced products to alleviate various foot problems. The source of the munificence is usually glossed over in college literature.'

I laughed. 'I'll bet. What did he get out of it, besides lots of favourable publicity?'

'How cynical you are. It gained his son admission to the college. Where I believe he lasted for two terms.'

'Just long enough for the last cheque to arrive. Ah, well.'

There was a queue forming at the front of the shop. It was time we vacated our seats. We made

21

our way through the crowd and walked back to the market. Elaine surveyed the busy scene.

'Trying to decide which stall tempts you?'

'That, and keeping an eye out for shoplifters and pickpockets. The market is a paradise for them. So crowded you're not really surprised if someone jostles against you, when your attention is on the decision between Brie and Stilton. See that pair over there?' She inclined her head.

I looked in the direction she indicated, but saw no one who looked suspicious to me. 'They all look alike – the young ones, anyway. Jeans and tees and backpacks.'

'Rucksacks, we call them. And the two I just saw look like all the rest. Except they're not students, and they're not carrying books in their rucksacks. They saw me spot them, so they won't try anything more today. They will have melted away by the time I could reach them.'

'You know them? They've been caught before?'

'I know the look. And they can spot a copper at fifty metres. If everyone's lucky, they haven't pinched anything yet today. But I wouldn't wager my pension on it. Now, is there nothing among all these treasures that you must take home with you?'

'There are at least a dozen things I want, but I should get back to St Stephen's and see what Alan is doing.'

'And mull over your problem.'

'Yes. Elaine, do you think I ought to tell some college authority about what I saw? Alan's more than half convinced I misinterpreted something quite dull and innocent.'

22

'Which you may have done. But you're not going to be easy in your mind until you're quite sure.'

'The longer I think about it the more confused I am. If it hadn't been for that smell . . .'

'Yes. Nothing else smells quite like blood, does it? Here, this is a shortcut.' She led me into one of the shopping malls, where the foot traffic was a trifle less frantic and bicycles were not allowed. Benches for weary shoppers were dotted here and there, and she steered me towards one of them.

'Let me tell you a story, Dorothy. I said yesterday that the multicultural aspects of Cambridge were both a blessing and a curse.'

'Your language was a little more diplomatic than that.'

'Andrews was listening. He keeps a close eye on me; doesn't trust me. Political correctness is his god. You saw how he reacted. But it's true, every word. One example surfaced during my first year on the force here in Cambridge. I had just risen from the PC ranks, a newly minted detective sergeant. That was a good many years ago, and women were not widely accepted in the police by some of their male colleagues, nor indeed by many members of the public.

'That was one reason why I was assigned to a messy case no one else wanted. It involved an incident in a small West Indian community in one of our suburbs. The first police on the scene couldn't communicate with the family. I do speak French, including some Creole dialects, and I'd had some experience with various cult religions,

23

which the first squad thought might be involved, so they sent me.'

'It was a murder?'

'Attempted murder. The victim wasn't dead yet, but the neighbours were convinced that he was being poisoned. I was to go in and investigate and report back to my superiors. They thought they knew who was responsible; they just wanted me to find enough evidence to bring him in.'

'And it wasn't that way?'

'To tell the truth, I'm still not sure. Certainly a man lay near death. He was conscious, barely, and what he told me, or what I think he told me – his speech was halting and his dialect not one I knew well – was that no one had been near him, no one had given him anything to eat or drink that could have been tainted, and he'd taken no medicine. He had no visible injuries. He had no symptoms of any recognizable disease. He'd been examined by a doctor – a white, English doctor – who could find nothing wrong. But he was certainly dying.'

'Just plain old age?'

'He was thirty-one.'

'What did the autopsy find?'

'There was no autopsy. The man disappeared.' She settled herself more comfortably on the bench. 'There he was, lying on his bed, taking a breath so seldom that I was sure each one was his last. I told his family I would send an ambulance for him, that he needed to be treated in hospital. They were very much opposed to the idea. They hadn't wanted me to interfere at all; it was a white neighbour who had called the police. I eventually insisted on the ambulance, made the call and went about my business. I told my chief that I could see no cause for the man's illness and no reason to suppose that the man the neighbours were blaming had anything to do with it.'

'And who was that?'

'A mountain of a man who more or less ran the community. The white neighbours were terrified of him, because he looked so formidable and spoke no English. They were sure he was a witch doctor. But I could communicate with him, and I was convinced that he was genuinely grieving for the dying man, who was his cousin.

'My superiors were not pleased that I hadn't arrested the obvious villain, but I was quite sure he was innocent, and there was certainly no evidence we could have taken to court. So I endured my dressing-down and went to write a report.

'The ambulance didn't get there for over an hour; there had been a big smash-up on the M11. When it finally arrived, there was no sign of the dying man. They called me back at once, because what there was sign of was blood, abundantly.'

I sat up straighter. 'They'd killed the man?'

'If they did, the blood had nothing to do with it. Of course, the gory scene brought the coppers out in force, and it didn't take too long to determine that the blood was from a chicken. It was daubed all over the house, on walls, windows, doors. And nobody was talking. They pretended not to understand any English, though most of them had a little. They pretended not to understand my French, though we'd communicated easily earlier. They wouldn't say what had become of the dying man. My colleagues and I made an extremely thorough search, then and on later occasions, but we found no body and no trace of where he might have gone.'

'This was how long ago?'

'A matter of twenty years. The West Indian community is gone now. There were only a handful of them, and the neighbours made them so unwelcome they eventually went elsewhere. I miss them. I used to go around occasionally when they were having a party. The music was wonderful.'

'But what do you think happened to the man who was dying?'

She was silent for a moment, then said, 'How credulous are you?'

'Not very. I like things to make sense.'

'Yes. So do I. But what I believe I saw all those years ago was a man dying because he believed someone had laid a spell on him. Note I didn't say *because of the spell*, but because he *believed* it.'

I nodded slowly. 'I've heard of such things. I do know from doctors and nurses I've known that a patient can will himself to live until some important event has occurred, and can also die much sooner than expected because he simply stops wanting to live. I can believe, just, that a death could be induced by the power of suggestion, if the victim's beliefs were strong enough. But what do you think happened to the man in the end?'

'I have a theory, based on not a shred of evidence. I think the family took advantage of the ambulance delay to try a desperate counter-spell, involving the sacrifice of a chicken. I think that it either worked, so that the man could be taken somewhere to recover, or else it didn't, in which case they must have spirited his body away to a hiding place until we, the interfering aliens, got out of their lives and they could proceed with their rituals. Shall we get back? It's nearly time for lunch.'

Four

Alan was waiting in our room to take me in to lunch with him, and pretended to be amazed that I brought no shopping bags back with me. 'What? No bankruptcy looming yet?'

'Not quite yet. I spent most of the morning talking to Elaine Barker. She's a very interesting woman, did you know?'

'Actually, I have met her only in passing through the years. I was retired before she began to be known as an up-and-coming officer.'

'I'll bet she's also known for making waves.'

'I've heard rumours. Her chief constable doesn't approve of her.'

'No. She has too many opinions of her own. Alan, I'm so glad your job never made you stuffy and pompous. I couldn't bear it if you'd turned into a Keith Andrews.'

'Not much danger of that, with you around. You remind me of Lord Peter's Bunter.'

'Why on earth? I can't tie a tie in a bow to save my life, I know almost nothing about wine, and I'm hopelessly ignorant about men's clothes.'

'Like Bunter, you "brace me with a continuous cold shower of silent criticism".'

'I do not! What a thing to say!'

We bickered happily across the college grounds. I was glad that our path did not take us near the Hutchins Building.

28

Luncheon was served cafeteria-style, and was excellent, catering for every taste from meat-and-potatoes to vegan. I was still full of croissants and took only a salad, but they heaped the grilled chicken on it so generously that I ate too much despite my good intentions. We had no assigned seats for the informal meal, so I had a chance to chat with several people I hadn't met. Elaine and her irritating boss were out of sight. I hoped he hadn't taken offence at her skipping his lecture, but decided not to worry about it. Elaine could defend herself.

The next conference session was immediately after lunch, but Alan walked back to the room with me to brush his teeth. 'What did you and Superintendent Barker talk about?' he asked through a mouthful of toothpaste. He rinsed it out. 'I'll wager I can guess.'

'And you'd be right. We didn't come to any starting conclusions, though. I did ask her if she thought I should inform the college authorities, and come to think of it, I don't believe she ever answered. We got off on other subjects.'

'I'm going to skip the second session this afternoon. It's about the latest technology, about which I know nothing and want to know less. Suppose we meet here around three, and then you and I can talk it over and make up our minds what to do about your uncomfortable discovery.'

I kissed him as he left the room. 'That's exactly what I've been wanting to do.'

I spent a long moment after he'd left looking at the very comfortable bed. A nap sounded like a lovely idea. But I'd slept late, and if I napped

I'd have a hard time getting to sleep at night. And naps, while delightful, are a dreadful waste of time. I splashed some cold water on my face, put on a jaunty red tam with a bright gold tassel, and set out, with no very clear idea of where I was going or what I would do.

I ought, certainly, to take a good look at the Hutchins Building. Somehow knowing it was built with corn-plaster money made it seem much less frightening. Still, would Alan want me going in there by myself?

I was waffling, and I knew it. I'd been doing things Alan thought I shouldn't for years, usually justifying my actions with some rationalization. This time I was just plain scared to go in there. I would never get that picture out of my mind – the starkly white, brilliantly lit laboratory with its nastily stained floor. And the smell.

Proust smelled madeleines, and the scent brought back his whole life. Or so I'm told. I've never been able to make my way through his book. But he was certainly right about odour being a powerful jog to the memory. Before I moved to England permanently, I'd be walking in my Indiana hometown on a damp, misty day, and smell diesel fumes, and instantly I was back in rainy London with a red bus going past.

I decided I was going to let Alan cut up any raw meat in our kitchen from now on. And I was *not* going in that building alone.

Fate took me in hand just then, and I've never been sure if it was a benevolent fate or the other sort. I approached the porters' lodge and the college gates, but couldn't get past for the crowd of people gathered there.

'Are we all here, then?' asked a strident voice in the middle of the group. 'All right, then, we're off. Now, remember that students are working here, and there is also a conference in session, so you'll need to be as quiet as possible. And please try to keep up. We want you to get a good picture of St Stephen's, but we can't have you wandering off by yourself.'

A tour of the college. What an opportunity! I had no idea what group was being shown the sights, but they seemed only loosely organized. No one would notice if I tagged along, would they?

I snatched off my hat and stuffed it into my purse. People notice hats, since so few women wear them these days. Me and the Queen, mostly. Without it, I'd be much less conspicuous. I smiled at the couple at the back of the group and followed them.

We moved at the usual pace of such tours: that of an elderly, arthritic snail. The tour leader had a most annoying voice and a most annoying attitude. Her assumption seemed to be that we were children of subnormal intelligence, to whom everything had to be explained in excruciating detail. I suffered through explanations of the way the college system worked at the great universities, from which I gathered that the group members were foreigners. Americans or Canadians, from the accents I heard. We were told all about the Hutchins family and their generosity, though the source of their wealth was not mentioned. I snickered to myself.

31

We were shown the residential buildings, for students and for guests. We were shown the chapel, which disappointed me. It was a bland place done in panelling and ivory paint, with no stained glass and little decoration of any kind. The guide explained condescendingly that it was used for non-denominational services which had not, for many years, been compulsory for the students. Perhaps that explained why the atmosphere of peace and blessedness was, for me, notably absent. It was just a building.

Our next destination was the Hutchins Building. We were warned again of the need for quiet. We were told that the rooms in the building were kept locked and were reminded again that we must keep together. We must not, in particular, enter any of the laboratories or interfere in any way with any of the work being carried out. 'Some of the experiments may be of critical importance to the pursuit of scientific knowledge,' the guide pontificated. 'Visitors are allowed only with the understanding that they will not be nuisances.'

I wondered briefly why visitors were allowed at all, and then scolded myself for my stupidity. Of course college officials wanted people to see the labs. This building was their showpiece, their prize pig. The handsome, beautifully equipped facilities would draw students, media attention, and perhaps donations.

And murderers? I buried that thought.

The guide led us into the building, not through the back entrance I had stumbled upon, but through the rather grand front door, from the

32

portico with its classical columns and pediment. The resemblance to an ancient temple was not accidental. This *was* a temple, I realized, a temple to science, a deity almost certainly ranking higher in this college's hierarchy than the God of the chapel. A bit ironic, that, in an institution named after St Stephen, the first of Jesus' followers to be martyred for his faith.

I tried to keep my bearings as we were led from one part of the building to another, so I'd know the one lab when we got there, but I've always been geographically challenged and I was soon hopelessly lost. Our guide droned on in a stifled whisper more irritating, if possible, than her stentorian tones. Doors were opened. We were invited to peek in, but never to enter. A lecture was going on in one room. It had to do with physics, I thought from the incomprehensible scrawls on the whiteboard. Another lecture room was empty. Two or three labs were peopled with students hard at work, hovering over microscopes or Bunsen burners or other equipment I couldn't identify. None of the rooms seemed to look exactly like the one I'd seen, but then none of them had a pool of blood on the floor.

It was the last room on the floor. I knew it the moment the door opened. No one was at work at any of the benches. The smell of blood was no longer present, but it entered my mind, if not my nostrils. I almost turned to run away, but I needed to hear what the guide said. Her voice was pitched a little louder, with no one here to disturb.

'This laboratory is devoted to zoology, the exploration of the animal world. I stress that no harmful experimentation is performed upon live animals. We of St Stephen's are devoted to principles of animal welfare. That is why most of our studies concentrate on matters at the microscopic level, research into the genome, certain aspects of the transmission of disease in mammals, a refinement of the system of blood typing . . .'

She lost me at the word 'blood'. So that was what it was about. A blood sample had somehow been spilled, and the white-coated person had simply left to fetch a bucket and mop.

Right.

When the group moved on to the next stop, I quietly melted away and went back to our bedroom. I remembered (for a wonder) to rescue the tam from my purse before it became terminally squashed, tossed it aside, and then lay down on the bed to think.

I wanted to believe the scenario I had conjured back in the lab. A harmless accident, nothing furtive about anyone's actions, no lurking disaster, no one – human or animal – injured or killed.

And yet.

How much blood did it take to perform tests on the genome? Or the blood type, or anything else the guide had mentioned?

I've had blood tests. Everybody's had blood tests. They find a vein and draw out a tube, or two or three, of blood, tape a cotton ball to the puncture, and send you on your way. At most they've extracted an ordinary lab test tube full of your blood, but it's usually much less.

The puddle on the floor was a whole lot more than that.

34

Of course, if you're donating blood, they collect a whole pint. Probably a half-litre in Europe? But they're careful with it. They don't go around spilling it on the floor.

I've given up trying to donate. I have tiny veins. They can't get more than about a tablespoonful. I can lie there for an hour. Or two . . .

'Wake up, darling.'

I shook myself and looked around, trying to remember where I was. What day it was.

Alan sat down on the bed and ruffled my hair. 'Coffee?'

'Mmm.'

Instant coffee isn't my favourite brew, but it does contain the necessary ingredient. One cup and I was restored to my right mind.

'I didn't intend to fall asleep,' I said sheepishly. 'I was thinking about blood tests, and drawing blood, and somehow . . .'

'You've been talking to someone about the research work at the Hutchins Building.'

'Not exactly. I went on a tour.' I explained. 'How did you hear about it?'

'I asked, of course. A policeman among policemen can ask all sorts of questions without raising an eyebrow, and we are presumed to be interested in anything touching forensic science.'

'And your deduction?'

He studied my face. 'Much the same as yours, I suspect, if you were having nightmares about it.'

'I wasn't having nightmares.' I thought for a moment. 'Come to think of it, maybe I was. I

35

was lying on a sort of dentist's chair thing, and they were drawing my blood, but something happened and it all got spilled, buckets of it, and they left the needle in and blood was spouting all over.' I shuddered. 'I'd forgotten until you said nightmare.'

'Sorry to make you remember. But you were thrashing about and sounding distressed when I came in, or I would have let you sleep. Something about the tour disturbed you.'

'Not the tour. It was just boring, most of the time. And at first I thought I'd stumbled on a reasonable explanation of what I saw. But when I got to thinking about it, I remembered what a lot of blood there'd been, and I couldn't imagine any experiment that would require so much.'

'I'm afraid I reached the same conclusion.'

I sagged back against the pillows. 'I think I need another cup of coffee.'

'So what are we going to do about it?' I asked briskly when the caffeine had done its work.

'I've had a few discussions with my colleagues about the relationship between the Cambridge City police and the university security forces. That's what this conference is about, you remember – police interactions with the community. You won't be surprised to know that, here as elsewhere, the lines of authority are a trifle blurry, and rapport can become a bit strained. It's no secret to anyone, probably to anyone in the world, that the university is vitally important to the economy of the city. Although there are also major businesses here, notably in the technology sector, still, for most of the world, the word "Cambridge" means the university. It's the university that generates the huge tourist influx, an invaluable source of income for the city.'

'Yes, OK, I get all that; you don't have to draw me a picture. The university has very important toes that no one wants to step on. So Elaine and her legions don't want to go marching in boots and all and demand an explanation. So now what?'

'I think we need to talk first to someone from university security. Superintendent Barker would know who might be the best person to approach.'

'Agreed. Are there going to be drinks before dinner tonight?'

'Not formally, but the bar in the conference common room will be open.'

'Let's corner her then. If we can pry her out from under from Andrews's eagle eye, I'll bet she'll want to help. Meanwhile, my dear, I'm awake and wired, and I haven't done that shopping yet. Do you want to come along to be a restraining force?'

'My dear, I may urge you on. I enjoy watching you shop.'

Which only proves what a peerless husband I have.

Five

I sailed out to cocktails in one of my new purchases, a floaty top in a black-and-white shadow print that made a white blouse and black pants look like the ultimate in chic. I had topped it with my favourite cocktail hat, a little black beret with a large sequined butterfly hovering over one eye, and I was very pleased with myself. My hair might be grey, my chin might sag, but I could still dress up, by golly.

'That hat,' said Alan, looking at me with amused fondness, 'is fantastic. In the literal sense.'

'A thing of fantasy. Yes. And fun. Shall we?'

St Stephen's, when doing the remodelling that enabled them to host conferences year-round, had thoughtfully provided a third common room in addition to the ones set aside for Fellows of the college and for students. Ours was fitted out with a bar, comfortable chairs, and a fire, which, on a chilly April evening, was most welcome.

We were among the first to arrive, so after Alan had fetched a Jack Daniel's for me and a Glenlivet for himself, we stationed ourselves in front of the fire in a good position to see later arrivals. It wasn't long before Elaine Barker appeared, fortunately alone.

Alan hailed her. 'Come and sit with us. And what can I get for you?'

She sat down with a sigh. 'Whisky. Neat.'

'They have several rather nice ones. Have you a choice?'

She waved aside any preference, so Alan got her his favourite, and we sat amiably toasting our toes.

'May I assume,' she asked after an interval, 'that this thirst for my company has something to do with your little problem, Dorothy?'

'It has everything to do with it. Not that we wouldn't have wanted to have a drink with you anyway, you understand. But Alan and I were eager to get you away from your boss and have a quiet word with you.'

'You'd better have it quickly, then. I got away from him, but he's looking for me. I didn't quite toe the accepted line in a few of my questions this afternoon, and he wants to help me see the error of my ways.' She upended her glass and set it down empty. Alan picked it up and went back to the bar.

I leaned closer to her. 'It's like this. Alan and I don't know quite how to proceed with looking into . . . with checking on what I saw yesterday.' I looked around and dropped my voice another few decibels. 'We don't want to upset any of the university authorities, but I don't quite see how we can get anywhere without talking to the security people, or to some of the people who use that building. Students, dons, whoever. Do you have any suggestions?'

'As a matter of fact, I do.' She, too, glanced around, and saw Alan coming back with her refresher. 'There is a student, a microbiologist whom I know quite well, who is working on his doctoral degree in that building. I trust him implicitly. He would be delighted to have a chat with you, and might prove to be quite helpful. His name is Thomas Grenfell. If you'll give me your mobile number, I'll see that he rings you.'

'I don't suppose he's any relation to the celebrated Joyce Grenfell?' I asked as I handed her my card.

'If so, it would be very distantly. I know his family. He is my nephew. There's Andrews bearing down upon us. I'm off.'

I raised my glass to Alan in a silent toast to the delightfully small world of English connections, and we strolled off to dinner.

Eager to hear from young Mr Grenfell, I woke early next morning and went to breakfast with Alan. As usual when confronted with an English breakfast, I ate far too much, almost all of it cholesterol. I always vow to resist temptation, and I always give in. The sausages were particularly good; I had two lovely big ones. And the bacon, and the grilled mushrooms . . .

'I'll walk it off while you sit and listen to lectures,' I said callously. 'It's a beautiful morning, and I still haven't walked along the Backs.'

'I don't actually have to attend any of the sessions except my own, my dear. Would you like some company on your stroll?'

'So long as we make it faster than a stroll. I really do need to work off some of those absolutely marvellous calories.'

The market was just getting under way as we

walked through. Shopkeepers were chatting with each other, exchanging good-natured jibes, swearing in rich Anglo-Saxon when a canvas curtain stuck and then pulled some merchandise to the ground when it gave way.

'How many centuries has this been going on, do you think?'

'I believe the market dates back to Saxon times, though it was held in small buildings back then. There was a fire at some point that destroyed the buildings, but not the market itself.'

'This is what I love so about England, Alan. One of the things, anyway. The continuity and stability. A market that's been here for a thousand years or so. There's a security about that, a sense of peace and assurance—'

A series of sharp yips accompanied a small dog chasing a cat pell-mell through the stalls. The cat screamed, hissed, and turned to confront the dog and deliver a sharp scratch across the nose. The dog yowled and ran away, and someone, presumably its master, called out furiously from one of the stalls.

'Peace and assurance. Yes, love.'

And then we were at King's Parade, and facing the magnificent east front of King's College Chapel. The morning sun shone fully on the wall of stained glass, the delicately carved golden stone, the perfect proportions. My eyes teared up; a lump caught in my throat.

Alan understands my reaction to perfect beauty. He took my hand, and we stood dumb until the dog we'd seen before came trotting over to see if our stillness meant we had a treat for him.

41

That broke the spell. I heaved a sigh of pure bliss, patted the dog with apologies for having nothing better than affection to offer, and was turning away when my phone rang.

The crush of tourists was mounting. I pulled the phone out of my pocket and sought a quiet corner in the doorway of a shop that wasn't yet open.

I glanced at the number before I answered. I didn't recognize it.

'This is Dorothy Martin,' I answered formally.

'Mrs Martin, Tom Grenfell here. My aunt asked me to phone you, something about a science lab?'

'Yes, and thank you for calling. The whole thing is a little complicated to explain over the phone. Do you have any spare time today when we could meet somewhere?'

'I'll be working in my lab most of the day. If you wouldn't mind coming there – it's in Hutchins – I could take a break around four thirty this afternoon.'

'That would be perfect! Which lab? And can you give me directions? I know where the building is, but the interior layout confuses me.'

'Ah, you've seen our labyrinth. Obviously designed by someone high on something or other. My lab-cum-office is on the first floor – second, to you Yanks – in the south-east corner. In the front door, take the stairs to your right, turn right and go down a corridor that ends at a forbidding-looking door. I'll be there to meet you.'

'Without a Minotaur, I trust.'

A chuckle at the other end of the line. 'I'll make sure he's properly caged. See you this afternoon, then.'

I related the conversation to Alan. 'You'll come with me, won't you? Or do you have to be somewhere then?'

'I'll come with you.' He gave me a quizzical look. 'You're uneasy about this, aren't you, love? I've never known you to be so apprehensive about pursuing an investigation.'

'I know. I usually just forge ahead regardless of the consequences. I don't know why it's different this time, but I'm truly scared of that building. Stupid, isn't it?'

'On the contrary, I'd say you were at last exhibiting some rudimentary concern for your skin. I applaud the change. Now, shall we explore the Backs?'

I admit I had only divided attention to give to the glories of Cambridge for the next few hours. We wandered along the Cam at the 'backs' of many of the ancient colleges. We returned to King's and checked out the times for Evensong. Today, Friday, it was at five thirty, so we wouldn't be able to make it. 'But there's one tomorrow,' said Alan consolingly, 'with an organ concert to follow. We'll get our music.'

We stopped in at Heffers, the wonderful bookstore near Trinity College, where I found a couple of new mysteries by favourite authors and had a pleasant chat with Richard Reynolds, who has an encyclopaedic knowledge of crime fiction. We skipped lunch at the college in favour of a salad lunch in a little café near the market, with our waistlines in mind. We did some shopping in the market, picking up a few small gifts for Alan's grandchildren, who had birthdays coming up, and

43

then went back to St Stephen's to rest our feet. I lay on the bed, but couldn't nap, though I wanted to. I suppose it was all that coffee. My mind kept going over and over that scene in the lab, which seemed permanently etched on my mind's eye.

At twenty past four, I couldn't stand it any longer. I swung my feet to the floor and put on my shoes. 'Alan!' I said urgently.

He put down the book he was reading (or nodding over) and stood up. 'Plenty of time, my dear.'

'I know. I'm antsy. Let's go.' I pulled on my bright tam for moral support, and we walked the few yards to the Hutchins Building.

It was a good thing, for the sake of my mental health, that young Grenfell decided to meet us at the front door. Even with Alan by my side, I would have been reluctant to try to find Tom's lab.

He was a very polite young man, and nice-looking. His beard was neatly trimmed; his hair only a bit longer than Alan's. Looking quite professional in his white coat, he shook hands with both of us as we introduced ourselves. He did smile a little at my hat, but he made no comment as he led us up the stairs to his workplace.

'What are you working on, Tom?' I asked.

He looked at me (and my hat) a bit dubiously. 'Um – carbon fixation and photorespiration.'

'My father and my first husband were both biologists, Tom. I do understand a little. That would have to do with photosynthesis, right?'

'Right.' He sounded surprised. 'Right. That is

– most people have never heard of photorespiration. I'm impressed. And here we are.'

We had arrived at the door at the end of the corridor. It was a plain, ugly panelled wood door with no window, no identifying information. I would have guessed it to be the door to a closet or a storage room of some sort. Tom fished out a key and opened the door on to a very small laboratory. Most of the light came from one window at the end of the room.

'We have to keep all the labs locked,' he said, sounding a little apologetic.

'Yes, I crashed a tour of the college yesterday and the guide told us about that. I wondered a little about the pathogens she mentioned.'

'There's no danger,' Tom assured us, 'unless someone goes prying around and opens lockers plainly marked as hazardous. But you never know what kids will do, if they've been drinking, or on a dare, or something. I guess, Mrs Martin, that's our Minotaur. I promised you it would be decently caged.'

He leaned against a tall stool in front of a very odd-looking collection of instruments. The only ones I recognized were components of a computer: screen, keyboard, mouse. 'Now, how can I help you? Aunt Elaine wasn't terribly forthcoming on the subject – sounded a bit mysterious, in fact.'

'It *is* mysterious, but before I go into it, what on earth is all that?' I gestured.

'Oh, haven't you ever seen an electron microscope before? We're very proud of it. It's absolutely the latest model and cost a bloody fortune. Oh, sorry.'

'It's all right. Americans scarcely think of the word as profanity. Now, as to what brought us here – Alan, do you think you could explain?'

He smiled. 'Still a little too sore a memory? I'll do my best. On the first day of my conference, Tom – the Wednesday, that would be – my wife wandered into this building by mistake while she was looking for me.'

'Easy to do until you learn the layout,' said Tom. 'They all look alike.'

'Precisely. At any rate, she found herself in a laboratory on the ground floor, near the back door.'

'It was bigger than this one,' I added. 'Quite a lot bigger. The tour guide said it's for work in micro zoology.'

'Ah,' said Tom. 'That's the demonstration room for second-year undergraduates. Hence the size. Group experiments.'

Alan quirked an eyebrow to see if I wanted to continue. I shook my head.

'The room was, I gather, deserted, but very brightly lit. She saw on the floor a good-sized pool of what she took to be blood.'

'It *was* blood, Alan. I'll never forget the smell.'

'She was a good deal disturbed. She left the room quickly to find me, but on her way out she heard a noise, turned and saw someone with a white coat like a lab coat disappearing through a door.'

'And I ran like a frightened rabbit,' I finished. 'Felt like one, in fact. A total coward.'

Tom was silent, considering. 'Mr Martin,' he began after a moment.

'Nesbitt,' Alan corrected. 'Dorothy kept her surname when we married.'

'Mr Nesbitt, then, my aunt told me you are a policeman. A chief constable, I believe?'

'I was. I've been retired for some time.'

'Then why did you come to me about this?'

That was one I could deal with. 'The situation is peculiar, Tom. I was the one who saw the . . . what I saw, and I have no authority anywhere. When Alan and some friends went over to take a look, the lab in question was in normal use, and there was no blood or anything that looked like it, there or in any other room they could get into. I could have imagined it all. I didn't, but there's no proof. I have nothing to take to the Cambridge police, in the person of your aunt, or to the university security people. And yet I know there is something that needs investigating. In view of the delicate political balance between town and gown, it seemed better to take a quiet, unofficial look before raising any red flags. Your aunt suggested that you might be of help.'

'I see.' There was a longer silence. Alan and I exchanged glances.

'Look, I don't mean to be rude or anything, but I've never met either of you. Aunt Elaine says you're trustworthy, but does she believe you? It's pretty incredible, you know.'

'I do know. She believes me anyway. She told me a story about her early days on the police force here that was pretty incredible, too. I think that's why she knows I'm telling the truth.'

'That one about the voodoo cult, or whatever it was? I always thought she made that up, as a ghost story to scare me when I was a kid.'

I hadn't told Alan the story. He looked at me oddly.

'That's the one. She didn't make it up, Tom. It happened. Strange things do happen, especially in a place that's as much of a melting pot as Cambridge. But I understand if you can't quite accept my word. It was worth a try.'

'I didn't say I wouldn't help.' Suddenly, he looked very young. 'I owe Aunt Elaine a lot. She's the reason I'm here at university, actually. If she says you're OK, then you are. No matter how weird it sounds,' he added with a grin. 'So what do you want me to do?'

That was the trouble. I hadn't the slightest idea. I looked at Alan.

'If I were investigating this officially,' said Alan, sounding very much like a policeman, 'the first thing I would order is a thorough testing of that floor for bloodstains. None are visible now to the naked eye, but I'm sure you know about using ultraviolet light to detect blood.'

'Only from cop shows on the telly,' said Tom, grinning again. 'Does it really work?'

'It does, though not in quite the way you might expect. The blood doesn't fluoresce under UV, but it shows very black, even if it's nearly invisible to the naked eye. You have the equipment?'

Tom nodded. 'The problem is going to be getting into that lab. Students – at least, graduate students – have keys to the rooms we use, but not to the rest. I could get in when the room is in use, but then I could hardly do any testing. I could see if I could wangle a key from one of my friends.'

48

'I'd like you to try it, if you can without landing in trouble.'

'That's really important, Tom,' I added anxiously. 'Staying out of trouble, I mean. It isn't just a question of getting into hot water academically for overstepping your bounds as a student. Where there is blood, there almost certainly was death. If it was a human death, then whoever is responsible isn't going to take kindly to anyone poking around. You could be in danger.'

The grin had gone. 'I understand. I'll be careful. What else?'

'If there are no obvious stains under UV light,' Alan went on, 'then you may have to do some close inspection on your hands and knees. The floor is of white linoleum, I believe, like this one. That's pretty impervious, but if we're lucky, some of the blood may have been spilt near a seam, where it could have run underneath. Dorothy, you're going to have to show him exactly where it was, as nearly as you can remember.'

I nodded, not looking forward to it.

'Then you'll have to inspect carefully, perhaps even scraping a bit with a clean knife.'

'I sometimes use sterile scalpels in my work. I can do that.'

'Good man. This is exactly what I would have my scene-of-crime officers do, but in this case, we can't call them in, or, rather, your aunt can't call them in. Not yet. If you can find evidence of blood, enough to warrant a test with Luminal, it will get us a good deal further on. Any questions?'

'No, sir.' Unconsciously, I thought, he had

responded to Alan's air of authority. 'Mrs Martin, could you bear to show me the spot right away? There aren't many people here just now, but I think I saw Bristow coming in to work in that lab, so we could get in. I could tell him I was showing you around the place.'

'Of course I will. It's foolish of me to be so skittish about it.' And Alan would be there. That would make everything much easier.

The building seemed to be deserted. At least it was very quiet. 'Tom, are we the only ones here? And your friend Bristow? I had an idea dedicated scientists worked all the time.'

'Friday afternoon,' he replied. 'Most of us take off, unless we've a critical experiment going that has to be tended like a dear little baby. And of course the animal-minders have to come in, but they usually just do a quick check of food and water and so on.'

We went back down the stairs. I was glad I was wearing sneakers. They squeaked a little on the stone treads, but they didn't clatter. Tom's shoes were rubber-soled, too, and Alan had learned the art of silence in decades of police work.

Why did I feel the need for caution in this nearly empty building? It was irrational, but still I clung to the banister, taking some of the weight off my feet, to quiet them still further.

Tom felt it, too. Perhaps my own unease was contagious. When we reached the ground floor, he pointed us in the right direction without speaking. I reached for Alan's arm and clung to it as a much better alternative to the stair rail.

I was prepared to feel queasy when we opened the door to the zoology lab, just as I had when the tour guide opened it.

What I wasn't prepared for was the sight of a white lab coat whisking out of sight through the back door.

Six

'Alan!' I said, clutching his arm frantically. I meant to speak in a whisper. I realized after a second or two that I had made no sound at all. I swallowed to try again, but my husband put a finger to his lips. He raised his eyebrows in an 'OK?' expression, and gently loosed my death grip.

I wanted him to stay with me, but, of course, he needed to get across the room and try to spot the person who had disappeared through that door. It was so much like my first experience in that room that my eyes turned involuntarily to the floor. To the spot where . . .

'X marks the spot,' I said with a near giggle.

'Steady, Mrs Martin.' The boy behind me grasped my shoulder. 'That was probably just Bristow, though why he'd leave, just as we came in . . . Anyway, your husband will be back in a tick, and I'm here.'

He was a child, no substitute for my stalwart husband. But he was a nice, kind child. 'I'm sorry. I'm not going into hysterics, really. It was just . . . seeing that person leaving the room, just as he . . . she . . . it did the first time. Not through the same door, of course. There are so many doors, aren't there? I'm not sure, anymore, which one . . . because I was standing back there, you see. Where he went out this time. And the puddle on the floor was . . .'

'I imagine it was about where that puddle is now,' said Tom, sounding grim.

That remark shocked me, at last, out of my babbling fit. 'Puddle? But there's no – oh.' I looked where he pointed, and there, sure enough, was a barely visible puddle. Not of blood, but what looked from here like soapy water.

I took a deep breath. 'We're too late, aren't we?'

'Looks that way. If that really was the spot.'

'I think so.' I was regaining my equilibrium. 'Tom, am I right that the door over there leads to a short corridor and then to an outside door?'

He nodded.

'Then I think that's the way I came in before. Could we go over and stand in front of that door? Then I'll be seeing things from the right angle, and maybe I can be sure about the . . . about the blood.'

Blood. Perfectly ordinary English word. Nothing to get upset about. Say it often enough and it becomes routine.

Right.

I wished Alan would come back. I wished he'd catch the phantom lab tech. If that's what he was. I wished I'd never seen this building, never come to Cambridge.

Or maybe not quite that. There was King's . . .

We moved around the room, staying as close to the edges as possible so as not to tread in any evidence that might be left. With lab benches up against nearly all the walls, it wasn't easy. I tried not to touch anything, but slow creeping creates balance problems for someone my age. I was glad of Tom's sustaining arm.

As we went, I counted doors. The one we came in. The one at the back that led out. One at each end of the room that led who knew where. It was through the one to the right of the main door that the lab-coated person had flown, Alan after him.

'I wish Alan would come back.'

'He is back,' said my husband in a normal tone of voice. He'd come in when I was looking the other way. 'The bird has flown. This place is a rabbit warren, if you'll forgive my saying so, Tom. My quarry could have gone in any one of three or four directions from the next room, and in several from each of those. He was just far enough ahead of me that I couldn't see a closing door, and they're all so blasted quiet I couldn't hear one, either.'

'He?' I asked.

'Or she. I've no clue.'

'We're out of clues here, too,' I said with a sigh. 'Our shy lab worker has been busy.' I pointed to the rapidly drying spot on the floor. 'That's where the blood was. He seems to have come back to finish the clean-up job.'

'And ran for the hills as soon as he heard us coming,' said Tom. 'I'd say that puts the lid on it. If that was Bristow, he couldn't have moved so quietly. He weighs around twenty stone. And none of the cleaners would be about just now. They come in at night. Something's sure rotten in the state of Denmark.'

'And there's a rat i' the arras,' I said, adding one more metaphor to the rich mixture. 'You're right. An innocent cleaner would have no reason to flee. But that's not evidence, is it, Alan?'

'Not even close. I had pinned my hopes on those blood stains, but clearly we have here a villain who watches the telly and learns therefrom.'

'But why did he – whoever – wait so long for the clean-up? It was there on Wednesday afternoon. This is Friday. Forty-eight hours. I know he did a lick-and-a-promise just before you and the others checked on Wednesday, but why wait for the thorough job?'

Tom frowned. 'The lab's in pretty constant use on Thursdays, but not on Fridays. I can't think why he didn't come back last night, or this morning.'

'Something else to do, something critical?' suggested Alan. 'He was in hospital. He was in jail. He was called out of town on an emergency of some sort. It could be anything.'

'So what do we do next? Should we – that is, should Elaine – be checking for missing persons, or hospital admissions, or a body? That blood had to belong to somebody.'

'Possibly an animal,' Alan reminded me. 'The fact is we have no solid evidence that there ever was any blood. I'm sorry, love, but although Elaine and I both believe you, she can't launch an investigation, risking both a good deal of expense and the possibility of town-and-gown umbrage being taken, based simply on your word. And that being the case, I suggest we ask young Thomas here to find us a good pub nearby and drown our sorrows, or at least take them for a moderate swim.'

I have always loved pubs. 'English pubs' is

redundant; only in England – or perhaps one could extend it to the UK – does the pub flourish. Attempts to import them to America have been abysmal failures. The atmosphere of a place that has been a centre of community life for at least three hundred years simply cannot be transported to a country as young as the United States.

Now that they're smoke-free, pubs are for me better than ever, although I admit that the ancient regulars befouling the air with their equally ancient pipes were a part of the ambience, and are missed by the real traditionalists. I'm as great a lover of Merrie Olde England as anyone, and as firm a defender of her institutions, but there are limits. I have an odd fondness for being able to breathe.

The pub Tom took us to was everything a pub should be. Near King's College, it was predictably crowded and noisy. It was old, and the owners had resisted the temptation to tart it up. There was a terrace sheltered from the street by greenery, but on this chilly April afternoon we found the interior more appealing. There was a fireplace with an inglenook, but the press of customers made the room quite warm enough without a fire.

Tom greeted friends as he made his way across the room to a single unoccupied table. 'What'll you have?'

I expressed my usual preference for bourbon. Alan asked for whisky and held out a ten-pound note. 'This round's mine,' he said, and Tom bowed a graceful thanks.

Settled with our drinks, Tom raised his pint. 'Here's to new friends,' he said somewhat solemnly, and we joined him in the toast.

56

'There's nothing quite like getting involved in a murder to cement a friendship,' I commented.

'Is that what this is? A murder?' Tom didn't bother to keep his voice down. The noise level was such that anything below a siren would go unnoticed.

'We don't know,' said Alan patiently. 'A pool of blood. That's all we have – or had. Now that's gone beyond recall.'

'As is your friend Bristow,' I said sourly. 'I'd very much like to know where he disappeared to.'

Tom pulled out his phone and poked at it, then held it to his ear. 'Matt? Grenfell. I thought I saw you at the labs this afternoon, but when I tried to find you, you'd gone. Oh. Oh, I see. And how is she getting on? No, nothing important. Later.'

He pocketed the phone.

'Had to leave to tend a sick mother, or girlfriend?'

Tom chuckled. 'Not exactly. He came to the building just for a moment to check on a pregnant guinea pig. She's doing well and not quite ready for her accouchement, so he left again.'

'Another red herring, then. Tom, you work in that building, even if not in that particular lab. You know the people working there – besides Bristow, I mean – and something of their projects, yes?'

He nodded.

'Can you think of any innocuous way a large quantity of blood could have been spilled on that floor?'

'No. I've been giving it some thought ever

57

since you told me. Sure, the zoologists work with blood, but they're tiny samples.'

'Human blood?' Alan asked.

'Not that I am aware. That kind of research is hedged round with all kinds of regulations, and rightly so. The possibilities for disaster are endless. No, they use the blood of lab animals. And before you get upset, Mrs Martin, they use tiny needles, and the quantity is so small the animals usually aren't even aware they've drawn it. Though a chap I know was bitten once by a rat. It thought it was about to be fed, and expressed its disappointment rather forcefully.'

He took a pull at his pint. 'How much blood was there, Mrs Martin? I know you've said quite a lot, but what does that mean?'

'Alan wanted to know that, too, and I'm sorry, but I can only tell the size of the puddle. I know from kitchen spills that a small amount of liquid can cover an amazing lot of floor, but blood is more viscous than water or wine or coffee or any of the other things I've been known to spill. The pool was about so wide.' I indicated about twelve inches with my hands.

Tom whistled. 'And it was fresh?'

I had a healthy swig of bourbon. 'Fresh enough that I could smell it.' Alan gave me a concerned look, but I was OK. Almost.

Tom drank his beer and brooded. I looked at my watch and raised my eyebrows at Alan. He shook his head, which could have meant a number of things. I finished my drink.

Tom stood. 'This is my round.'

'No, thank you,' I said.

Alan stood, saying, 'I do really have to get back to the conference. The speaker at dinner tonight is an old friend, and I should be there.'

'But we can't just let this drop!' Tom was now almost as concerned as Alan and I.

'No,' I said, putting my hand on his arm. 'I have no intention of letting it drop. But until one of us has a better idea of how to pick it up, we might as well let it stew.' My, but I had a fine line in mixed metaphors today!

'I'll ring you tomorrow,' said Tom, 'after I've had a better chance to think about it, and nose around a bit.'

'But be careful!' I said, just as Alan said, 'Use all due caution, mind you.'

Tom grinned. 'I have a healthy regard for my own skin, you know. I'll not go and do something stupid. But what you need at this point is inside knowledge, and as I see it I'm the only man who can get that for you. And the drinks tomorrow are on me!'

We hurried back to St Stephen's by the most direct route, not lingering to look at King's or any of the other ancient colleges. I was sorry. I needed that dose of antiquity to offset a modern world that was altogether too much with us.

Seven

I indulged in the conference breakfast with Alan the next morning before making my escape. I was very glad there were no scales anywhere on which I could weigh myself. At the rate I was eating, I'd have gained ten pounds by the time I got home.

The earliest we could expect to hear from Tom would surely be late morning, if he was like every other college student I've ever known. So I told Alan I'd decided to get some exercise and some culture at one go, and planned to visit the Fitzwilliam Museum.

I'd heard a lot about the Fitzwilliam, but on previous visits to Cambridge it was never a high enough priority to warrant skipping other attractions. This morning it seemed a good place to while away some time and perhaps take my mind off the mysterious pool of blood. So I pulled on my tam, unfolded my map (which was becoming somewhat tattered), walked south on King's Parade until it became Trumpington Street, and there it was – a magnificent neo-classical building that reminded me of the Capitol in Washington, DC, minus the dome. Like the Capitol, it was approached via an impressive staircase, and though there were prominent signs pointing to the disabled-accessible entrance, I defied my years and minor aches and pains, climbed the stairs, and stepped inside.

And inside . . . oh, my! I simply stood and stared.

An imposing double staircase, with treads of white marble and railings and balusters of polished purple and golden stone, led up to a doorway supported by two Grecian-style caryatids, the whole surmounted by a heraldic shield, presumably that of the Fitzwilliams. It was supported not by the traditional lions, but by two large birds I couldn't identify, although to my untutored eye they looked like ostriches. Surely not! There's something intrinsically comical about an ostrich. I couldn't imagine anyone choosing them as part of a family's identity.

Beyond the dazzling doorway I glimpsed a warm red wall and a gorgeously carved ceiling, and by craning my neck I could see the frame of a picture or two. A gallery, then.

A dome topped the entrance hall, and behind the reception desk on the main floor were dark green marble columns flanking the entrance to more galleries.

'Excuse me.' The voice behind me sounded impatient, and I realized I was blocking the way.

'Oh, sorry!' I stepped aside. 'It's just that . . . I've never seen . . . well, it really *is* amazing, isn't it?'

'Your first visit, madam?' The man behind the counter sounded mildly amused.

'Gosh, how could you tell?' I grinned at him. 'Just because I'm totally discombobulated? Truly, I've never seen anything like this. It wouldn't matter if you had nothing on display at all; the building itself . . .' I waved my hands around,

61

nearly beaning the woman who stood beside me. She took a hasty step back.

'Oh, good grief, I *am* sorry. I'll settle down and behave, I promise. Where would you suggest I go first?'

'What is your main interest? Painting, sculpture? Porcelain, pottery, glass? European, Asian?'

I could hardly tell him my main interest was in killing time. 'I'm not really sure. Such an embarrassment of riches . . .' I remembered in time not to wave my hands around again.

'Here's a gallery guide, then. Note that flash photography is prohibited, but you can take pictures without flash in most galleries. Just ask any guard if you have questions.'

I didn't have a camera with me, and if my tiny, antiquated flip-top cell phone was able to take pictures, I certainly didn't know how. I smiled at the nice young man, clutched the floor plan and headed up the stairs, because how could one see that magnificent flight and not climb it?

I'm sure the art on display was wonderful, but its setting was so superb as to overwhelm the paintings. I wandered from one gallery to the next, marvelling at a carved plaster ceiling here, a stained-glass window there, an inlaid floor, an elaborate lintel.

I was in such a state of artistic satiation that I forgot about everything else until my phone rang, to my embarrassment. I'd neglected to turn it off, a thing I always try to be careful about. I ducked around a corner and eventually fished the thing out of my purse. It had stopped ringing by that time, so I looked at the display, which showed a number my phone didn't recognize. Almost certainly Tom Grenfell. I was really going to have to program him in. A quick check of the floor plan showed me there were no lavatories on this floor, or indeed on the main floor. I'd have to go outside, or all the way down to the lowest level, to find a place where I could ring back and talk without disturbing everyone else. There was, it appeared, only one elevator, several galleries away. I headed for the staircase without a thought to its beauty, but only its utility as the most direct way out.

If it hadn't been for the railing, I couldn't have saved myself. At least a foot wide, it afforded no handhold, but I was leaning on it for support as I went down the stairs at the nearest approach to a run I could manage.

The shove came from one side, not directly in my back. Again I was fortunate. A direct push would have sent me somersaulting down those marble steps, and I would almost certainly have been dead by the time I hit the bottom. The shove against my shoulder pushed me hard against the railing. I was leaning on it already. My body spun to meet my hand and arm, and I found myself on my front, slipping down the glassy marble as if it had been an oiled slide and I a small naughty boy. I fetched up against the broad flat marble post at the bottom, teetered there for a moment, and then slid inelegantly to the floor.

I'm sure a degree of pandemonium must have ensued, but to tell the truth I missed most of it. I wasn't exactly unconscious, just somehow not quite there for a while. When I was once more aware of my surroundings, someone had spread a blanket over me and was taking my pulse.

'Who pushed me?' I croaked.

Nobody took the slightest notice. 'Did you hit your head?' asked the pulse-taker.

'No. I don't think so. It doesn't hurt. Someone gave me a shove—'

'Are you dizzy at all?'

'Of course I'm dizzy! I have mild vertigo, and I've just taken a wild ride. Look, someone needs to look for—'

'Look straight at me, please.'

I glared at her. She shone a flashlight in each eye. I put up a hand to shield them, growing more irritated every moment.

'Probably no concussion,' she said briefly. 'No broken bones. She should lie still for a while, in view of her dizziness and confusion. I don't think she needs to go to hospital, if you've a quiet place where she could stay for an hour or so.'

I sat up and threw off the blanket. 'I do not need to lie down, and I am *not* confused. How many times must I tell you that someone tried to push me down those stairs? If I'm not dead, it's no fault of his. Help me up; my titanium knees don't like getting up off the floor.'

'Now, now, you shouldn't—'

My fury helped me to stand up on my own, if awkwardly. 'Don't tell me what I should and shouldn't do! And don't treat me like a child.' I patted my pocket. 'Where's my phone?'

'We found this, madam,' said the nice young man from the reception desk. 'I'm afraid it's seen better days.'

It was in pieces, shattered beyond repair. As *I* might have been if all the saints hadn't been looking after me. I muttered under my breath words I don't usually say out loud.

'Someone call my husband.' I gave them his mobile number. 'Chief Constable Alan Nesbitt. He's attending the police conference at St Stephen's College, if he doesn't answer his own phone. Tell him to get here as soon as he can.'

Though, of course, by now it was far too late even to attempt a search for whoever had tried to kill me. He'd have mingled with the crowd and vanished before anyone had any idea it wasn't a simple accident.

The museum people and that nurse or doctor, or whatever, were quite sure it was an accident and I was merely raving. I sincerely hoped that among the painful bruises I was certainly developing was one that would show the mark of a homicidal hand.

I still felt dizzy, and every part of me felt sore, but I was not about to let that officious medical person dictate what I would do. 'I will wait for Alan right here,' I said firmly, 'and I would rather stand than sit, thank you, unless there's a well-cushioned chair somewhere. I fell rather hard on my sit-upon.'

Turning my head carefully to avoid making the dizziness worse, I looked at the stairs. Somehow they didn't seem nearly as attractive as they had earlier.

The nice young man materialized again, pushing before him an upholstered chair he had found somewhere. Like my phone, it had seen better

65

days. The cushions were a bit lumpy, and the wood of the legs was scuffed. 'From the staff room,' he said. 'It's a trifle ratty, but it's comfortable.'

I collapsed into it gratefully to wait for Alan.

It wasn't a long wait. In fact, he appeared before I thought it possible, charging in the front door of the museum rather like a raging bull.

'Don't hug me, love,' I warned. 'I don't think there's a square inch of me that doesn't hurt. How did you get here so fast?'

'I was down at King's. When I tried to call you and got an "out of service" message, I was sure something was wrong, and went looking for you.'

'It might have meant I'd forgotten to charge the phone,' I pointed out, serene again now that he was there.

'But it didn't. Dorothy, what happened?'

'Someone tried to push me down the stairs. No one here believes me, but that's what happened.'

'She was running down the stairs,' said the officious medical person with a sniff. I had hoped she had left.

'You saw the incident?' said Alan in a voice that ought to have frozen her solid.

'No, but I talked to several people who did.'

'And you are an employee of the museum?'

'Certainly not, and I don't care for your implication. I walked into the museum, saw that there had been an accident and offered what assistance I could.'

'You are a doctor, or a nurse?'

She sniffed. 'I am trained in first aid.'

'As am I. May I ask why you took the word

of passers-by about what happened to my wife, rather than her own word?'

'Well! Anyone could see that she was raving. She was disoriented and in pain, and, by her own admission, dizzy.'

'She is also an excellent witness, and an entirely truthful person, as I have reason to know. I don't know if she told you that I am a senior policeman. Did it occur to no one to investigate this so-called accident?'

'Well, really! I was *trying* to be helpful!'

I was actually beginning to feel a little sorry for the woman, annoying though she was. 'Alan, I was just a little woozy at first. I suspect that by the time I said anything, whoever did it was long gone. But I wasn't running. You know I don't run anymore. I was hurrying, I admit, because – oh! Alan, Tom tried to call me. I'm sure it was him, and I couldn't talk to him in here, so I was trying to get outside, and now my phone's smashed to bits and I don't have his number and—'

'All right, darling, all right. We'll sort it out. The question now is what to do with you. Can you walk?'

'Not very far. Nothing's really wrong with me, but I'm a mass of bruises and pretty uncomfortable.'

'Then let's get you back to St Stephen's in a taxi.'

'Um – if you wouldn't mind, sir.' It was the nice young man again. David something, I saw on his name badge. 'When there's any kind of accident here at the museum, we like to have a

67

doctor see the victim, just to make sure there are no serious injuries. We can have someone take your wife to the doctor we prefer to use, unless . . .'

Alan studied him. He must have been satisfied with what he saw, because he nodded. 'As we live in Belleshire and know no doctors hereabouts, that will be fine. I was going to have someone at college recommend a doctor, but this is quicker. Dorothy?'

'Fine with me.' I was suddenly very tired.

The doctor poked and prodded. I yelped. He pronounced me unharmed except for all the bruises, and tried to prescribe some pain meds, which I refused. 'I can't take them. They make me sick. I'll just have to cope, with the help of ibuprofen.' All I actually wanted to do was lie down on a soft bed with a mild sleeping pill and drift away to a place where I didn't hurt all over.

'You'll be stiff as a board when you wake up,' said Alan when I told him.

'I'll be stiff as a board no matter what I do, and at least I'll have an hour or two of respite. I'll deal with the outcome later. Just get me to bed, Alan.'

He grinned and gave me his best imitation of a leer, but I hurt too much even to smile in response.

I didn't take a pill, after all, but I still slept away the afternoon. I was, as predicted, so stiff when I woke up that I could barely move. Alan was there.

68

'Shouldn't you be doing something official?' I tried to sit up.

'I've explained to the conference chair. I'm not letting you out of my sight, my dear, so you may as well resign yourself to my company. Do you think you could get into a bathtub? Hot water would help.'

'Maybe if I had a shower first to loosen things up a bit. Oh, Alan, I do hurt!'

'I hurt just looking at you. Those bruises ought to be in the *Guinness Book of Records*.'

'I always did bruise easily. I don't even want to look at myself. I don't think I can get out of this blasted bed without help.'

Alan was as gentle as a big man can be, but I was panting from the effort by the time he got me upright. He gave me his arm to get to the bathroom and then helped me out of my clothes; I couldn't manage by myself. Pulling off my shirt, he paused and then turned my back towards the mirror.

'Dorothy, do you have a hand mirror with you?'

'A little one in my purse. But I told you I don't want to look at myself.'

'You'll want to see this.'

'Alan, I'm cold!'

'I'll only be a moment.'

He rummaged in my purse and came back with the tiny round mirror. 'Look at your left shoulder blade, or just above it.'

I looked, and gasped. There, in tasteful shades of red and purple, was the distinct image of a palm and five fingertips.

Eight

'Proof!'

'It looks very much like it to me. And if it won't offend your sense of propriety, I'm going to snap a picture, just for the record.'

'Nothing very improper about a back. Be my guest.'

He took a quick couple of shots with his mobile. 'Now, into the shower with you before you add hypothermia to your other woes. Do you need assistance?'

'Just stepping over the edge of the tub. But aren't you going to do something about this?' I tried to gesture with my head towards the revealing bruise, and let out a yelp as sore muscles protested.

'I'm going to phone Superintendent Barker while you're in the shower. I talked to her earlier, while you were asleep, but I want her to know about this evidence.'

'Isn't she still at the conference?'

'She is. I told you I'm not leaving you. She can come here. Someone's tried to kill you once. I'm not giving them a second chance.' He turned on the shower and adjusted the temperature. 'OK, one leg. Steady! T'other leg. There you are, darling. Give a shout when you need to get out.'

The hot water was wonderful. I wasn't able to do much actual washing; twisting was painful,

70

and the pressure even of a washcloth on the bruises was a bit much. There wasn't a lot of healthy skin between the purple patches, but I did my best and trusted to the water to sluice away most of the grunge.

I turned off the water, wrapped myself in the bath sheet that Alan had left on a convenient hook, and was about to try to extricate myself with the aid of the grab bar when Alan came back into the steamy bathroom.

'Ready for that bath now?'

'Alan, I can't. I do feel much better, but the idea of sitting on hard porcelain . . .' I shuddered. He surveyed the relevant portion of my anatomy and nodded.

'I take your point. Let me help you into your nightie and dressing gown, then. Superintendent Barker is on her way over with some lunch for both of us, if you can bear to sit long enough to eat it.'

'Oh, you missed your lunch, didn't you?'

He grinned. 'Too busy rescuing a damsel in distress. Now, if you'll just move that arm a little – there you are. Warm enough?'

'Toasty, thank you.'

His phone tootled. 'That'll be the superintendent, I expect, wanting me to let her in.'

It wasn't. I could hear the agitated male voice myself, though not what was being said. Alan's responses were limited to variations of yes and no.

He chuckled as he put the phone back in his pocket. 'Young Tom. Did you hear?'

'Not quite.'

'He's just heard from his aunt about your fall and is somewhat distressed. He wanted to come over, and I said he could. If you're not too terribly uncomfortable, I thought we could have a conference, the four of us.'

I headed back to the bathroom for more ibuprofen.

When all were assembled, the room, though a nice one for two people, seemed crowded. Alan insisted that I take the one chair, well padded with pillows. Alan and Elaine perched on the beds while Tom sat cross-legged on the floor in a position I hadn't been able to assume for at least thirty years.

'Now,' said Elaine, when Alan and I had eaten our salads and crusty rolls, 'Alan tells me you were pushed down the stairs, and have the bruises to show for it.'

'It certainly looks like a handprint to me. Alan can show you a photo. I do bruise easily, or it might not have come through so clearly. I doubt my attacker took that into consideration.'

'But, Aunt Elaine, what are you doing about it? It's perfectly obvious that someone's trying to kill Mrs Martin because of what she knows about whatever's going on in the Hutchins Building, and here we sit talking about bruises.'

'Simmer down, boy! Nothing's perfectly obvious, as you put it, except a bruise. It could have been an accident.'

I shook my head. 'I was pushed, Elaine. Hard.'

'Were the stairs crowded?'

'Moderately, I think. That's why I was edged right up against the railing. I was trying to hurry, to get to a place where I could phone, and the way was clearer over there at the side. Besides, I thought it would be easy to slip on all that marble, so I wanted to be careful.'

'And some rude person wanted to push past you, and pushed your shoulder to get you out of the way. And then when he saw the disaster that resulted, he got out of there as fast as he could.'

Tom and Alan and I began to protest. Elaine held up a hand. 'I don't believe it happened that way, either. I believe it was deliberate. But you do see that my scenario is just possible.'

I kept my mouth shut. Tom glowered. But Alan slowly nodded his head. 'You're quite right, Superintendent.'

She gestured impatiently. 'Elaine. Or am I to call you "Chief Constable"?'

'Elaine, then. And tying the incident to the Hutchins business is a stretch.'

'Damn it all, what other reason could anyone have for trying to kill a nice lady like Mrs Martin?' Tom was getting red in the face.

'Again, I don't say you're wrong,' said Elaine with maddening calm. 'I don't say we shouldn't approach an investigation from that angle. I do say we can't regard anything as obvious at this stage.'

'You are going to investigate, then?' I shifted in my chair. The effect of my shower was wearing off and the pillows weren't much help. If my bones and muscles were capable of moaning, they'd be setting up quite a chorus.

'Certainly! Disappearing bloodstains in a college are one thing. An assault on a visitor in my city is quite another. The Fitzwilliam is on my beat, Dorothy. It won't be simple, because their CCTV isn't working just now, so there won't be any firm evidence. But believe me, they'll cooperate to the hilt with anything I want to do.'

I got it after a second. 'Because the alternative is an accident for which they might be sued.'

'Precisely. You look terribly uncomfortable. Should you take a painkiller and go to bed? We can take our consultation elsewhere.'

'I can't take pain pills, at least not the kind that really work. And I want to be in on this. They're my bruises, after all. But I admit I can't sit here much longer.'

They tucked me into bed, with all the pillows the room afforded. 'I feel like some Renaissance monarch conducting a levee.'

Alan bowed. 'Would your majesty care for some coffee? Or tea?'

'No, it might keep me awake. Don't mind me. Carry on.'

'Then let me tell Mrs Martin what I was going to say when I tried to phone her.' Tom settled himself on the chair I'd vacated, sitting backwards and leaning his arms on the back. 'See, I've been talking to some of the other students. No, don't look at me like that, Aunt Elaine. Of course I was careful. Nobody could have had any idea what I was after.'

She looked dubious, but said nothing.

'Actually, I mostly listened. You know the canteen in Hutchins? At least, it's not a real canteen, just a kettle and a fridge and some vending machines. We bring our own coffee and

74

tea and that. Anyway, most of the students take a break there around eleven, so I went in and started them talking about famous university pranks.'

'Pranks!' I said indignantly. 'It was no prank back there at the museum!'

'No, but hear me out. I just thought it was a good way to get them talking. Well, the other doctoral student who was there looked down his nose, implying that we're all far too mature and studious and high-minded and all that rot to play games. In fact, it is usually the undergraduates who get up to that sort of thing, and almost always the English ones – or the Irish. Two of the Asian undergraduates were there, and they just looked confused. They're terribly earnest – they may never have heard of university students acting silly. So I primed the pump, talking about the cars they've hung from the Bridge of Sighs, and the various things up on the pinnacles at King's. I said I thought those were fairly obvious and crude, easily done and not up to the standard of today's students. With almost the whole Easter term to work in, they ought, I said, to come up with something truly imaginative, truly worthy of a group of scientists – maybe even something involving blood.'

We waited.

'And that, friends, is when the room went silent. Just for a moment it was like a morgue. Then it broke and the chaps started chattering again, talking about things we might do, or saying the whole idea was ridiculous with examinations ahead for some of us, and then everyone left to get to work, but two or three left ahead of the rest, sort of not part of the group, you know?' He sat up in his chair and gestured vehemently. 'And I'll swear to you, all of you, that those men knew something. I know you'll say this isn't evidence, Aunt Elaine, but what I think is that the whole bit about the blood was a prank gone badly wrong.'

'No. Not evidence. But suggestive, I'll agree. Who were the students who left?'

He sagged back. 'That's just it. I don't know. I can't be sure. People had been moving about, getting coffee and snacks, talking to each other. You know how it is in a break room. I didn't see anyone's face when everybody got quiet. I'd spilled my coffee, and by the time I looked up, things were back to normal. It was only for a second or two. And then I was just seeing general movement out the door, people's backs.'

'And I suppose all of those backs were in white lab coats.'

He shrugged ruefully. 'They were. Required garb when we're working.'

'That's no help, then,' said Alan. 'In fact, although your experience is certainly suggestive, again it proves nothing. I presume you can give your aunt the names of all the people in the room at the time?'

Tom looked even more apologetic. 'I didn't know them all. Some had only started working in the labs this term, and, as you know, that began just a few days ago. But if I give you the names I know, between them you might come up with a list of everyone.'

'And thereby warn them all that they might be suspected of something,' said Elaine. 'I can think of no more certain way to turn them all into clams.'

'In any case,' said Alan, 'it might be more useful to know definitively which students were *not* in the room at the time. This must have been only a few minutes before Dorothy was pushed down the stairs, if you phoned her immediately.'

'I waited till I was certain they were all gone, and then I went up to my own lab for some privacy. When I didn't get an answer the first time, I didn't leave a message. I was trying to be careful. I waited a few minutes and then called again, and that was when I got the "not available" message, and I started to worry.'

'So let's work out the timing,' said Alan, tenting his fingers in a gesture that always reminded me of Alistair Cooke. 'How long was it from Tom's call till you were pushed?'

'I have no idea. I wasn't looking at a clock. I do know I started down the stairs right away.'

'While your phone was still ringing?'

'Oh. No. Let's see. I heard it making that peculiar noise. I can't think why they can't make them sound like real telephones.'

'They can,' Tom put in. 'When you get a new one, I'll program it for any ringtone you like.'

'Oh, yes, actually I did know that. That they can sound like almost anything, I mean. I have an American friend who makes hers play Tchaikovsky at Christmastime. One of the dances from *The Nutcracker*.'

'If we could get back to the subject at hand,' said Alan with forced patience. 'You heard your phone ring.'

'Burble, is more like it. All right, Alan, I'll come to the point. I heard it and I was upset because I'd forgotten to turn off the sound. So I hunted for it, and of course it was at the very bottom of my purse. It had stopped ringing by the time I found it, but I thought it was probably Tom, so I looked around for a place where I could call him back without bothering everybody. The nearest place I could think of was outside, so I headed for the stairs. I'd gone down only one or two, I think, before . . .' I stopped, feeling suddenly wobbly. The memory of that moment of sheer panic was strong. I had, I realized, been quite sure I was about to die.

'Yes, all right, love. So in fact it could have been as much as five minutes from the call until you started down the stairs.'

'Not that long, I don't think. Maybe two or three. Hear the phone. Rummage for it in my purse.' I mimed the action. 'Ring, ring, ring. Where is the dratted thing? Ah, there. It's stopped. Who was calling?' I peered at the imaginary phone. 'Don't know the number. Probably Tom. Where can I go to call him back? Rummage for floor plan.' I pawed at the duvet. 'Find plan. Study it. Darn. No restrooms except in the basement. Have to go outside. Make my way through the crowd to the stairway.' I walked my fingers across the duvet. 'Reach over and more or less drape myself over the railing. How long was that?' Alan had been looking at his watch.

78

'Not a lot more than a minute. Double it to allow for the difference between real and reconstructed actions, and I'd say three at the absolute outside. Now, how about your end, Tom? How long between the departure of the last of the break-room party and your phone call?'

Tom went through a similar dumb show. 'Perhaps five minutes, sir. I had to climb those stairs, and I didn't care to take them at a run, in case anyone was watching. I didn't want to appear hurried. Then I had to find your number on my phone, Mrs Martin. Not more than five minutes, I should think.'

'That would give a student eight minutes at most to get from the Hutchins canteen area to the top of the stairs at the Fitzwilliam Museum. Could it be done?'

'At a dead run,' said Tom, frowning. 'But—'

'But—' said Elaine at the same moment.

'But it makes no sense.' I overrode both of them. 'The – call him X, for want of a better term – X would have had to know who I was and that I was getting dangerously close to something he didn't want known. Which, heaven knows, I'm not. Getting close to anything, that is. Then he would have had to know I was at the Fitzwilliam, out of all possible places in Cambridge.'

'You told no one where you were going? Except me, I mean.'

'No one. I didn't see anyone to speak to.'

'Then it seems reasonable to deduce that it was not one of the students with whom you had your little chat, Tom, who attacked Dorothy.'

79

'If, in fact, she was attacked,' murmured Elaine.

I pretended not to hear her. 'So if we're going with this scenario, it means that someone else involved in what Tom's calling this "prank gone wrong" somehow knew me, thought I knew too much, et cetera. Someone who wasn't in the canteen with Tom this morning. But the only student I've actually met over there is Tom. So how could anyone – in this city I've visited only two or three times in my life – pick me out of that crowd as his victim?'

'My dear,' said Alan gently, as Elaine said, 'My dear woman!' with a snort.

'What?'

'I think they mean your hat, Mrs Martin,' said Tom, trying not to snicker.

'Oh, my hat. Alan, my hat!' I sat straight up, a move I regretted. 'Where . . . ?'

'I brought it back, love. I'm afraid it fell under the staircase, or was kicked there. It's a bit dusty, and somewhat the worse for wear.'

I collapsed back on to the pillows. 'Salvageable?'

'Well . . .'

'I loved that hat. We got it in Scotland, remember? That little shop in Edinburgh. I suppose it was a trifle conspicuous.'

'Dorothy, apart from the mortar boards or Tudor bonnets some wear for graduation ceremonies, almost no one in Cambridge ever wears a hat. *Any* hat is conspicuous, and when it's red and gold, of course it's noticeable.'

'So,' said Elaine, 'X knew the person wearing that hat was the nosy American lady who was prying into some sort of mess, and decided to take direct action. Spur of the moment. No real way to trace him or her. Dead end.'

'But it has to be someone who knows about the blood on the floor, knows I saw it. Someone, in short, who knows I could somehow be dangerous. And I've told only the people in this room. You told your two buddies, Alan, the ones who went with you to look. Did you or they say anything to the student who you talked to there?'

'Of course not.' Alan did his best not to sound offended.

'Sorry, love, I had to ask. So how did anyone know what I saw?'

'The phantom in the lab coat,' said Alan. 'The one who keeps disappearing. He must have seen you that first day. You weren't sure, as I recall. And then, of course, on Friday, you were there snooping again – and wearing your hat.'

'So that must mean the blood on the floor was vitally important – to conceal it, I mean. And that means . . .'

'Yes,' said Elaine. 'I will get the search started. Missing persons reports, serious injuries, deaths at hospitals. Starting at that end might give us something to work on. Get some rest, Dorothy.'

Nine

That was when Alan shooed them away and let me (at last) take that sleeping pill. I drifted away into blessed oblivion until the next morning, waking only a couple of times when my bladder made demands I couldn't ignore. Even then I didn't wake fully, only enough to make my painful way to the bathroom and back. Every time, in the dim light that came through the blinds, I saw Alan watching me from his pillow. He had meant it when he said he wasn't letting me out of his sight.

In the morning I felt a little better. Every part of me still complained, but not quite as loudly. Perhaps the grumbling voices were drowned out by the bells.

Bells?

Our house in Sherebury is right next to the Cathedral Close, and the bells on the other side of the wall have become so much a part of our lives that we don't always hear them. But these sounded different. I opened my eyes and saw Alan getting dressed.

'Bells?'

'Still not quite awake, darling? Yes, bells. It's Sunday, you know. The various churches and chapels are saluting the Sabbath. Are you feeling well enough to go to church?'

'Oh, Alan, let's. We still haven't heard the

King's choir. Do we have time to get there?'

'Masses of time. Can you totter to breakfast with me, or shall I get someone to bring some to us?'

'I think I can just about make it that far, and I may even be able to dress myself.'

'That's progress. I'll stand by in case a helping hand is needed.'

I needed only a little help from Alan, though I'm afraid some operations did elicit a certain amount of profanity. I wasn't very comfortable once I was dressed, and I've looked better. 'I feel naked without my hat, and it's the only casual one I brought,' I grumbled.

'We'll find you another. At the moment what I want to find is sustenance. Come, love. We'll take it slowly.'

Everyone at the conference had apparently heard about my 'accident'. We'd agreed to let them think that, at least for now. Alan and Elaine had both quailed at the thought of an entire conference of police officers jumping on our problem. 'If this is meant to be about community relations,' Elaine had said, 'the concept would be ready for burial long before we caught our mysterious X. I've nothing like enough evidence yet to trample on the town/gown division of powers.' So Alan and I responded pleasantly to the sympathy and offers of assistance and well-wishing as we walked to the dining room, and kept our mouths shut about our suspicions.

Alan got my food for me. He had seated me next to Elaine, who acted as substitute watchdog until he returned.

'Feeling a bit better?'

'A bit. I can move without wanting to scream.'

'Good. Coffee?'

I accepted coffee with thanks, and took a reviving sip. 'Oh, that's good. I don't know what genius first figured out that you could take some red berries that didn't taste very good and roast them and grind them and pour hot water over them, but I owe whoever it was a great debt of gratitude. *Skoal*.' I raised my cup.

'You are feeling better. More sleuthing planned for this morning? Not that I know quite where you'd begin.'

'Nor do I. Alan and I are tending to our neglected souls this morning. And, I must admit, to our ears. We're going to the Eucharist at King's. We've been intending to get to Evensong all week, but things kept happening.'

'Things like almost getting killed.' She looked around. Nobody was paying any attention to us. 'You could have been, you know.'

'I know. If I'd fallen the other direction and bumped my head all the way down those stairs . . . but I didn't. And I honestly wonder if X intended to kill me, or to frighten me, or just to put me out of commission for a while.'

'He didn't succeed in any of those goals, thank all the gods at once,' said Alan, arriving with my food. 'Unless you count one wasted afternoon and evening as a "while".'

'He frightened me, for sure. But he didn't scare me off. I'm more determined than ever to get to the bottom of this, even if I'm moving a little slower than usual. I very much wonder what X intended to do with me out of the way that would have been more difficult with me around and snooping.'

'We might have had a better chance of finding out,' said Alan, 'if we had acted as if you were seriously injured. Now that you're visibly among the living, right here in the college, word is going to get around. Our servers here are students, you know, and they talk.'

'Well, I refuse to worry about it just now. I have wonderful food before me, and it's a glorious Sunday morning, and I intend to put my troubles behind me for a few hours.'

For an Anglican lover of choral music, there can be few more blissful experiences than a service of Holy Communion at King's College Chapel. It's all there. Splendidly soaring architecture, brilliant stained glass, probably the finest choir in the world and the stately cadences of the Book of Common Prayer combine in what can be a perfect worship experience.

We lingered in the chapel even after the last notes of the postlude had died away, unwilling to break the spell. Finally, some tourists began to wander and chatter, and we reluctantly got up to leave. I grunted as I rose, and staggered a little. 'Alan, I didn't even notice how uncomfortable those choir stalls are until just now. It was all so lovely, and they even had my favourite hymns.'

'Perhaps we'll stay on a few days and come back for Evensong a time or two. Would you like that, or are you yearning for home?'

'Yes to both. I do long for my own bed,

especially with all these aches and pains, and I miss the animals, of course. Which reminds me, I should call Jane and make sure they're all right.'

'You know quite well they're being pampered within an inch of their lives. Watson's enjoying playing with Jane's dogs, and the cats are sleeping everywhere they're not allowed and eating all their favourite treats.'

'I know. But I still miss them, and I hope they miss us.'

'They'll tell us they did when we get home, whether or not. So you'd like to leave tomorrow morning?'

'Not really. I've got to hear this choir again. And—'

'And we've unfinished business. I'm sorry to remind you.'

'It's all right. Right now I feel I can face anything.'

'The exaltation will wear off, you know.'

'I know. It always does. So let's strike while the iron is hot, so to speak. I want to get a really thorough look at the whole Hutchins Building. We got distracted on Friday. Do you think any of the rooms will be unlocked on a Sunday?'

'If not, I imagine Elaine can work out a way to get us inside. You're not going to go all wobbly again, are you?'

'No. I'm feeling invulnerable. My guardian angel is back on the job. And besides, you'll be with me.'

'Glued to your side, my love. But let's get a taxi. I don't want to waste your strength, or your angel's patience, on a walk through these incredibly crowded streets.'

The taxi dropped us off at the college gates. Alan extricated me, groaning, from the back seat and then said, 'Look, love, there's no point in you walking all the way to Hutchins and then back to our room if we can't get in. Do you think you can bear to sit on this bench for a moment while I phone Elaine and ask her to meet us there?'

The bench in question was stone. There was no question. 'No. I wouldn't last five seconds. There's no terrific hurry. Let's just go to the room. I can take some ibuprofen and lie down for a little while to ease the memory of choir stalls out of my bones. Meanwhile you can see about getting us into the labs.'

As I lay letting the pills do their work and my maltreated body began to quiet, my mind began to work, chasing loose ends here and there, trying to come up with some sort of scenario that would explain phantom blood stains and an attack on me.

Alan got off the phone and reported. 'Elaine had some news, if only negative. There are no reports of missing persons that could match with the timing of the blood on the floor, and no one has been admitted to local hospitals with wounds that could produce that much blood. So no help there. She also reminded me of what Tom told us: that the rooms in Hutchins, except for the lecture rooms, are routinely kept locked. Lecturers have keys, but they wouldn't be in on a Sunday. Some of the graduate students may be, I imagine.'

'So can we get in, or not?'

'Perhaps. Of course, Elaine's position would allow her to march in and demand that the building be unlocked for us, but . . .'

'Politics.'

'Yes. We still have no concrete evidence to support the idea that a crime has been committed.'

'Meanwhile, someone is getting away with – perhaps not murder, but something very nasty. I feel it in my bones, Alan.'

'Your poor, mistreated, aching bones! We'll get in eventually, love. Elaine happens to be a good friend of the master of St Stephen's College. She's going to ply him with sherry after lunch and persuade him to let us have a private tour.'

'I don't want a "tour". I want to be able to poke around and see if I can't find something incriminating.'

'Ah, but this is no ordinary tour. Our guides will be Elaine and her nephew.'

'Oh, well, that's different. But Alan, I've been thinking. If the Hutchins security is so tight, how was it that I could get into the lab that first afternoon?'

'Someone was either very careless or very careful. If you need to get away fast, or if you need to remove a body, you don't want a locked door to slow you down. Now, love, if you'll promise to stay in this room with the door locked, and not allow visitors, I really should put in an appearance at the conference. It's nearly lunch-time and there'll be some mingling. I've been neglecting my duties shamefully.'

'I promise I won't let in even the distinguished

gentleman with the ribbon of some foreign order. Really, I'll be fine, Alan. Go and mingle.'

'Shall I fetch you for lunch, or can you find your own way?'

'You won't believe it, but I'm truly not hungry. You can bring me a roll or an apple or something. I'm going to read one of my new mysteries.'

I'm sure Alan expected me to nap, and to tell the truth I expected that, too, but after reading a few pages, I fell to musing about my problem.

A prank gone badly wrong. That's what Tom thought, and now that Elaine had found nothing . . . But what sort of a prank would involve a large quantity of blood?

I let my mind freewheel. Blood. What did that suggest? Images of a cape and fangs floated across my mind. Vampires. Vampires were popular just now in the more sensational kind of fiction. Vampires and – what were they called, the 'undead'? Zombies – that was it. Where did the ideas of these mythical creatures arise? Was Bram Stoker the first to conjure up a Dracula figure, Mary Shelley the first to think of bringing a dead man to hideous life? Surely not. The concepts must go back to folklore origins some-where. Vampire bats. Did they get their name before or after the vampire legends arose? Bats. Spooky creatures, though helpful. They eat mosquitoes. The ones that don't suck blood, that is. Of course, mosquitoes suck blood, too. Blood. Blood can carry disease. Pathogens in the lab. Blood. Bats. Belfries.

I nearly jumped out of my skin as my hair was brushed lightly.

89

'Didn't mean to startle you, love. Did you have a nice nap?'

'I . . . what time is it?'

'Ten past one.'

'Oh, then I can't have slept very long. I didn't know I'd fallen asleep at all. I was thinking about blood and zombies and vampires and bats, and I was sure I was about to figure out something important . . . but I guess . . . oh, well.'

'Never mind. How are you feeling?'

I wiggled experimentally. 'Not too bad, except for my posterior. I have a feeling it's going to be sore for quite a while. That marble floor at the Fitzwilliam didn't have a lot of give to it.'

'I brought you some salad. They kindly gave me a plastic box to put it in.'

I sat up and slid my feet to the floor. The fresh vegetables smelled good. I pulled a pillow over to the desk chair and gingerly sat down to eat. 'Did you mingle successfully?'

'I suppose. My mind was only half on my business, though. The other half was occupied with our problem, and from what you say, I have the feeling we were pursuing the same line. Blood. What could blood have to do with anything, in a facility where it is present only in minute quantities, if at all?'

'Especially, what could it have to do with a student prank? And my thoughts were leading me, before I fell asleep, to vampires and zombies.'

'Very useful.' Alan's voice was arid in the extreme.

'No, but it is, actually. Or it could be. Because

90

vampires and zombies are the stuff of legend, of folklore, of superstition. Do you remember Tom mentioning that story his aunt told him, about a voodoo cult?'

'Vaguely.'

'I don't think I ever passed it along to you, but it had to do with a small West Indian community right here in Cambridge, and a man who disappeared. And there was quite a lot of blood involved, though not human blood.' I told the story as best I could remember it.

'Hmm.' Alan made one of his noncommittal, all-purpose sounds that always annoy me.

'If you don't believe me, ask Elaine.'

'I didn't say I didn't believe you. You'll admit, though, it takes a bit of believing.'

'The point is that the incidents she described did happen. You can make whatever deductions you like, but the story serves as undeniable evidence that a particular strain of superstition, or religion – or whatever you want to call it – did exist in ultra-civilized Cambridge, England, as recently as twenty years ago. Who's to say it doesn't still exist? The university brings people here from all over the world. To a certain extent, they bring their culture with them.'

'So you're suggesting that the blood you saw had to do with some religious ritual?'

'I'm not suggesting anything except a line of thought that might be worth exploring.' I impaled the last piece of cucumber and wiped my mouth free of salad dressing. 'And speaking of exploring . . .'

91

'Yes, Elaine should call soon. She was leading the master off to his fate as I left the dining room. Meanwhile, I may have a little snooze myself.'

Ten

I'd slept enough, so I picked up my abandoned book and tried to immerse myself in it. For once, though, fiction failed to capture me. The real mystery I was involved in was more interesting. I followed paths of thought down unproductive byways for quite a while, and was just wondering what on earth was keeping Elaine so long when Alan's phone rang (or whiffled, or whatever these things do). He was still snoring, so I picked it up and answered.

'Dorothy, Elaine here. I need to speak to Alan, please.'

That was odd. Why couldn't she talk to me? I nudged him awake and handed him the phone.

His end of the conversation consisted mostly of monosyllables. Finally, he said, 'Sorry, I can't. I'll explain in a bit.' He rang off.

'Can't do what?'

'Keep you out of it. There's been a crisis, love. I know nothing more than that. Elaine wants me at the Hutchins Building immediately, and she asked – no, she *told* me to have you stay here. "Where she'll be safe," she said. You heard my reply. When we get there, I'll explain that we come as a pair.'

I just looked at him for a long moment, remembering all the times in the past when he had tried to keep me out of trouble, tried to protect me, shield me, wrap me in cotton wool. He still wanted me safe – witness his insistence on not leaving me alone – but he'd learned that I needed to follow my own way.

'But get a move on, love! Whatever's happened, it's urgent.'

'Alan Nesbitt, I do love you.' I put my shoes on, reached for my hat, remembered it had met its fate, and followed Alan out the door, feeling vulnerable, like a knight without his armour.

There was a service drive leading to the side door of the Hutchins Building, the one I had blundered in on that first memorable occasion. I hadn't noticed the drive then, but now it was occupied by two cars so blandly inconspicuous that they had to belong to the police. No flashing blue lights, no markings, but somehow they looked very official. Alan and I looked at each other. 'Something very serious, then,' I murmured, and he nodded. We avoided that door and went to the imposing front one. It was locked, but Alan had barely raised his fist to knock when it opened. A uniformed constable stood aside to let us in. 'Mr and Mrs Nesbitt?'

I let that go. It was close enough.

'Superintendent Barker is waiting for you in one of the labs, sir. I'll show you the way.'

'No need, constable. We know the way. At least, if it's the zoology lab.'

'Yes, sir.'

'It would be,' I whispered. 'What *is* it about that place that makes it the focus of everything?'

Alan didn't answer, but he grasped my arm firmly. 'Thank you, constable. Carry on.'

I was glad of Alan's presence. Whatever awaited us in that ill-omened room, I wasn't at all sure I wanted to see it, but with Alan, I thought I could manage.

Prepared for almost anything, I opened the door to the lab, Alan close behind me.

What I was certainly not prepared for was nothing.

There was no blood on the floor, at least that I could see. There was no body on the floor, as I had half feared. The lab was in perfect order, its only occupants Elaine Barker, looking very official, and a man I recognized as the master of St Stephen's, who had welcomed us that first evening of the conference.

They were conversing in low tones, but they stopped and looked up as we entered. I expected Elaine to greet us, and when she did not, there was something in the quality of her silence that put me on full alert.

Alan gave my arm an encouraging squeeze and moved away from me. 'Alan Nesbitt, sir,' he said, holding his hand out to the man.

'My apologies, Alan,' said Elaine, finding her voice. 'This is Dr Robert Everidge, master of this college. I don't believe you met him earlier. Robert, Alan Nesbitt and his wife, Dorothy Martin.'

The men shook hands and murmured something polite, and even in the midst of my growing unease, I could be amused at the niceties of English manners. If the sky were falling, one would take time to introduce Chicken Little to all the others before taking cover.

Elaine continued. 'Alan, I hope I didn't sound too – er – distraught on the phone just now. The situation may not be as serious as I fear.' She paused to clear her throat and, I thought, to get firm hold of her composure. 'The fact is, however, that Tom seems to have disappeared.'

I would have burst into speech, but Alan gave me a look of warning and I managed to keep still. We waited. Elaine bit her lip and continued.

'We walked over here, Dr Everidge and Tom and I. Robert could let us into this lab, as he has a master key, and Tom has only the keys he needs for his work. There seemed to be no one else in the building.'

'Is that unusual?' I asked, after consulting Alan with raised eyebrows.

'Normal on a Sunday afternoon,' said the master. 'Even scientists do take some time away from their work, and it's a lovely day to go out on the river.'

I nodded, and Elaine went on. 'Of course, I had told Robert all that had happened, starting from your experience on the first day of the conference, Dorothy. He agreed that an investigation was in order, but preferred, as I thought he would, that we keep it private for a start. So we got into the building, and Tom said he wanted to pick up his notes from his conversation with the students. He's very methodical, you see. He'd written it all down.'

I groaned. 'And kept it in his lab, right here in this building.'

Elaine bristled a little. 'Locked up, of course. He's neither careless nor stupid.'

This time it didn't take Alan's look to keep me silent, but I couldn't stop my thought processes. Locked up, right. In a desk drawer or a filing cabinet with a lock that could, I was sure, be picked in about two seconds flat, once someone got into the lab itself.

Alan was speaking. 'I'm assuming,' he said mildly, 'that he couldn't find the notes.'

'I don't know. He didn't return.'

Oh, dear. This was not good. I still kept my mouth shut.

'You have looked for him, of course.' Alan was reverting to policeman mode.

'Robert and I searched the building. When we found no trace of him, I phoned him. No ring; apparently, he'd turned it off. By that time I was seriously concerned, so, with Robert's permission, I called in a few constables. They are trained in search procedures, as you would know, Alan. They found no trace of him, nor any indication that anyone had been subjected to force.'

'That would seem to mean, then, that he left the building voluntarily.' Alan frowned. 'Why would he do that, without letting you know? He doesn't strike me as an irresponsible young man.'

'He isn't. Not at all. He has always been most considerate. I can think of only one thing that would induce him to behave this way.'

'He was following someone, or something.' I spoke with certainty. 'He didn't want to waste time phoning you, or else he didn't want to be overheard.'

'I think so. A person, or some sort of indication. Probably a person, or he would have told us. And that unfortunately means . . .'

She lost control of her voice, and Alan finished for her. 'That means he could be in danger.'

Elaine nodded. The master frowned. 'But Elaine, would Tom do something so foolish as to pursue someone who might be . . . well, unbalanced, or even criminal? He has always struck me as a sensible sort.'

'Sensible, intelligent, yes.' Elaine was in command of herself once more. 'But he has also been, from a child, headstrong and impulsive. He's so very bright that he always thinks he knows best. He's sure that no one can do the job, whatever it is, as well as he. I have to admit that he's often right about that.'

'But not always.' Alan sounded sombre, and I realized he was speaking now not only as an experienced policeman, but as a father and grandfather who had done his share of worrying about his offspring.

'All right,' I said with a brisk assurance I didn't feel. 'Let's think logically about this. If Tom decided to follow someone, who might it be?'

Elaine looked a bit cross. 'Someone he thinks is involved in this series of peculiar events, of course.'

'Yes, that's a given, but I mean, who would that be? One of the other students, right?'

'We don't know that.' Elaine was frowning now.

'We don't know anything,' I retorted, 'but we can make a reasonable guess. Tom thought from the beginning that we were dealing with a student prank gone wrong. When he began talking about pranks to some of his fellow students the other day, he got a reaction, though he wasn't sure where it came from. What are the odds that he saw one of those students doing something suspicious and decided to follow him to see if he couldn't learn something?'

'Something suspicious,' said Alan in flat tones. 'What, for example?'

'How would I know? To me, a non-scientist, almost anything anyone would do around this building could look suspicious. But suppose . . . suppose one of the students working in the plant sciences, like Tom with photosynthesis, was doing something with a lab animal – a rat or whatever. Wouldn't that look a little strange?'

'Unless they were playing with it.' Alan was, it seemed, determined to play the sceptic.

I shuddered. 'Perish the thought. Play with a rat – ugh! And I don't think lab rats are meant to be played with. Anyway, that was just an example. I don't know enough of what goes on around here to know what might be suspicious. What we need to do – that is, if you agree, Elaine – what I suggest we do is find a student who is absolutely to be trusted, and take him, or her, into our confidence. We could find out more about what work is going on here, and perhaps who's doing what, and that might lead us to Tom. Does that sound reasonable?'

Alan grimaced. 'There's one big, obvious flaw.'

'Exactly,' said Elaine. 'How do we know what student might be perfectly trustworthy? Tom would know, but . . .'

99

'I have a suggestion,' said the master, clearing his throat. 'Perhaps you've forgotten, Elaine, if you ever knew, but a young friend of mine is one of the students here. An undergraduate. Brilliant boy, with a good future in the offing. His name is Terence Faherty, and he is, in fact' – more throat-clearing – 'looking to be my son-in-law once he has taken his degree and found a job.'

Alan and I exchanged glances. I knew we were thinking the same thing. If we'd gone to this man at the very beginning, instead of taking feeble stabs at solving the problem ourselves, we might have had all the answers long before now.

Elaine was plainly thinking the same thing. 'Oh, Lord, Robert, I did know about Terence, but I had forgotten. Stupid, stupid, stupid. Do you happen to know where he's to be found just now?'

The master allowed a small smile to break through his concern. 'Given that it's a fine Sunday afternoon, my guess would be on the river. With my daughter. Shall we?'

'Perhaps we could simply phone him,' Elaine suggested. 'I really do want to find Tom as soon as possible.'

'My wife tried to phone him this morning, to invite him to dinner tomorrow. He seems to have forgotten to charge his phone, not for the first time, and Jennifer has mislaid hers, also not for the first time. I understand your anxiety, Elaine, but I truly think searching the river is the quickest way at this point.'

It should have been a lovely stroll to the Cam. St Stephen's is not on the river, but many of the

100

older colleges are, and the presence of Dr Everidge would have given us access to the boat landings normally off limits to the public. But we were in a hurry, and I was in no shape for a walk. We all piled into Alan's car, drove as close as we could to the public landing near Trinity College and walked the rest of the way. Leaning heavily on Alan's arm, I felt like an old lady, and was consequently in no sweet temper by the time we arrived at the boats.

Or, rather, boat. A solitary punt was floating at the dock, or whatever the landing place was called. It was very low, the seats a bare few inches above the floor of the boat. The deck, I suppose. I looked at Alan. 'I can't possibly get into that thing,' I said. 'And even if I could, I couldn't sit. My knees won't bend that much. I'll have to wait here for you.'

But the boatman wasn't about to let a customer get away. 'Ah, madam, I have the perfect solution.' From some recess behind him he produced a miniature chair, rather like the booster seats restaurants sometimes provide for children. 'We'll put you just here, in front of me, where you can see everything in perfect comfort. If these gallant gentlemen will assist me . . .'

And before I could protest further, I found myself more or less lifted into the punt and seated on what was, amazingly, quite a comfortable perch. 'Now, you'll want to hold on to the gunwales – the sides of the boat, madam. You're sitting above the usual level, and if some lout were to bump us – you see?'

Alan seated himself next to me. What with the extra width of my chair, it was a tight fit for his

101

solid bulk, but he managed. 'I'll keep her safe and secure,' he said, reaching up to take my hand.

My ruffled dignity was somewhat eased. It was plain I wasn't the first feeble old lady he had transported. 'Onward and upward, then,' I said. 'Excelsior!'

Elaine and Dr Everidge took their places at the front of the boat. Before the boatman pushed off, the master said, 'Unfortunately, we're not here entirely for pleasure today.'

'No, Dr Everidge, sir?'

The 'small world' phenomenon again. Plainly, the boatman was a student, or a former student, and knew the bigwigs of the colleges.

The master took it in his stride. 'No, we're looking for a pair of students, Terence Faherty and my daughter, Jennifer. Do you know them?'

He shook his head. 'I don't know many of the students who are up now. I took my degree several years ago. We'll just head up the river, shall we, and see if you can spot them?'

He pushed away from the landing place and began to pole the boat slowly upstream. It looked so easy; all the same, I wouldn't have wanted to be standing there on the flat back of the boat, steering around the heavy traffic with nothing but his long pole – and his own weight, I suppose – for navigation.

'You have a degree from one of the colleges here?' I asked.

'And what am I doing punting tourists for a living? It's a reasonable question.'

'Oh, dear, I didn't mean it that way.' But I had, I realized. 'How very rude of me. I'm sorry.'

'Don't be. I often wonder myself. The truth is I read philosophy at King's. Although I scan the adverts every day, there are very few openings for philosophers.'

'And yet you stay here in Cambridge.'

He shoved off a punt that was ready to collide with ours, with a word or two to the boatman (in this case, a woman), and poled a few yards farther up the river before he answered. 'Yes, I stay here, doing odd jobs and still dreaming of real employment. I've not been giving you a proper tour, because Dr Everidge knows it all, and you've other things to think about. But look about you, and then ask yourself why I stay.'

I looked. There, drifting past in utter serenity, was the incomparable King's College Chapel. Across the river, a swathe of green looked like a bit of a child's brand-new paint box. Overhead, the pale blue sky was rimmed with the bright new leaves of willows. We passed under a footbridge so beautiful it brought a lump to my throat. Everywhere, the sound of laughter vied with spring birdsong. For a little while I could forget the urgency of our errand. I had to clear my throat before saying, 'Yes, I see why you stay. Even if it means surviving on beans on toast for a while longer.'

'And beer. Don't forget the beer. Yes, sir?'

Dr Everidge pointed, and my nerves tightened again. 'Can you put in here for a moment?'

'Only for a moment, sir. I'm not allowed to moor on college grounds, and that proctor is giving me the evil eye.'

A woman in a billowing academic gown was,

in fact, walking purposefully along the riverbank, bearing down upon our punt.

'Don't worry,' said Dr Everidge. 'Er – what is your name, by the way?'

'Denton, sir. Sam Denton.'

'Good afternoon, madam,' he said to the approaching proctor. 'I'm sure you won't mind if my friend Sam allows us to stop here for a moment. The fact is I want a word with my daughter, and I believe I see her just through there.'

'Of course, Dr Everidge,' said the proctor icily. 'He mustn't tie up, mind.'

'Certainly not.' If he had been wearing a hat, he would have doffed it. The proctor stalked off, furious at being deprived of her lawful prey, and I was reminded of the hapless proctor in Sayers's *Gaudy Night*. That was set in Oxford, and in the 1930s – almost another world – but some things remain the same.

Sam jumped out and held the boat steady, since there was in fact no place to tie up, even if he had been inclined to ignore the regulation. The other three scrambled out; I stayed where I was. I wanted to hear what the master's prospective son-in-law had to say, but there was no way I was getting out of that rocky boat.

The pair who had caught the master's eye were sitting on a bench by a green lawn. College buildings loomed in the background. I didn't know which college, nor did I care. This boy might hold the key to all the distressing events of the past few days. I waited impatiently for everyone to come back.

They were too far away and there was too much background noise for me to hear what they were saying, but it was plain from the body language that they were not eager to abandon their leisurely Sunday afternoon pursuits. However, the boy needed to be deferential to his fiancée's father, and the girl was being pleasant enough about it. The little group walked down to the riverbank.

Although dressed in the universal student grunge, the young couple were both attractive. The boy, even if his name had been Joe Smith, still could have been nothing but Irish, with abundant dark hair, a ruggedly handsome face, deep blue eyes, and the kind of light, clear complexion that any girl would kill for. The girl was slim and lithe, and as tall as her companion. Her soft, fine brown hair blew about her face in the slight breeze, flirting with her little upturned nose.

They were near enough now that I could hear.

'Our punt's moored along there,' said the boy, pointing upriver. 'I'd better go and get it and then join you at your landing.'

'I'd rather you came with us,' said Dr Everidge firmly. 'You can fetch your boat later. We'll all fit in if you don't mind close quarters.'

I doubted that the two young people would mind close quarters.

Eleven

'Now, Terence,' began Dr Everidge when we were all settled and on our way back down the river, 'we seem to have misplaced one of our students.'

'My nephew, Tom Grenfell,' put in Elaine. She didn't quite succeed in keeping the tension out of her voice. 'You know him, I think.'

'Yes, of course. Not well, though. I'm only in my second year, you know, and he's working towards his doctorate. What do you mean, you've misplaced him?'

'He met us at one of the labs today and went to his office to fetch some papers, and didn't return. He sent no message, and we have been unable to reach him by phone. We hoped you might have some idea where to find him.'

Terence was facing me at the other end of the boat. I could see that he was bewildered. 'I don't really know him enough about him even to guess, Mrs – er, Ms—'

'Barker. Elaine Barker.'

Neither Terence nor Miss Everidge – Jennifer – showed any recognition of the name. Well, when I was their age, I certainly didn't know the name of the chief of police in my small Indiana town. One usually doesn't, unless one has been the victim, or the perpetrator, of a crime. I was finding it hard not to explain the whole situation to Terence, but Sam's presence made that impossible. I wished I had an oar so I could speed the boat a trifle.

However, progress down the river was quicker than up, especially as, with the afternoon wearing on and the air taking on a distinct chill, many of the punts had left the water, allowing Sam to steer a straight path to his landing place.

I had a hard time getting out of the boat, even with strong arms to help. My knees had stiffened in the confined quarters, and my various bruises were all screaming. Why is it, I thought resentfully when I finally landed safely on my feet, that Miss Marple never seemed to have any of these troubles? She was at least as old as I. And stayed that age for many years.

I hobbled to the car. Without any discussion, Elaine and young Terence climbed in with Alan and me, leaving Dr Everidge and his daughter to walk back to the college.

'All right, Terence. You're wondering what this is all about, and why we dragged you away from your pleasant afternoon with your girl. My name is Dorothy Martin, by the way, and this is my husband, Alan Nesbitt. We're staying in St Stephen's for a conference.'

The light began to dawn on Terence's face. 'A police conference. I've seen the signs. Are you all with the police, then?'

'I am,' said Elaine, not mentioning her rank. 'Mr Nesbitt is a retired chief constable, and Mrs Martin is' – she hesitated for a moment – 'has been deputized for a special problem. It concerns St Stephen's, and particularly my nephew and others in the biological sciences.'

'I *told* them!' Terence began, and then shut his mouth firmly.

'Yes. Exactly. I can understand that you have no wish to betray your friends, but this has become a police matter, and I'm afraid I have to ask you to tell us what you know about any . . . er . . . unusual activities recently at the Hutchins Building.'

I turned around, wincing, to look at the boy. His face had taken on that blank aspect that I knew so well from my years in the classroom. I had taught sixth-graders, but the 'I don't know nothin', I ain't sayin' nothin'' expression doesn't change with added years. I said, 'Terence, we do understand. But you need to know this. Tom Grenfell is missing and may be in great danger. I myself was subject to a painful attack yesterday, perhaps intended to be murderous. We *must* get to the bottom of this, and the sooner the better. If you can help at all, I hope you will.'

It hung in the balance. If Terence hadn't been engaged to the daughter of the master of his college, he might have held out. But he was, so his personal as well as his academic future was at risk.

'Oh, hell!' he said at last. 'Yeah, OK, I'll tell you what I know. But could we go someplace besides the college? I wouldn't want . . .'

'To be seen talking to the police,' Elaine finished. 'I understand. Alan, could you find a place to park? Go on, Terence.'

Alan said, 'Just a moment, Terence. I think it will be useful if my wife tells you what she knows about this affair. It's her story, for the most part,

108

although it certainly has wider implications.' He headed the car out of the city centre and found, by some miracle, a place to stop and talk.

I concentrated on remembering accurately. 'It began on the day we arrived at St Stephen's – last Wednesday. Alan took off for the conference rooms, and I got lost looking for him and ended up in the Hutchins Building, in one of the labs.'

'Oh! So it was you . . .' His voice trailed off.

'So you do know something about that. You know what I found there?'

'I've heard rumours,' he said cautiously. 'Tom was asking questions in the break room, you know.'

'Yes, I do know. At least, he wasn't exactly asking questions, was he?'

'No, he was skating around it, but we were all pretty sure what he was talking about.'

'We were afraid of that,' said Alan with a sigh. 'He may not be quite a subtle as he likes to think.'

'Fool boy!' said Elaine explosively. 'Sorry.'

'Yes. Well. I suppose you know that it began as a student prank. There've been some good ones in Cambridge over the years, but nothing really memorable lately. And we're all scientists, and reasonably bright, so we wanted to do something scientific, not just something stupid like what's been done before. So, as we're in the biological sciences, we thought of perhaps doing something pretty spectacular along the lines of bringing the dead to life.'

'I'd have thought,' said Alan mildly, 'that sort of thing would be more appropriate to one of the theological colleges.'

109

Terence flushed. I'd have bet that he did that easily, with that almost transparent skin, and that he hated it. 'It wouldn't have been real, you know. We thought we'd use a lab animal. We could concoct something that would make the rat or guinea pig seem dead. No vital signs at all.'

'Shades of *Romeo and Juliet*,' I murmured.

Terence flushed again. 'You mean, it's all been done before. But that was just a sleeping draught, and fictional. Juliet would have had a pulse – slow, perhaps, but detectable. Anyone with any sense would have seen through the ruse, even if she was in a tomb. This, though, would really have worked. At least, we thought it would. We've come up with a chemical that puts the animal in such a deep coma that there isn't a heartbeat, or not one that can be heard or felt. We thought we'd put him in a cooler for a while so he'd feel cold to the touch, and for realism we'd fake some sort of injury and splash some blood around.'

'Blood,' I said, suppressing a shudder.

'Where were you planning to get the blood?' Elaine sounded a lot like a suspicious Rottweiler.

'Make it, of course! It wouldn't be real blood. Kensington Gore isn't that hard to make, and it's very realistic. But . . .' He wound down again.

'But something went wrong,' I said. 'What I saw . . . and smelled . . .' This time I couldn't stop the shudder.

'Yes. The smell. That doesn't matter on the stage, and obviously not in the movies. But up close, someone would notice. So one of the students, a guy named Mahala, wanted to use chicken's blood. He knew where he could get a chicken. He's from West Africa somewhere, and they sometimes—'

'Use chicken's blood in their religious rituals,' I said. 'Am I right?'

'If that's what you call it,' said Terence dubiously. 'He told me a bit about it, and it doesn't seem much like religion to me.'

'You're Catholic, of course.'

He nodded.

I thought fleetingly about getting into a discussion about the Mass, and the Body and Blood of Christ, but instantly dismissed the thought. This wasn't the time for abstract theology. 'So your friend brought a chicken to the lab,' I prompted.

'He said he would. I wasn't very happy about that. Fake blood is one thing. Killing a real chicken, just for the sake of a prank . . . I'm a vegetarian, you see. I don't believe in killing animals for food, or any other reason, really. So when he said he couldn't get the chicken, and brought a cat to the lab instead—'

'A cat!' Alan and I spoke together. 'But that's insufferable,' I said. 'He killed a cat?'

'I don't know,' said Terence. 'That's when I told them I would have nothing more to do with the project. I guess in his country cats are nothing, but I like cats. Even a chicken was bad enough, but a cat . . . I like cats,' he repeated, with a slight air of apology. In this Sceptred Isle, the dog is the reigning species, followed closely by the horse. Cats are pleasant enough creatures, but less highly regarded than their canine and equine friends. Alan and I – and, apparently, Terence – feel differently.

'Did you do anything to stop it?' Elaine was growling again.

'Actually, I . . . I tried to steal the cat and set it free. Mahala had brought it in a cage, and I thought it would be easy to let it out. But I couldn't find even the cage. I don't know what he did with it, or with the cat. And I don't actually know anything about the blood in the lab. Except when I heard about it . . .'

I swallowed hard, hoping I wasn't going to be sick.

'When did you try to find the cat?' Elaine's tone had moderated a bit.

'What's today? Sunday? It would have been sometime last week. Tuesday night, that was it. Because I worked late that day in the lab, and was almost the last person to leave the building. When I'd seen the cat, it was in its cage in the break room. That door is never locked, so when I left the lab, I went in and looked everywhere. The cage wasn't there. I couldn't get into any of the other labs, of course, but I did just look in the animal rooms – where they're kept, you know – and the lecture rooms. No cage, no cat. So I thought perhaps Mahala'd thought better of the whole thing and taken the beast home, or wherever he found it. But then . . .'

'So we still don't know the source of the blood in the lab,' said Alan. 'It's a great pity it was cleaned up before it could be tested. However, that can wait. What's important now is to find Tom Grenfell. Terence, this is what we're thinking. We had planned a conference, since the attack on my wife had made this officially a matter for the police, and we wanted to poke around the place, see what we could find, plan a strategy.'

'Wait. The attack on your wife. You've said that before? What attack? When?'

'Yesterday,' I said. 'I was pushed down the stairs at the Fitzwilliam. That doesn't matter now. Go ahead, Alan.'

'It does matter, though, not only because you were hurt, but because it was what finally made an investigation possible. As I said, we were all to meet – Superintendent Barker, Dr Everidge, Tom, my wife and I – at the Hutchins Building. Tom came quite some time before Dorothy and I got there. He told the others he was going to his own lab, to pick up some notes he had made about the matter. He didn't come back, nor did he answer his phone. He couldn't be found after a thorough search of the building, so we tried to work out where he might be. It was my wife who suggested that he might have seen someone doing something suspicious and followed him – or her, of course. We'd like your reaction to that, as well as any leads you could give us. What, and whom, might he have seen?'

Terence's face had turned even paler than normal. 'I don't know. He couldn't have got into any labs except his own, unless someone was working there. Most of the doors have small windows, you know, but they're really only big enough to see if the lights are on, unless you move up quite close. And from the zoology lab to his – you met him in the lab where everything's been happening?'

Elaine nodded.

'From there to his, on the first floor, there's nothing much to see. He's at the end of a corridor, and the rooms on either side are lecture rooms or storage rooms. I can't think what he could have seen that would send him haring off like that.'

'The window!' I said suddenly. 'He showed us his lab one day, and his door doesn't have a window it in, but the room itself does. What's the view from there? What could he have seen?'

'Let me think. It's at the end of the first floor, over a side door. He could have seen someone walking to the building, I suppose, though nobody much comes on a Sunday afternoon, except to tend the animals. They have to be fed regularly, of course.'

I wasn't paying attention. 'Or,' I said, 'he could have seen someone leaving. Maybe with something he shouldn't have had.'

'Like,' said Elaine, 'an animal cage.'

'The cat!' Terence was excited.

'Alive – or not,' said Alan.

Twelve

'Mahala!' said Terence.

'Where would he have gone?' asked Elaine urgently.

'I don't know where he lives. Here in town somewhere, not in college.'

'His address will be on record at the college.'

'Wait a minute,' I said. 'Did Tom know about the cat?'

'I don't know. Or wait. He didn't seem to know anything about the proposed prank, that day in the common room.'

'He did or he didn't,' said Elaine, 'but Mahala and the cat seem to be our only leads at the moment. Let's find Mahala.' She called Dr Everidge. 'He'll find Mahala's address and meet us at the college gates. It may take him a few minutes. The staff isn't in on a Sunday, so he'll either have to search the office himself or call someone in.'

We were silent. I could feel Elaine's frustration at further delay. 'Will he get a phone number, too?'

'I don't know if Mahala has a phone,' said Terence. 'I know he doesn't have a mobile. He's very poor.'

So much for that.

We waited at the college gates for only a few minutes, but each one passed like an hour. We had stopped in an area where lingering was clearly prohibited, and only the presence of the superintendent of police kept us from being ticketed. At last Dr Everidge came out, almost running.

'I left my car at my lodge. This was quicker. Can we all fit?'

'I can get out, sir. That is, unless I'm still needed.'

'You stay where you are, Terence. I want you to identify Mahala for me. I have a vague idea who he is, but I want to be sure.'

His home turned out to be a cottage on the outskirts of town, at the end of one of the bus lines. It was the sort that tourists find pretty and quaint, thatched roof and all, but there were signs of neglect and dilapidation. The garden was full of weeds and some trash, and I was willing to bet that the plumbing left a great deal to be desired. The whole place looked unloved and, indeed, deserted.

'I don't think anyone's at home.' Elaine was the one who said it, but we all felt it.

'Stay here,' said Alan in his policeman voice. I was happy to comply. I didn't care for the house or the neighbourhood, and I wasn't eager to deal with someone who might have killed a cat.

'I don't see a cage,' said Elaine.

I didn't know if that was a good or a bad sign, and made no reply.

It took Alan only a few minutes to check the house and return to the car. 'How recent was that address?' he asked Dr Everidge.

'It could date back about eighteen or nineteen

116

months, when he began his studies at St Stephen's. Or actually when he was accepted as a student, which would have been some time before term began.'

'It is certainly no longer valid. There is no furniture in the house, one of the back windows is broken, and I saw a squirrel in what must have been the larder. No one has lived here for some time.'

And that took us firmly back to square one. We looked at each other blankly for a moment. Then Elaine opened the door and levered herself out of the crowded back seat. 'Neighbours,' she said, and strode off towards the next house.

Alan shook his head. 'It's worth a try, but I doubt a woman – and a white woman at that – will get much change out of the people around here. A young black constable would have better odds, I believe.'

'I could try,' said Terence. 'I'm young and male, at least.'

'No,' we said in chorus.

'You keep forgetting, Terence,' I added, 'I think we *all* keep forgetting, that was real blood I saw. We're almost certainly dealing with a killer, perhaps of a cat, not a person, but at least someone whose respect for life is somewhat questionable. We don't know for sure that it's Mahala, but it isn't wise for you, who know him, to go talking to his neighbours, who might well be a lot more sympathetic to him than to you.'

'Then let me go and talk to his friends. Or at least his fellow students. He doesn't have many friends at the college. He's sort of . . . odd.'

'You know where they'd be?' I asked.

'I know their favourite pub. At this hour on a Sunday, most of them are there; I'd put money on it.'

Alan and I looked at each other. Dr Everidge said, 'That's an excellent idea. As soon as the superintendent comes back, shall we all go?'

'I'm going to beg off, if it's OK with the rest of you,' I said. 'The day's gotten away from us, and I don't think I'm good for much more.'

Alan gave my hand an understanding squeeze.

It would be fruitless to describe our wait for Elaine. She was thorough; I gave her that. We sat in the car wishing we could think of something more productive to do and, in my case, wishing I could take a hot shower and a nap to ease the growing discomfort of my abused body. 'I'm getting too old for this,' I murmured once to Alan.

'You'll never be old,' he replied. Which was sweet, but didn't make my bruises feel any better.

When Elaine came back, it was to report about as much success as we had expected. 'Not much joy,' she said briefly. 'The closest neighbours agree that no one has lived here for months, but they can't, or won't, say how long, or where the former residents might have moved to. No one stays here long if they can get away was the general feeling. I must say, I can understand. Nevertheless, they know something. It may or may not be relevant, but I'm going to send a constable out. There's a young man, new on the force, who's terribly keen. His parents are from Nigeria. He might be able to glean a few answers.

Meanwhile, if we can't find Tom soon, I'm going to have to call his mother. I'm not looking forward to that.'

'You've tried calling him again.' It wasn't really a question. Of course she had.

She just nodded. 'He never turns off his phone. He lives by that thing. He lost it once and nearly went mad. Something's wrong, or he'd answer.'

Of course, that jollied up everyone's spirits no end.

We told her our plans for the pub. 'I'll drop you on the way back to the college,' Alan told Everidge. 'I need to get this woman to bed.' And then he heard how that sounded, and that lightened the mood a little.

We dropped them as close to the pub as we could get – it was in one of the little pedestrian passages near the Market Square – and went back to St Stephen's, which was beginning to feel very much like home. Once I'd taken an ibuprofen and Alan had me settled more or less comfortably, he stood, irresolute. 'I don't know what's best. Tonight's the last official session of the conference,' he said. 'Dinner is formal, and there's a panel discussion afterwards, in which I'm meant to participate. I've been among the missing for so much of the time, I really should go. But I'm almost as worried about young Tom as Elaine is, and I might be able to steer a pub conversation in a useful direction. What do you think?'

'When is the dinner?'

'Drinks at six thirty, dinner at seven.'

'That leaves over an hour. You could go to the

119

pub, see what you can find out, and still get back in time to dress.'

'And you? Are you up for dinner?'

'Not a long formal one with speeches. Let me just lie here and veg for a while, and you can bring me a sandwich or something.'

'Try not to worry too much, dear heart. There's nothing either of us can do just now for Tom, so put it out of your mind if you can. Elaine's doing all she can.'

'Can she call in the forensics people now? To the lab, I mean.'

Alan sighed. 'If it were my call, I'd send them in. There are too many unexplained incidents clustering around that lab, and Tom's disappearance is very serious. And we still don't know what we're dealing with – a prank or something much more serious. But Elaine's position is difficult, with the political balance to be taken into account.'

'You had a university to contend with, when you were policing Belleshire.'

'The University of Sherebury, my dear American, is a fine institution, but it's hardly Cambridge. One treads lightly in this country when dealing with a world-famous establishment that's been around since the thirteenth century.' And seeing the expression on my face, he added, 'Isn't that one of the reasons you love England? Our respect for ancient traditions and foundations?'

'I suppose. Alan, go away and leave me in peace. At the moment I'm thoroughly sick and tired of this ancient foundation.'

I do get testy on the rare occasions when I

don't feel good. Alan patted my hand and quietly left the room.

As the pill began to work, I relaxed a little. Ever since my tumble down those unyielding marble stairs, I'd been feeling like an old crock, which is unusual for me. True, in years I'm getting up there, but I try to stay active, and most of the time I feel about twenty years younger than my birth certificate indicates. It's all a matter of attitude.

Very well, then. My attitude needed some adjustment. For a start, I needed to figure out why I was floundering so in this investigation.

I let my mind relax into free fall, let thoughts and ideas waft around, making no attempt to organize or make sense of them. Ancient institution. Discretion. Danger. Blood. Pain. Danger. Cats. Occult religions. Danger.

Was I letting the memory of blood, the fear of danger, keep me from accomplishing anything?

No. I sat up straight, and then lay back down as my bruises objected. No, it wasn't fear that had put me in a straitjacket. It was that damnable discretion.

I'm a great admirer of Dorothy L. Sayers, and my very favourite of her novels is *Gaudy Night*. Her semi-autobiographical character Harriet Vane is asked to investigate a series of nasty practical jokes at Shrewsbury College, Oxford (based on Sayers's own college of Somerville). As the incidents get uglier and uglier, Vane becomes more and more impatient with the wishes of the college administration that the matter be kept under wraps, for the sake of the college reputation. She understands and to some extent sympathizes – it's her college, after all, and she has no wish to bring it into disrepute – but she chafes under the restrictions.

I could understand the problem here, too. In the long run, though, I thought St Stephen's would suffer more if it became known that they had covered up criminal activity. Furthermore, this wasn't my college, but the bruises and nightmarish memories were mine.

Something else was knocking around in my brain, seeking admission. I tried to focus and couldn't bring it to the front. I closed my eyes. Maybe if I let it alone, it would appear.

College. Sayers. Vane. Blood.

Aha! I sat straight up again, regardless of the aches and pains. In another of Sayers's books, *Have His Carcase*, Harriet Vane found a corpse with its throat cut, apparently very recently dead, with blood dripping all over the place. A huge part of the investigation focussed on the time of the murder, trusting in Harriet's firm statement that the blood had not clotted.

Wouldn't that be a big flaw in any plan to use real blood for the students' prank? It would clot almost immediately, wouldn't it?

Or was there something that could be added to the blood to keep it liquid, at least long enough to play the joke?

Certainly the blood I'd seen had looked to be liquid, but I had been too squeamish to go near enough to see.

I added these questions to the many I needed to ask somebody very soon. Making up my mind, I got up and headed for the shower.

When Alan returned, he found me struggling into the 'little black dress' that is my standard dressy travel attire. Made of some miracle fabric that refuses to wrinkle, it fits in such a way as to cover a multitude of sins and can be dressed up or down with scarves and jewellery. Someday it's going to wear out, and I shall be bereft.

'Oh, good. Help me with this, will you, Alan? My bruises scream if I bend my arms enough to get into the blasted thing.'

He pulled it over my head and gave me an approving pat. 'You've changed your mind about dinner, then?'

'And drinks. Did you learn anything useful at the pub?'

He was shrugging out of his shirt. 'Nothing to the point. Terence is still at it, but it's slow going. Some of Tom's friends are there, but since we don't know who might be involved in his disappearance, we have to be careful about how much we tell them.' He headed for the bathroom.

'I'll get your dinner things out,' I said, trailing after him. 'And, Alan, you'll be annoyed with me, but I've made a decision.'

'And that is?' He turned on the shower.

'I'm going to dive into this investigation with both feet. I'm past caring how many toes get stepped on in the process. Whatever is going on has to stop!'

He didn't respond until he'd completed his very quick ablutions. 'Then you'll be happy to know,' he said, drying off, 'that Elaine and the master have agreed on the same course of action. Elaine is at the Hutchins Building even as we speak, with her minions, doing a thorough forensic search of that laboratory. Where's my hairbrush?'

I handed it to him.

'And the constable she mentioned,' he went on, 'the Nigerian, has been dispatched to question Mahala's neighbours. Tom's disappearance has galvanized her into action. The master is going to make a little speech about it at dinner, asking for cooperation from all police forces.'

'And high time, too!' I was relieved that I wasn't going to have to quarrel with Alan. 'Now, I'm going to wear this lacy sort of jacket thing with this. Do you think pearls with it, or shall I trot out your lovely diamonds?'

By which he understood that I had got over my resentment of his condescending remark about Americans. He gave me a peck on the cheek, and I searched my luggage for my jewel case.

Alan seldom wore his dinner jacket. English social customs have become much more informal than they once were. In his youth, Alan had told me, black tie was *de rigueur* for any evening occasions that did not require top hat and tails. Now most men wore ordinary suits in the evening, but I was delighted that he was dressing up for once. He looked perfectly splendid when he had fastened the last stud and tied the tie. I told him so, and he preened a little.

'Are you sure you can walk as far as the dining hall?' He held the door for me as we left the room. 'I could probably scare up a wheelchair somewhere.'

'Don't you dare! I've been feeling old, and a wheelchair would be the last straw. No, I'll get there on my own two feet if it kills me. We can go slowly and pretend we're admiring the college grounds.'

They were worth admiring, actually. Even in the few days since we had arrived, the trees had burst into full bloom, and the flower beds were rioting with all sorts of spring colours. At a slow pace, with Alan giving me plenty of support, I actually enjoyed the walk. Once we arrived, Alan found me a comfortable chair and brought me a watered-down glass of bourbon. I gave it a dubious look.

'Because you're on painkillers, love. Mild ones, but it's not a brilliant idea to add too much alcohol to the mix.'

'Oh, you're right, I suppose.' I looked around the room. It seemed to me that the ranks had thinned a bit. 'Do we have some teetotallers in the group?' I asked.

'What? Oh, I shouldn't think so. Anyway there's tonic and orange juice. No, I believe some of those from far-flung districts have left already, perhaps needing to be at their desks bright and early tomorrow morning.'

I nodded. 'And Elaine doesn't seem to be here.'

'Still over at the lab, darling. But steel yourself. In her stead, here comes Andrews.'

I took a quick gulp of bourbon and looked up with a beaming smile. 'Mr Andrews! How lovely to see you! I'm afraid I haven't been able to attend very many of the conference events. I hope it's been successful for you?'

'Er – yes. Mrs Nesbitt, I need a word with you.'
I upped the wattage of the smile a trifle and
gave a coy little giggle. 'Oh, dear, you must have
me confused with Alan's first wife. He was a
widower when I met him, you know. Did you
ever know Helen? I understand she was a lovely
woman. I do feel so lucky to have found Alan
after I lost my own dear first husband. Have you
a family, Mr Andrews?'

'Yes. Now, about this trouble you're stirring
up—'

'Oh, how nice. Children?'

'Three sons, grown now. I must tell you—'

'Oh, but how wonderful. My first husband and
I were never able to have any children, and we
so wanted them. That means, of course, that I
don't have the blessing of grandchildren of my
own, but I've become honorary grandmother to
Alan's, and I do enjoy them so much. Everyone
says that the joy of grandchildren is worth every
moment of the problems and worries of raising
children, but I'm lucky enough to have the one
without ever having suffered through the other.
I'm sure you agree?'

'My grandchildren live in New Zealand, Mrs
Nesbitt. I have seen the oldest only once, the
others never. You must understand, madam—'

'Ladies and gentlemen, your attention, please.
May I have your attention, please?'

The chief constable continued to talk, in a
hoarse undertone, but I made a pretty shushing
gesture and shifted in my chair so my back was
to him, my attention directed towards the speaker
at the front of the room.

126

It was the chairman of the conference. 'In a moment we'll go into dinner, ladies and gentlemen, and a splendid dinner it is, I assure you. However, before we go in, Dr Everidge, Master of St Stephen's, wishes a word with us. Dr Everidge.'

He was wearing full academic robes. With their rich colours, he eclipsed the sombre black and white of the other men in the room. He wanted to impress the group, and he did.

'I regret that I have been unable, since your conference began, to give it the attention I would have liked. I repeat now my delight that such a distinguished assemblage has honoured St Stephen's with your conference, and I hope very sincerely that your time here has been both pleasant and productive. But it is on another subject – a distressing one – that I speak to you this evening. With such illustrious representatives of our police forces gathered together, I cannot help but enlist your aid.'

He leaned towards us to emphasize the importance of what he was about to say. 'I'm sorry to say, ladies and gentlemen, that one of our students here at St Stephen's has disappeared today under disquieting circumstances. We have tried without success to find him. I fully understand that there are rules about the designation "missing person" and that the disappearance of this young man does not fall under those rubrics. But because of various recent events, I believe that it is truly urgent that we find him as soon as possible, and I am asking your aid in doing so.

'I've prepared a summary of the circumstances I mention. I've given your chairman enough

127

copies for each of you, and I hope you'll take them with you when you leave St Stephen's, and will exert whatever efforts you can in our aid. I am aware that there will be a certain amount of unpleasant publicity for the college when some of this news becomes public. It can't be helped. I know that you are all concerned with the interaction between the police and the community, and I trust you to do what you can to minimize the talk, but lives are more important than reputations. I will deal with whatever arises. Now, please accept my heartfelt thanks, my apologies for intruding on what should be a festive occasion for you all, and my wishes for a splendid evening.'

There was a startled hush when he'd finished, and then a movement towards the chairman, who started handing out the sheets of paper. I was a little startled at the prompt response.

'They're the police, love,' Alan reminded me quietly. 'They're trained to deal with crises, and most of them love their work. They'll want to get on this right away.'

Chief Constable Andrews was still at my side, looking as though someone had smacked him with a two-by-four. I smiled again. 'But, Mr Andrews, I kept interrupting you. I'm so sorry. You were saying?'

Thirteen

'You should have been a speaker at the conference, love,' said Alan in an undertone as we headed for the dining hall. 'You handled Andrews beautifully!'

'It's a good thing Dr Everidge spoke when he did. I was running out of things to drivel on about. Wasn't his face priceless, though, when the master took the wind out of his sails?'

Our meal was superb, but I didn't pay it the attention I should have. I was plotting my actions the minute we had finished eating. I was going to the Hutchins Building to help Elaine search.

Alan couldn't come with me. He explained that he really had to stay for the closing panel. 'I'm by way of being one of their star turns, you see. And then I want to pop over to the pub again and see if Terence has come up with any bright ideas. I may be late getting back.'

'I understand. I'll be fine, as long as Elaine and some of her minions are there, too. Now that I don't have to fret about stepping on anyone's toes, I can wander where I want and poke into anything I like.'

'Bearing in mind, always, the rules about disturbing evidence.'

I just gave him a look.

It wasn't so easy to get away after dinner. Dr

Everidge had named Alan and me in his handout, and too many of the conferees wanted to ask us about what had happened. The questions were to the point, and we were glad they wanted to help, but I was glad when the chairman finally herded the last of the stragglers into the conference room and I was free to go.

Alan had asked – well, had bribed – one of the servers, a student, to go with me. I chafed under the restriction, but it was probably wise. Our progress was slow. I still couldn't walk without some pain, and sitting through dinner on a straight chair hadn't helped, but I had taken took another couple of pills and forged ahead. I did wonder for a moment what happened if one took too many ibuprofen, and then decided to stop wondering. I had more important things on my mind. Like whose blood I'd seen, and where Tom and Mahala were.

I was glad to see a constable still at the door, keeping people out. He had been given orders to admit me, though. 'Superintendent Barker would like to see you, madam. She's in the zoology laboratory.'

Of course. Where else? I sent my student escort on his way with thanks and went to the lab.

The room was a scene of purposeful activity. Figures in white suits and booties were doing mysterious things to various surfaces, including the floor. I stopped in the doorway, and Elaine came to join me.

My first question was 'Any word from Tom?' She shook her head.

'We'll hear soon,' I said, meaninglessly. Elaine

rightly ignored me, and I hurried on. 'Have your people found anything yet?'

'We won't know for certain until they get back to the lab – the police lab – with samples. Certainly they found traces of blood in various locations, including the floor, but until it's analyzed there's no telling what it means. Animal blood is used in research here.'

I nodded. 'You know what the master told us all tonight?'

'He told me what he was going to say. None too soon.'

'Indeed. Everyone was most interested. I don't know if anything will come of it, but at least now we're free to investigate as we will. I've come to ask your permission to roam around the building and see what I can find, if anything. I'm not trained in search procedures, of course, but I'm sometimes good at spotting odd things.'

'And you know enough to leave those odd things as they are.' It wasn't really a question. She called one of her minions over. 'James, get a set of gloves and boots for Mrs Martin. She's going to do some snooping in the rest of the building.'

James looked startled. I was pretty sure he would have had something to say if the order hadn't come from the big boss. He said nothing, but returned with the necessary items.

'Will I be able to get into the various labs and offices and so on?' I asked as I put them on.

'Everything is unlocked for the moment. Robert arranged that. Would you like someone with you?'

131

I considered that for a moment. 'I'd rather go alone. I can think better that way. Surely the guard at the door is a guarantee of safety.'

'There are no guarantees in a building like this. Too many cubbyholes. But we did a quick patrol before we started to work. It's your choice.'

'Then I'll go on my own. Thanks, Elaine. I'll report back if I find anything of any interest at all.'

I had, of course, no idea what I was looking for. Not knowing what was going on in these labs, I didn't know what I should expect to find there, and what was peculiar.

But I had visited many laboratories with my father and Frank, and of course had worked in them in high school chemistry and physics. I knew the basics. I could have used Tom to show me around and tell me what was what, but the point of the exercise was to find and, if necessary, rescue Tom.

Slowly, bitterly regretting my age and present decrepitude, I climbed to the top floor to work my way down.

It turned out that the top floor was where most of the animals were kept. The first room I encountered was full of rats. I nearly screamed and slammed the door shut.

I pulled myself together. This would never do. True, I *cannot* like rats. Their pointed faces, their long sharp teeth, their beady little red eyes, those horrid pink naked tails . . . ugh! I've never even been able to bear opossums, which look to me like giant rats. And these rats seemed really big to my prejudiced eyes. But they were safely

132

caged. They appeared to be asleep. They paid me not the slightest attention, anyway, as I sidled nervously into the room.

I didn't turn the lights on for a moment. The corridor lights had been more than enough to show me the rats, and what was I afraid of, anyway? That the rats would rise up in revolt if they could see me?

There was probably nothing to see in here, but I intended to look. I turned on the light.

Once my heart stopped pounding, it occurred to me that I could usefully check to see if any cage was empty. I didn't know, of course, the full complement of rats here, but an empty cage that showed signs of recent occupation might be interesting. That blood had to come from somewhere.

All the rats seemed to be there, however. Not hundreds, as my first fright had suggested, but a round dozen, one in each cage. Which was precisely twelve too many, but never mind. All the animals seemed to be in good condition. They were plump – very plump – and they truly were much larger than any I'd ever seen in a pet store. Their white coats were glossy. They were well kept, too, in clean plastic cages with full water bottles, clean bedding and no spilled food anywhere. There was little odour, amazingly.

Still no sign of interest from the rats. Good! I ventured farther into the room. Besides the two shelves of cages and a shabby wooden desk against one wall, there were two cupboards near the end of the room. I supposed they would contain food, water and bedding for the animals, and that, indeed, was what I found along with cleaning supplies and a box of disposable rubber gloves. Nothing out of order, nothing at all interesting. I took one last careful look at the sleeping rats, trying to spot any signs of injury. Nothing. Just clean white fur.

One of them had awakened. It looked at me with what I could have sworn was intelligent interest, and spoke briefly. At least I suppose it spoke. It opened its mouth, but if it squeaked, the sound was pitched too high for me to hear.

'Shh!' I said. 'I don't have anything for you, and you'll wake the rest of the nursery. Goodnight.'

Gratefully, I turned out the light and gently closed the door, passionately hoping there were no more rats in the other rooms.

The inhabitants of the next room were much more to my liking – adorable, fluffy little guinea pigs. Unlike the rats, which had been isolated in their cages, these cute little critters were housed in groups of four. Their cages were of clear plastic, like those of the rats, but much bigger and a different shape, about twice as long as they were wide. And unlike the rats, the guinea pigs were all wide awake and talking.

'Are you talking to me or each other?' I asked one in the nearest cage. That increased the noise level in the room. 'I can't feed you, you know. I don't know how much you're supposed to get, or when, and I'd be in deep trouble if I disrupted your schedule.'

The squeaking died down a little. I wondered if the little fur balls realized the human voice was unfamiliar, not the one by whose hands they were usually fed.

'I wouldn't hurt you for the world, so you can rest easy,' I said as I walked around the room counting cages and inhabitants. Small animals in motion can be surprisingly hard to count, even only four at a time, and each cage had a sheltered area that I had to investigate carefully to see if it was or was not tenanted. I went around twice, coming up with a different count the second time, then twice more, writing down the results this time. The last three times agreed.

And they were one pig short.

Twelve cages. Forty-seven guinea pigs. Not forty-eight.

That could mean something, or nothing. Maybe there had never been four of them in that top cage nearest the window. Maybe the missing one was in some lab somewhere, engaged in furthering scientific knowledge for the benefit of mankind.

I didn't want to think about the alternative. I would, I think, have been more or less unmoved had I thought a rat had died. The thought of a guinea pig being murdered, though . . .

I scolded myself. What, after all, was the difference? The guinea pigs were cute – that was the difference. Beauty is a great thing in this world, but it's not the main thing. Rats are just as much God's creatures as their more attractive cousins, I thought piously, and are, I believe, more useful in the lab because of their relatively high intelligence.

I still grieved for the missing guinea pig.

But it might well have been a cat. *Had* been a cat, as far as I knew. Furthermore, and at the top of the importance scale, Tom was missing. That galvanized me. Time was getting on, and I'd better do the same and hunt for anything else to report to Elaine. 'Goodnight, babies,' I said, very glad there was no human around to hear me talking to lab animals, and resumed my rambling.

In and out of storage rooms and offices, labs and cage rooms. One set of cages held snakes. It was warm enough in there that they were awake, blinking at me and darting their forked tongues. I was in and out of there in record time. Count the snakes, check out the storage cupboards, escape.

I had finished the second floor (as the English reckon them; the third, to me) and had made my way down to the next before I found anything else significant, and then I nearly missed it.

It was in one of the labs. This one was labelled *Pathogens in use. No admittance.*

There had been, in one of the storage areas, a box of surgical masks, or at least face masks of some sort. I went back and put one on, feeling very silly, and opened the door of the 'no admittance' lab.

To my untutored eye, it didn't look much different from any of the other labs. There were work stations with hoods along one wall, presumably for working with the aforementioned pathogens or other dangerous substances. There were two cupboards very much like those in the other labs and the animal rooms, except one of these was locked with both a key and a sturdy padlock.

I was beginning to tire, and growing less and less hopeful of finding anything of any importance. That locked cupboard, for example. If I

136

had something I needed to hide, what better place than among nasty microbes? It would take a braver heart than mine to open that door, even if I had the keys.

But the point, as I hitched one hip up on a high stool and thought about it, wasn't to find something hidden. The forensics people would do that, far more efficiently than I could even attempt. No, I was looking for something *wrong* – that was the only word I could come up with. Something that didn't fit, that wasn't right. That missing guinea pig, perhaps.

I wished I could find him, or her as the case might be. I devoutly wished I could find the cat. I didn't want either of them to be the source of the blood in the lab. More than anything else, I wished I, or someone, could find Tom.

Maybe the students Terence was talking to, at the pub, would come up with something. Maybe Terence would come away with nothing but bitter regrets, tomorrow morning, about all the beer he'd drunk.

Maybe it was time I stopped dilly-dallying and continued my self-appointed task. Just this one more search, I promised myself, and then I'd ask one of those nice policemen to escort me back to my room and my comfortable bed.

A quick look around the room showed me nothing that seemed out of place or out of the ordinary, assuming I had known what 'the ordinary' was here. Wearily, I went to the unlocked cabinet and opened it. Storage, as I had expected. Neat shelves of rubber gloves and face masks like the extremely uncomfortable one I was wearing. A small stack of clean Petri dishes – good grief, I hadn't seen those since college biology classes. Didn't know they even still used them. These looked a little different somehow, though. There was a sign propped in front of them reading *NOT STERILE*, so I ventured to touch one with my gloved fingertip. Aha! Plastic, not glass. I wondered how they went about sterilizing them. Maybe they didn't. Maybe they just bought them sterile and threw them away after they'd been used. But in that case, why these non-sterile ones in here?

Was that enough of an anomaly that I should mention it to Elaine?

Probably not, but one never knew.

Spurred by finding one thing of possible interest, even if it wasn't exactly earth-shattering, I ventured to explore that cupboard a little further. There was a shelf full of chemicals in bottles and boxes. All were neatly labelled, but most had only the chemical symbols, not English words. I'd forgotten, years ago, all the chemistry I ever knew. Anything more complicated than H_2O or NaCl defeated me, and most of these labels were very complicated indeed.

Elaine and her crew would sort those out. Next shelf. Assorted lab glassware. Test tubes in half-full boxes. A few flasks. Rubber tubing in various lengths. Top shelf. Miscellaneous cleaning supplies.

I began to think that this was the equivalent of my kitchen 'junk drawer', where one tossed things that might come in handy someday, but usually didn't. Remembering that I sometimes found lost treasure at the back of that drawer, I rummaged in my purse for the little flashlight I always carry, hoping my fall at the Fitzwilliam hadn't broken it. No, there it was at the bottom, still working. I shone it at the backs of the shelves, just to be able to tell myself I was being thorough.

It was just a gleam of light. Something shiny at the back of the next-to-bottom shelf, something about the size of a pen or pencil. It looked as though it had rolled to the back and fallen into the crack where the shelf didn't quite meet the back of the cabinet. I couldn't tell what it was; at least half of it was sunk in the crack. Feeling guilty for moving anything, I nudged aside a bottle of Lysol that had drifted there from the top shelf by mistake, and tried to take a closer look.

And dropped the flashlight.

I didn't even stop to find it. I didn't close the lab door behind me. I pelted down the stairs as hard as a woman my age and build could be expected to pelt, back to the scene of the crime.

Elaine was leaning against a door frame, looking weary. Her normally tidy grey hair was standing up as though she'd been running her fingers through it. She saw me as I skidded through the door, and stood up straight.

'Come quick!' I called, breathlessly and ungrammatically. 'I think I've found it!'

'*It*? What?'

'Maybe a murder weapon! I don't know. I didn't touch it, but it looks an awful lot like a scalpel – a knife of some kind, anyway – and it's got blood on it!'

Fourteen

There were a lot of assumptions in that remark. I'd never seen a scalpel in my life, only in pictures and on television, and stains that are more or less brown can be anything from chocolate to dried apple juice to just plain rust. I thought I was justified, though. Combine a sharp instrument – and the thing I saw was certainly sharp – with obvious stains, not to mention recent events, and the jump to my conclusions wasn't all that far.

Elaine didn't get excited. She beckoned to one of her team and the two of them followed me up the stairs. 'You didn't touch anything?'

'I moved a bottle of Lysol to get a better look at the thing. It's at the back of a shelf. You'll see. And I only moved it an inch or so. The shelf is dusty. You can see where it was.'

Elaine only grunted.

'There's something else, too. One of the guinea pigs is missing. At least, there are four in all the cages except one; it only has three. I don't know if that means anything, or if there were only forty-seven to begin with.'

She didn't even grunt at that. I decided not to mention the Petri dishes.

She and the forensics person – I didn't know the person's name or even sex, as the garments worn were concealing in the extreme – strode into the lab. 'Stay here,' said Elaine, and I stopped. 'It's in the open cabinet?'

I nodded. 'Next-to-bottom shelf, way at the back on the right.'

They stood in front of the cabinet, peering in. The one in the white coveralls pulled a large flashlight out of a hidden pocket and shone it inside. She (I had decided to call it 'she') nodded to Elaine. 'Yes, a scalpel,' she said. (I was right. The voice was female, though low-pitched and rather grating.) 'Expensive, stainless steel handle. Disposable blade, I *think*.'

'The shelf is adjustable. Go ahead and remove it if you need to, to retrieve the thing. Do you want help?'

'Yes, send Steve if he's not busy with something else.'

Elaine came over to where I was standing in the doorway. 'You heard. Well done, Dorothy. We'd have found it eventually, but the sooner the better.' We walked down the stairs.

'What does it mean?'

'No idea. We have to get those stains analyzed first. If they match the ones from the floor downstairs, and they're both human, then we could have a very nasty case on our hands. But it's far too soon to make guesses about that. Now, what did you say about a guinea pig?'

'Only that there's one fewer than I'd have expected. It may have died a natural death, or been taken home by one of the students to pamper it a bit, or maybe it never existed – was never here, I mean. But the fact remains that there's one cage with only three, and all the rest have four.'

'Hmm. Any sign of trouble in their dormitory, or whatever it's called?'

'None that I can see. All the little residents seem quite happy and lively. They chirped at me quite a lot when I was in there. I got the impression they expected me to feed them.'

'Probably. I had a guinea pig when I was a child, and, as I recall, she always expected me to feed her. They graze all the time on hay, but they love fruit, too. I don't know what the lab ones are fed.'

'I knew I was sure to give them the wrong thing, so I didn't give them anything. They seemed annoyed. Oh, Elaine, they're such cute little beasts! I do hope nothing awful has happened to one of them. Or to the cat.'

'Or,' said Elaine with a sigh, 'to Tom.' She went into the lab, found the one apparently called Steve, and sent him upstairs. Then she spoke to the crew at large. 'You can carry on here as long as you need to, and then I'm afraid you need to spread out to the rest of the building. We'll have to get everything done tonight. I'm going to close off the area until we determine whether or not we're dealing with a crime, and that won't be until we get the analyses back from the lab. Unfortunately, however, we'll have to allow at least some of the students into the building – those who have an experiment at a critical stage, and, of course, the ones who look after the animals. So cover as much ground as you can tonight. When you've finished in here, go up to the pathology lab on the first floor. We've found something interesting in there; Nora and Steve will tell you about it. If you find something that leads you to another room, follow it. This is an exhausting business, and possibly to no purpose, but we have to be sure. Thank you all, and thanks especially to those of you who came in on your day off.

'I'm off now to talk to some of the students. I'll want to see your reports on my desk in the morning. Goodnight.'

We went to the front door of the building and were let out by the vigilant constable. 'I'm off to the pub,' said Elaine, smothering a yawn. 'Terence and Robert may have had some luck by now. Are you coming?'

'No. Alan may be there, if he's finished with his panel, but me, I've reached the end of my energy. I'm going to bed. Maybe in the morning my brain will be working again. Right now I can't seem to make any connection between missing animals and a missing nephew, and blood on the floor and a hidden scalpel.'

'You're not alone, my dear. I'll see you in the morning, then?'

'I don't know what Alan's plans are. The conference is over, but we'd like to stay on in Cambridge for a while, if we can find a place to stay.'

'I'll ring you, then. With good news, I hope.'

'I hope so, too. But remember I don't have a phone at the moment; you'll have to call Alan. And would you mind dreadfully seeing me back to my room? Since my experience at the Fitzwilliam, I've become a little wary about going places by myself.'

'Of course. My car's that way, anyhow.'

We said goodnight at the door to my staircase, and I went in to my room and my long-awaited bed. Alan wasn't back yet. I wanted to talk to him, and hear what he had learned, but once I was in bed with a sleeping pill it was a lost cause.

Alan greeted me in the morning with a cup of coffee he'd made in the room, and an almond croissant he'd found somewhere. The coffee wasn't wonderful, but it was hot. I took a few sips and then stretched experimentally. 'Hey! Nothing hurts very much!'

'Much as I hate to say it, my dear, it's a sign of age when that is cause for rejoicing.'

I would have thrown a pillow at him if not for the cup of coffee in my hand. 'The voice of experience?' I said instead, and got a grin in return.

'As soon as you've completed re-entry,' he said, nodding at the coffee cup, 'we should trade reports. You were dead to the world when I came in.'

'I was wiped out last night, for sure. And I've got lots to tell you, but do we need to pack first? I don't know what time we have to get out of here.'

'We don't. Don't forget this accommodation is reserved for guests, and the porter told me last night that no conference is booked in for more than a week. So I told him we wanted to stay for at least a few days.'

'Meals?'

'I bought us two meal tickets. We get them

144

scanned whenever we use them. That gives us the flexibility to eat here when it's convenient, or elsewhere when not. You understand we'll be having student fare, not the posh meals that were provided for the conference.'

'That sounds perfect. What a relief! I was afraid we were going to have to find a hotel or B & B somewhere, because I simply refuse to go home with the big mess unsettled.'

'Not to my liking, either. So. Would you like a somewhat heartier breakfast before we tell all?'

'No, this is fine. I've been eating far too much, anyway.' I lay back against the pillows, luxuriating in the relative absence of aches and pains. 'OK, who goes first?'

'You do. My titbits aren't of great interest.'

'Oh, dear. Well, one of mine is, or could be. Alan, I found a bloody scalpel!'

He looked taken aback for a moment, and then smiled. 'I assume that's a literal description, and not your opinion of the thing.'

'Oh, I always forget. Yes, literal – I wasn't swearing. Although, in fact, it may not be blood at all.' I told him all about it. 'I hope they'll find it is blood, though. Then I'll feel we're getting somewhere at long last. Oh, and Elaine's crew turned up traces of blood on the floor of the lab, too. *The* lab, I mean. *My* lab.'

'Ah. Vindicated!'

'Yes, and it does feel good. Honestly, I'd almost begun to wonder if I'd had an especially nasty and vivid dream. Oh, and speaking of nasty, one of the lab animals may be missing – a guinea pig. Maybe not, but there was one fewer than I

145

expected.' I explained that, too. 'I wouldn't mind so much if it had been a rat, but those guinea pigs are adorable. And don't give me the lecture about all creatures great and small. I've already delivered it to myself. The fact is I can't bear rats.'

'Nor can I. The wild ones are the worst, but even in a cage – Elizabeth had a pet rat when she was ten or so. Or two, actually. They're social animals and like to have a companion. When she asked for them, her mother and I had a conference and then told her that she could have them, on several conditions. One was that she kept them out of our sight at all times, another that she alone was responsible for their care. She was diligent about that part, but the more adventurous one of the pair escaped from its cage a time or two. Helen wasn't best pleased the day she found it under our bed.'

I shuddered. 'I'd have screamed the place down. Of course, I've always had cats, which would, I think, have meant a short life indeed for an escaped rodent.'

'They don't live a terribly long time in any case. I think Elizabeth was twelve when Gregory and Wilberforce both died, and by that time she was mad about horses and didn't mind too much. Helen and I were profoundly grateful. Anyway, I assume Elaine is looking into the case of the missing guinea pig?'

When I had recovered from 'Wilberforce,' I replied. 'Maybe, when she has time. I think she's a good deal more concerned about the case of the missing nephew.'

'Yes. Which brings me to my news, or lack of

146

it. As soon as I could get away after the session last evening, I went back to the pub. Everidge was still there.'

'I'd have thought that might put a damper on the students. The master of the college and a high-level policeman joining them for drinks.'

'We didn't sit actually *with* the students, but at the next table. The students were far too wrapped up in their own conversation to notice a pair of old fogeys like us.'

'And was their conversation productive?'

'Not very. When the barman called time and everyone left, Terence sat with us over coffee for a few minutes to report. Elaine was with us by that time, plainly tired and distressed, and nothing the boy said made her feel any better. He'd been hard put to bring the conversation around to Tom without spilling a few too many beans, but eventually he mentioned Mahala – hadn't seen him of late, wondered what he was doing, that sort of thing. The boy is not popular in his college, Terence said. Thinks himself better than the rest, keeps himself to himself.'

'A chip on his shoulder.'

'More like a plank, apparently. Thinks they despise him for being a foreigner, when they simply dislike him because he's unpleasant. Or so Terence says. He may not be entirely disingenuous, or he may not understand his own motives completely.'

'So he introduced him into the conversation,' I said impatiently. 'And?'

'Not much, as I said. One of the students said he'd seen him that morning, from a distance.'

'Seen him where?' I asked eagerly.

Alan sighed. 'In the market. No help at all. Sorry, love.'

Fifteen

'Well, at least he's still alive and in town. And that means . . . What does it mean?'

'Not a lot, except that we may be able to find him. I'm sure Elaine is on it, and she has the official resources we do not.'

'And if we find him, we'll know more about Tom.'

'Perhaps. There may be no connection at all.'

'True.' After a moment I kicked the covers out of the way and struggled to an upright position. 'It's high time I was up and dressed. I can't think properly when I look like a lazy bum.'

I showered, dressed for a chilly morning and decided I was ready for a real breakfast, whether or not I needed it. Some protein, I rationalized, would help my brain function. 'I don't suppose the dining hall is still serving?'

'I'm afraid not. But the University Arms isn't far away, and they're bound to do a good breakfast.'

After I'd lovingly tucked myself around an excellent kipper, a poached egg on toast, some grapefruit, and a cup of very good coffee, I felt much livelier. 'Fish is brain food, and this seems to have done the trick.' I pointed to the denuded skeleton on my plate. 'I've had an idea. Not earth-shaking, perhaps, but anyway a glimmer.'

'More than anyone's had so far,' said Alan. He sounded grumbly. I ignored that; he was just feeling frustrated.

'Well, what I've thought is we've been approaching this from the wrong end and with the wrong attitude. We're working from what has happened, from the end results, and we've been thinking like investigators. But we don't know enough about the situation to make much progress. So I think what we need to try to do is think like students. We still don't know if we're dealing with a prank, or what, but let's begin with the notion of some spectacular student nonsense, and go from there.'

'Dorothy,' said Alan heavily. 'It has been decades since either of us was a student. And though you were a traditional student, I was an adult and already a policeman when I pursued my university work. I can't possibly get into the mind of today's students.'

'Nor can I. Especially since I'm American and went to an American college – rather different from Oxbridge, as you reminded me the other day. No, my idea was – ta-da! – Nigel.'

Alan's face changed from grumbly to thoughtful. 'You know, that's not a bad idea at all. He actually attended King's for a while, didn't he?'

'Until he was thrown out for some infraction. I don't remember what. The point is he's still young and will remember what it was like here. And he has a decent imagination. I'll bet he could come up with any number of ideas.'

'Right.' Alan stood. 'Let's phone him now.'

'I don't have a mobile anymore, remember?'

'Then it's time we got you one, a proper smart-phone this time. Hie us to the market.'

It was another gorgeous day, the sort that puts the lie to my theory that it rains all the time in England. It does actually rain quite a lot, particularly in the low-lying fen country near Cambridge. But that makes us appreciate the fine days that much more.

I thought about Nigel Evans as we made our way to the market. I'd met him my first Christmas in England, when I was newly widowed and immersed in self-pity. He was a student at Sherebury University at the time, and the prime suspect in a murder case I'd become involved in after literally stumbling over the body in the Cathedral. Half English, half Welsh, he had a brilliant mind, a lovely singing voice, a temper, and (now) a wife and two children and a fine job in computer services at the university. He was a close friend, and I thought the ideal person to help us 'think like a student'.

Before anything else, I expressed the urgent need for a hat. I really do feel only half-dressed without one. I wasn't sure I'd be able to find anything but a baseball cap, as ubiquitous (oddly enough) in England as in America, but one stall offered a nice line in straw boaters. They're meant for men, but I found quite a jaunty one that fitted perfectly and made me feel like myself again. Alan shook his head a little at the price, but smiled at my appearance. 'I'll have to keep a closer eye on you than ever, love. There will, of a certainty, not be another woman in Cambridge wearing one of those. Possibly not in all of England.'

'Good. Now we can buy me a phone.'

We found one not in the market itself, but at a shop nearby. I watched as the young clerk tried to explain its many functions to me, and was daunted. It's not that I'm opposed to technology as a matter of principle. Alan and I each have a computer at home, and we use them regularly for all kinds of things. But I'm old enough that I still consider a phone as a means of talking to someone from a distance, and the concept of this small device as a computer, a camera, a map, a dictionary, and whatever else . . . well, it intimidated me.

'Wait a minute,' I said, holding up my hand and interrupting the nice young man's rapid spiel. 'Just show me how to make a phone call. At the moment that's all I need. I can learn the rest later.' *If I want to*, I added silently.

'Sure,' he said. 'First you'll want to program in your numbers from your old mobile.'

'My old phone was smashed to bits a couple of days ago. And I must say I sorely miss it. It was so simple!' I ended on a near wail, and the clerk finally realized I was a refugee from the age of dinosaurs and took pity on me.

'I understand,' he said kindly. 'All right. Look. Is there a number you often call, that you can remember?'

Alan pulled out his phone, with Nigel's number showing on the display. I read it off to the clerk.

'Oh, great! I can transfer the data on his phone to yours, if it's OK with both of you?'

152

'Amazing. Yes, please. I can delete anything I don't want. At least if you'll show me how to do that.'

'Right. Now turn on the mobile. That's this button here.'

I turned it on. A keyboard appeared on the screen.

'Touch the numbers you want to enter.'

I did that.

'Touch this, and your call is on its way.'

I gazed at the screen.

'No, hold it up to your ear.' He managed not to roll his eyes, but I could see it was a struggle.

Aha! It was actually ringing, with a clearer sound than I'd ever had on the old phone. Nigel didn't answer, though; the call went to voicemail. I left a brief message asking him to call me back and then asked the clerk, 'Quick! What's my new phone number?'

'Don't worry. It'll show up on your friend's phone. Press here to end the call, and I'll show you how to find your number.'

We were able, right there, to buy a few minutes of time I could use until we worked out what network I wanted to join, and we walked out of the shop, my phone in my purse and a jumble of instructions in my head. Alan, I think, was slightly amused, but I was feeling rather battered.

'Don't worry, love,' said my dear husband. 'I'm sure it's a bit confusing at first, but if six-year-olds can master the wretched things, so can you.'

'Six-year-olds,' I retorted, 'do not have seventy years of habits cluttering up their brains. They don't even know what a dial phone looks like.

For that matter, they don't know what a clock dial looks like. The other day I said something about "clockwise" to the teenager at the till in Tesco's, and I might as well have been speaking Swahili.'

A burst of loud and rather tinny rock music assaulted my ear. I looked around to see who was rudely playing a radio at such a volume.

Alan cleared his throat. 'I think it's your mobile, darling.'

I managed to fish the thing out of my purse before it stopped making its dreadful row. Alan touched the place that allowed me to answer.

'Dorothy? Nigel. Sorry I couldn't answer before. I was just putting Greta Jane's carrycot in the car for Inga. Today's her one month check-up. Can you believe it?'

'You'll turn around and blink a few times, and she'll be sixteen and pestering you about learning to drive.'

'Isn't it terrifying? Nigel Peter's starting school next term, and I was putting *him* in his carrycot only yesterday or so. I'm beginning to feel like an old man.'

'Are you staying with him while Inga deals with the baby?'

'Only temporarily. I'm due back at the uni in a few minutes, so I'm taking the Nipper to stay with Jane until Inga can pick him up.'

'Oh, dear, this isn't a good time, then. Nigel, Alan and I need your help, or your advice, or – well, what we really want is to pick your brain, I guess. It's a long story.'

'Right. Can you give me a précis, and then we

can talk late this afternoon? Will that work?'

'Um. OK, there's a lot to tell you, but the root of it may be a student prank here at St Stephen's. You're not so far removed from your student days, for all you're the father of two. Think about the very best prank you can come up with, using a bunch of very bright students in the biological sciences.'

'Biologists. Hmm. That makes it harder than, for example, engineers or mathematicians.'

'You studied history, as I recall, and I'll bet you had some ideas.'

'I'll say we did! There was the time—'

'Daddee!' came a wail from the background.

'Pipe down, monster,' said Nigel affectionately. 'I need to go, Dorothy. Let me ask one question. Am I allowed to imagine calling in students in other fields to help?'

'I hadn't thought of that, but I don't see why not.' Further childish distress sounded. 'I'll let you go. Call as soon as you can. Thanks so much, Nigel!'

'No good,' I reported to Alan, who wasn't surprised, having heard my end of the conversation. 'He's buried in work and the demands of fatherhood. He'll think about it and call back this evening, but we need ideas right now. It wouldn't be so urgent if it weren't for Tom. I wish, just for once, we'd get a piece of luck!'

Looking back on it, I was certain that my wish had served as a prayer, one that was answered immediately. I didn't see it that way at the time. I was standing stock-still in one of the crowded pathways of the market, and a teenager absorbed in her mobile cannoned into me and pushed me into a display set out on a stall.

I wasn't hurt, or not much. Some of the bruises from my fall raised fresh protests, but no new damage was done. I was mightily annoyed, however, and so was the owner of the stall, who spoke with inventive profanity about such-and-such so-and-sos who didn't mind where they were adverbially going.

Alan agreed, though in somewhat seemlier language. 'You're all right, love?' he asked.

'More or less. I hope I haven't damaged any of your stock?' I asked the proprietor. I looked at what I had fallen into – a bin full of what seemed to be small mechanical toys.

'No worry, madam. This lot is the cheap end of the line. Now these in the back, they're the real thing. Cost a pretty penny, these do.'

I felt I owed him a few minutes of attention, though I wasn't really interested. 'I see,' I lied. 'Those certainly seem to be better made. And bigger.'

The man looked at me pityingly. 'They're real! Those in the bins, they're only plastic models. These work!'

'I'm afraid I don't understand.'

'I think,' said Alan, who had been studying the display with some interest, 'that what Mr . . . er . . .'

'Levenger.'

'What Mr Levenger means is that his more expensive wares are robots, real ones that actually perform.'

156

That sparked a little mild interest. 'Oh, really? What do they do?' I had once seen a small version of R2D2, the adorable little robot from *Star Wars*. The one I'd seen could dance around and make various noises in response to voice commands, but it seemed of little use beyond entertainment. Cute, though. The ones in this display were very odd-looking, resembling nothing so much as large fantastical insects.

'These, madam, are meant to be used in the home. This one can retrieve objects from under furniture. This one is designed to clean, dust and polish surfaces, and will not fall off edges nor knock over objects on the surfaces. This one can actually carry objects up and down stairs! And this is the only place you can get them. They're quite new, designed by a team of students here in Cambridge.'

I took a discreet look at the price tag on the surface-cleaning one, and when I had my breath back decided that sponges and dust rags weren't all that hard to move back and forth. 'Well, very interesting,' I said. 'The wave of the future!' We managed to escape fairly gracefully.

'Good grief, Alan,' I said when we were out of earshot, 'did you see what he was asking for those absurd little gimmicks? For that money I could hire a housekeeper to do all those things seven days a week, and do them better.'

'They're gimmicks now, but people will buy them, all the same, just because they're exactly what you say: the wave of the future. Robotics studies have grown exponentially in recent years, and robots have grown more and more useful in areas like industry and the military. They can do jobs that are far too dangerous for humans, like minesweeping, for example, or handling hot metals in steel work.'

I shuddered a little. 'Yes, well, they're also used for jobs that aren't so pretty. I was reading about one that's used on board ship. It's like an intelligent cannon. It fires itself and even chooses the target. That's coming awfully close to the fictional kind that can think and take over the world.'

'Mmm,' said Alan, which is almost as annoying as 'yes, dear'.

'Anyway, I'm not going to spend hundreds of dollars on something that looks like an aluminum praying mantis and does what I could do better, if I could get down on hands and knees anymore. And leaving aside silly robots for the moment, do you have any suggestions about our problem? Since mine can't be followed up until later.'

'As a matter of fact, I do. Are you really undamaged by that young idiot who ran into you?'

'I'm fine.'

'Up for a bit of a walk?'

'How much of a bit?' I replied cautiously. I've learned over the years that English ideas about walking can be quite different from mine.

'Down past the University Arms and through Parker's Piece, that green park behind the hotel, to the police station. I'd like to talk to Elaine, find out what they know about the blood samples from the zoology lab, see if she's heard any more from or about Tom, and so on.'

The day was growing warmer, almost hot in

the sun. My nether parts were beginning to ache rather badly, and I'd already done as much walking as I wanted to this morning. 'If it's all the same to you, love, could we drive there instead?'

He grinned and led me to a little outdoor café a few steps away. 'I have another idea. Why don't I phone Elaine and see if she can join us here for morning coffee?'

I sat down gratefully. The chairs were cushioned, and not too uncomfortable. I ordered two coffees while Alan was being shunted through layers of protective secretaries. The coffee had arrived by the time he rang off.

'No joy,' he said with a sigh. 'She can't get away. She can see us for a few minutes if we go to the station, though. I hate to suggest that I go alone, but . . .' He made a gesture of resignation.

'No, look.' I took a swig of coffee. 'Where's the nearest place you can drive to?'

'King's Parade, probably, but I can't park.'

'I can walk that far, and there are some benches in front of King's College. Why don't I wait for you there?'

'So long,' he said firmly, 'as I escort you there, and you promise not to move an inch till I pick you up.'

We asked for paper cups for our coffee, paid and took off as rapidly as I could manage. 'And speaking of blood,' I began as we walked. 'Though we weren't.'

'Not here, I think,' he said. 'After we get in the car.'

'Well, remind me. My mind is too full of shards these days.'

It was delightful to sit in the sun in front of one of my favourite buildings in the world, or it would have been if the bench hadn't been such sturdy concrete. I reneged slightly on my promise not to stir, and stood to take off my sweater and fold it into a somewhat lumpy cushion. In the warmth of the sun, my posterior needed its comfort a whole lot more than my arms and shoulders. But I was still very glad when Alan rolled to a stop a few feet away, and I was able to exchange the bench for a well-upholstered car.

Sixteen

We probably could have walked almost as quickly, and we certainly would have taken a more direct route. Cambridge is a very old city, parts of it Roman. The streets were not laid out with modern transport in mind. They are winding and narrow and have a tendency to come to abrupt ends at pedestrianized zones. Many are one-way. All are filled to clogging point with motor vehicles of every kind, with bicycles, with mothers pushing prams, with pedestrians. The students all have loaded backpacks and their faces are, almost to a man (or woman), buried in their mobiles. Add in the cars that are double-parked to let off or take on passengers, and the odd dog or two trotting along the kerb, and you have a traffic nightmare of epic proportions.

Alan is a temperate man, of both behaviour and speech. He said nothing as he threaded through the maze, doubling back when a street took him the wrong way, stopping to wait for halting buses, for pedestrian crossings, once for a wedding party spilling out of a church into the street, but something about his silence told me I'd better keep quiet, too. We could talk about blood later.

Eventually we fetched up at the police station, and Alan pulled into the car park. I let out the breath I hadn't known I was holding. Alan rolled

161

his window down to speak to the constable who was approaching with a frown on his face.

'Sorry, sir, but this car park—'

'Is reserved for police personnel. Yes. I am Chief Constable Alan Nesbitt, here by appointment to see Superintendent Barker. Where would be the best place to leave my car? And would you like to take the keys?'

'Yes, sir. That is, no, sir, keep them. Your car will fit just there, if you will. That is . . . I trust you won't be a long time?'

'Less than half an hour, probably. I believe the superintendent is very busy, and I don't want to take too much of her time. Thank you, constable.'

I grinned at him as we got out of the car. 'You don't often throw your title around.'

'My former title. My dear, that young man should be happy my title was the only thing I threw. I was not in a mood to be trifled with.'

We found the front door and walked into the station, a modern building that looked, from the outside anyway, more like an ordinary office building. I could see from his face that Alan was prepared to do battle with functionaries, but the desk clerk had apparently been warned. We were shown immediately to the superintendent's office. She gestured to us to sit down while she finished a phone call.

'That was the lab,' she said, nodding at the phone. 'Our lab, that is, not one at St Stephen's. I pushed hard for immediate results, and they responded nobly. The critical thing is that the blood found on the floor of the zoology lab, and on the scalpel, is indeed human. I'm going to have to close off the whole building as a crime scene.'

'But the animals—' I protested. I was thinking of those cute guinea pigs.

'I'll have to see to it that their cages are taken elsewhere. I need to phone Bob Everidge straight away, and then launch enquiries about missing persons, hospital admissions, and so on, so if you'll excuse me . . .'

'Just one quick thing, Elaine,' said Alan. 'Have you heard anything more from or about Tom?'

She shook her head as she picked up the phone.

Well, that was that.

Alan drove us back to the college, each of us silent in our own thoughts. When he had dropped me at the gate and gone to park the car, I went to our room, padded the desk chair with a pillow from the bed and pulled my little notebook out of my purse. Alan walked in to find me at one of my favourite occupations – making lists.

'Ah, I wondered when you'd get around to it.'

'It's past time. We've been floundering. It's time to get organized.'

'What have you decided on thus far?'

'Well, we don't have easy access to the Hutchins Building anymore. No one does, except for the police. And whoever takes the lab animals away.'

'That'll be police, too. Some constables will be assigned that chore. They can be trusted to keep their eyes open and not exceed their brief.'

'In other words, they won't pull any funny stuff.'

163

'My dear Yank, have you taken, this late in the day, to reading hard-boiled crime novels?'

'That isn't even medium-boiled, my dear Brit. Just standard American. I only hope they pick constables who aren't afraid of rats and snakes. All right. So we can't check out the building, and there's no real reason for us to get in on the act, anyway. Elaine's minions will do an excellent job of that, I'm sure. I do have one important question for Elaine, the one I was going to ask you earlier, but I don't think she needs to be bothered about it right now.'

'And that would be?'

'The blood. The blood I saw, I mean. Alan, I can't swear to it, but I think it was still liquid. Now that would mean either that it was really fresh, or that something had been added to it to keep it from clotting. They can do that, can't they?'

'Yes, of course. Hospitals and clinics have to, in order to make sure the blood they draw for tests and so on stays liquid.'

'It never meets the air, though, at least I don't think it does. Straight from vein to vial to the lab. So is there something they could put in it to keep it liquid even in the open air? Because if not, this idiotic prank the students were planning wouldn't have worked.'

Alan shrugged. 'Yes, a question that needs to be answered. Although, as I've said before, since you could smell the blood you found, it was certainly fresh. But you're right: not something for Elaine just now.'

'Well, we could have asked one of the forensics

people at the conference if I'd thought of it soon enough. Or I could phone our doctor. But our immediate need, if Tom is to be found, is not scientific detail, but a better insight into the human end of things. So the only thing on my list, for a start, is to talk to Terence and his girl-friend, Everidge's daughter.'

'Then we'll need their phone numbers. I can't bother Elaine about that just now either, and Everidge is going to be up to his ears dealing with the repercussions of crime-scene tape around a college building, with all that implies.'

'Yes, I thought of that. But if you show your identification, I'll bet Everidge's secretary, or whoever keeps the college records, would give you Terence's number, and he can put us in touch with his fiancée. He'll be at something of a loose end, with no work to be done in the lab, so I'm sure he'll be happy to talk to us.'

'As a second-year student, he'll have other studies to worry about as well.'

'Of course he will, but do you know, at the moment I just don't care about those other studies one bit!'

'And you, a teacher!' He shook his head in mock horror. 'Very well, I'll see what I can do. What other assignments do you have for me?'

'None until I do some more thinking. I'm going to play with my new phone for a little while and see if I can't figure out how to make it do the handstands I understand it's capable of.'

'Mind you don't set off a nuclear explosion by mistake. I'll be back. Oh, and what do you want to do about lunch?'

165

'When do they serve here in the dining hall?'
'I'll have to check. It's not a long period. Twelve till half past one – something of that sort.'
'Let's do that, then. What time is it now?' I don't like wearing a watch.
'Your amazing new mobile can tell you that, my dear.'
He left the room quickly.

I sighed, fished my phone out of my purse, and prepared to do battle. It was easy enough to find the time of day. It came up on the screen as soon as I turned the thing on. But then I decided to experiment a little and see if I could do some research.

Working out how to use the thing as a computer was harder. I punched various little pictures on the screen, some of which seemed to me to be highly obscure, none of which took me to anything resembling a computer.

Eventually, I found Google. I've used my computer at home enough to know that it'll find you anything from a recipe for sticky toffee pudding to newspaper articles in Russian. It works a little bit differently on a phone, but I finally found what I was looking for: websites about famous student pranks. Of course, I still didn't know if a prank was involved in our problem, but it couldn't hurt to cover all the bases.

Alan walked in just as I pulled up a promising site. Unfortunately, it was about American colleges, and was rather disappointing, noting such stunts as filling dorm rooms with ping-pong balls or shaving cream.

'I have the phone numbers,' said Alan rather smugly. 'The secretary gave me Jennifer Everidge's as well.'

'The old Nesbitt charm at work?'

'Of course. Shall I ring them up now, or would you rather have a bite to eat?'

'Call on our way to lunch. Then if you have to leave a message, we won't have wasted time. Alan, can I save this thing?' I pointed to the site on my phone.

'I think so.' He took the gadget, pressed and poked and swiped his hand up and down, performed other mystic rites, and handed it back to me. 'I've saved the search. You can come back to it.'

'Can I turn the blasted thing off now?'

'You don't want to. Just leave it alone. The screen will go dark, but the phone will ring if anyone calls in.'

'That's another thing we've got to do – change the way it rings!'

'One hurdle at a time, love. Let's go and find some lunch. Do you have your meal pass?'

Alan called both Terence and Jennifer. Both calls went to voicemail. He gave my number and his, and we sat down to lunch, not as elegant as the conference meals, but well cooked and sustaining. My phone set off its horrid jangling just as we were finishing our rice pudding.

It was Nigel. 'Hi, Dorothy, just a quick question. I've had a little time to think about your problem, though I've not come up with anything definite. But am I right in assuming that your students have lab animals?'

'Yes. Rats and snakes and guinea pigs.'

'Good. Got to go. I'll call after we get our particular beasts settled for the night.'

'Wait, Nigel. What's the word on Greta Jane? Is she growing properly and all that?'

'Blooming. Sound of wind and limb. Especially wind. I'm surprised the neighbours haven't complained about her lung power. Later.'

The next phone to ring was Alan's, with its much more subdued tones, as we were walking out of the dining hall. Alan mouthed to me that it was Jennifer Everidge on the line.

They spoke briefly before Alan punched off and turned to me. 'She's with young Terence.'

'No great surprise.'

Alan grinned. 'No. They would like to meet us at the Eagle.'

'Is it my sort of pub?'

'It's quite pleasant, and on a fine afternoon it won't be terribly crowded, or not with students, at least. Such students as aren't devoted to tutorials or the other duties of the academic life will probably be on the tennis courts or the river. I believe it's the oldest pub in Cambridge, and some famous people have frequented it, so there may be tourists.'

'I'll chance it.'

'Can you walk that far?'

'You know, I think I can. I'm back almost to normal, and I put on my most comfortable shoes.'

'Good. *Avaunt!*'

We stopped at our room so I could change into a cool blouse and put my hat back on, and then set out. The pub, when we got there, was not the tarted-up sort with baskets of flowers hanging everywhere, but it was, as Alan said, quite pleasant. Just an honest pub, bigger than most, and with a remarkable array of beers, if the pumps ranged along the bar were any indication. I opted for a half-pint of mild, and planned to give most of it to Alan. I needed my wits about me.

Terence's eyes widened, possibly in disbelief, as he caught sight of me in my hat. Jennifer smiled. 'I've never seen a woman wear one of those before,' she said a little shyly, 'but it suits you. I might just have to buy one for myself.'

'I hope I'm not breaking some unwritten Cambridge rule by wearing one. Sort of like a college tie, you know, that no one except a member of that college should ever, ever wear.'

'If you are, love,' said Alan, arriving with our beer, 'you'll be excused on the grounds of being an ignorant American. Cheers.'

He let us each have a refreshing couple of swallows before putting his own glass down and surveying the room. It was just crowded enough, just noisy enough, to give us a reasonable measure of privacy. 'Now. We are, Terence and Jennifer, on serious business here. Tom Grenfell is still missing, still not answering his phone. And as you've probably guessed from the security zone established around the Hutchins Building – if your father hasn't told you, Jennifer – it has been declared a crime scene. Yesterday Superintendent Barker supervised a forensics team to collect various samples, and it was found that human blood had been spilled on the floor of the zoology laboratory. In connection with the other events surrounding that building, Elaine deemed it essential that it be sealed off.

'You know that I am a retired policeman. I can tell you that it is extremely unusual for a murder to be assumed without the presence of a body. There are extenuating circumstances here, however, chief among which are the attack on my wife and Tom's disappearance. So, as is sometimes said in church, I require and charge you both that you declare anything you might know or even suspect about these matters.'

The two youngsters looked at each other. Jennifer spoke first. 'We don't really *know* anything, Mr Nesbitt. We'd have told my father if we did. We have some ideas. Only . . .'

'Only they are just ideas, and they may not be true, and we don't want to get anybody into trouble.' Terence looked unhappy.

'The sentiment does you credit,' I said before Alan could start the civic responsibility lecture he'd used so often when he was an active policeman. 'This is a small and tightly knit community here at the university, and a well-respected one at that. No one wants to spoil relationships with unconsidered gossip. But this is a special case. Your fellow student is missing and may have come to harm, Terence. Your father's college, Jennifer, has already been pushed into the eye of the media, most unfavourably. And a human being, almost certainly someone who is a part of this university community, has been at least injured.' I took another swallow of my beer before I could continue. 'I must tell you both that there was quite a lot of blood on that floor, before someone cleaned it up. This was not a case of a cut finger.'

Another wordless communication between Terence and Jennifer, and the girl nodded sharply. 'Yes. That's what I told him. We have to tell, Terence. We *must*.'

We waited.

'It's about Mahala,' Terence said at last.

'Do you know where he is?' asked Alan. I gave him The Look. *Let him tell it his own way*, I said silently.

'No. Not even where he might be.' He finished his beer. 'It's hard to tell this, because, you see, I'm not all that keen on Mahala. It isn't a race thing, truly. There isn't a lot of prejudice in Cambridge, anyway, with students here from all over the world. It's just . . . no one likes him, really. He's brilliant and works hard, but he rubs people up the wrong way. No one wants him for a partner in lab work; he gives the other person all the dirty jobs and takes all the glory if the task goes well. And then he hates sport, never even goes punting. He just doesn't fit in.' He looked at his empty beer glass. Jennifer slipped away to the bar.

'This all happened two or three weeks ago, what I'm about to tell you,' Terence went on. 'Near the beginning of term. I overheard him arguing with one of the first-years. They were in one of the animal rooms – where they're housed, you know – and as it was a warm day, the windows were open. I was outside, just under the window, and I didn't mean to listen, but they were shouting, having a real ding-dong.'

171

Jennifer set down a tray with fresh glasses all around. I smiled and shook my head, but I helped her pile the used glasses on the tray.

'I'll tell the rest,' said Jennifer. 'Terence always sticks at the middle of the story, because he hates telling tales. It was an argument over the lab rats. The one student – Terence doesn't know who it was – was saying that Mahala was feeding them too much, and the wrong sort of food.'

'Wait a minute,' I interrupted. 'You're saying Mahala works with the rats. Does anyone know what research he's doing with them?'

'He's very close-mouthed about it,' said Terence. 'His professor would know, of course, but he's in America just now lecturing at – would it be Columbia University? That's the one in New York?'

I nodded, and Jennifer continued. 'Anyway, the other student challenged him, and Mahala claimed he knew what he was doing, that it was part of a special experiment in breeding, and the other student could . . . er . . . keep out of what wasn't his business.'

'And that's all?' asked Alan after a pause. 'No sounds of the argument turning violent?'

'I don't know. I didn't hear anything, but I left pretty quickly. I don't like conflict.'

'And you're sure Mahala was one of the two involved?' Alan continued. 'You didn't see him?'

'I didn't need to see him. His accent is quite distinctive.'

'Like his manner,' said Jennifer. 'And manners. He really is the most horrid little toad.'

'And you don't know who the other person

172

was? You said he was a first-year student.'

'I can't be sure about that, but it's usually the first-years who do the routine work of looking after the animals. I might know his voice if I heard it again, but there was nothing special about it.'

'No particular accent?'

'None that I could hear.'

'And when did you say this happened?'

'I don't remember exactly, except it was in the first week of term.'

'But you're sure the argument took place in one of the animal rooms?'

'I'm sure. It was the rat room. I've checked since. I was reasonably sure before, since they were talking about rats.'

I remembered something. 'You know, Alan, when I saw the rats, they seemed awfully big to me. I thought lab rats might be bigger than the ordinary ones people get as pets. It could have been my imagination, though. I was pretty scared of them; maybe that made them look huge.'

'It's not your imagination, Mrs Martin,' said Jennifer with a little shudder. 'They really are far bigger than the usual rat. Terence showed me. They're creepy, if you ask me.'

'Well . . . but, just feeding them more wouldn't make them bigger, would it? Fatter, yes, but bigger?'

'No,' said Terence and Alan together. The younger man deferred to the older. 'I told you, Dorothy, that my daughter had pet rats. She decided they weren't growing fast enough and started feeding them more. They rapidly became

173

obese, sluggish, and not very healthy, but only girth increased, not length. Helen and I put a stop to the overfeeding when we happened to see them one day and noticed what sort of shape they were in. Neither of us could bear the things, but we didn't approve of cruelty to animals, which was what this amounted to.'

'You're quite right, Mr Nesbitt. Mahala must be giving them growth hormones or something of the sort. And he did mention selective breeding.'

'But you say he's a first-year student. Would he have had time in just a few months to make much difference in the rat population?'

'Oh, dear. I must have given the wrong impression. No, Mahala's in his second year. And rats breed fast, you know. They can have as many as five litters a year, with maybe seven to ten babies, or even more. So if he chose the biggest and fittest from those litters—'

'Wait! If he bred siblings to each other, wouldn't he get a lot of undesirable traits?'

'But he wouldn't do that. He'd choose several of the biggest males and females in the lab, those with different blood lines, and raise several different litters. Then he'd repeat the process. He's a git, but not a stupid git. And whatever he's been doing, it's working. Those rats are at least twice the size they ought to be.'

'Yes, well.' Alan cleared his throat. 'This is very interesting. And if you'll tell me the name of Mahala's professor, I'll try to phone him and learn more about the rat project. But none of it is perhaps directly relevant to our problems, the most immediate of which is the whereabouts of Tom Grenfell.'

'Yes, but it *is* relevant, Alan,' I said. 'It may not tell us where Tom is, but it tells us where Mahala is, or will be soon.'

Seventeen

They looked blank.

I beamed. 'He'll be looking after his precious rats, won't he?' I probably sounded a little smug. 'He'll go to the Hutchins Building, and when he can't get in, he'll raise all kinds of stink until he finds out where they're being kept. So all we have to do—'

'Is find the constables delegated to move the animals, and tell them to be on the lookout for an angry West African student. Does he have a surname, by the way?' Alan had picked up his phone and was punching buttons as he spoke.

'Probably, but I've never heard it,' Terence said, but Alan shushed him as he spoke into his phone.

'We're just in time,' he said as he put the phone down. 'Elaine has dispatched the constables and they should have just reached the college. She's having them notified to watch for Mahala.'

I breathed a deep sigh of relief. 'And once we find him, we can pressure him to tell us where Tom is.'

'If he knows.'

'He knows something,' I retorted. 'He's deeply involved in the prank thing. I'll bet good English money that he knows all about how it went wrong, and I'll bet he has a pretty good idea what Tom's doing about it.' I reached for the beer Jennifer had brought. 'I think I do want this, after all.'

176

I had taken one good swallow when Alan's phone jingled. He glanced at the display and shook his head. An unfamiliar number, then. 'Nesbitt here. I see. Yes. Where? No. I'll be right there.'

'They have Mahala. I told the constable to keep him under observation, but not detain him. Not yet. Terence, would you have any reason to want to speak to him?'

'No, sir. As I said, I steer away from conflict, and I don't care for that boyo.'

'Phone one of us if you think of anything at all relevant, or even peculiar. Dorothy?'

The pub was in a pedestrianized area, but there was a cab waiting at the end of the street. Alan grabbed it. 'St Stephen's, and as fast as you can.'

The cabby allowed himself one sarcastic snort, and set off through the madhouse of traffic.

The one-way streets were in our favour this time, and the taxi could use streets forbidden to private cars. He got us to the college gates faster than I would have dreamed possible, and Alan rewarded him with a hefty tip.

We were met at the gate by one of Elaine's constables.

'He's still there?' was Alan's first remark. Which told me how concerned he was. He almost never neglects the courtesies.

'He is, but we do need to hurry, sir.'

'Where are we going?' I said, trying to keep up with Alan's lengthy stride. 'Slow down a little, will you?'

'Sorry, love. We don't know how long Mahala can be expected to hang about.'

'Go ahead, then. I'll follow. Which building?'

'Library,' the constable called back to me, 'lower ground floor.'

I walked as fast as I could, but Alan and the constable were soon out of sight around the corner of a building. I stopped a passing student to ask where the library was and limped along in the direction indicated, thinking how much I hated the infirmities of age. *It's only because of that fall*, I told myself. *You're pretty spry most of the time*. And then I remembered that the word 'spry' is only ever used to describe the elderly, and was annoyed all over again.

When I reached the library, Alan and the constable were standing just outside, talking, or rather listening, to a dark-skinned young man. He was tall and wiry, and at this moment extremely angry.

'You have no right to detain me! I have done nothing wrong, nothing illegal. I must tend to my animals. You will ruin months, years, of work! It is always the same. Persecution, persecution everywhere I go!'

The constable put out a hand to restrain him. That was a mistake.

'You will not touch me, pig of a policeman! Pig! Pig! I am in this country legally. You will leave me alone.'

'Mr Mahala,' said Alan with quiet force, 'we wish to speak with you about some incidents at the Hutchins Building. We can do it in civilized fashion here at the college, or we can do it at the police station. The choice is yours.'

'You have no right! I have done nothing!'

178

'We have every right. Constable?' He raised his eyebrows and made a gesture with his head. The constable reached for his handcuffs.

Mahala looked frantically to left and right, but before he could decide which direction to run, Alan had grasped his arm. 'Don't be a fool, man! I don't want to put you under arrest, not just yet, but if you attempt an escape I'll have no choice.'

I stepped into the scene. 'Now look here, young man! Behave yourself! The idea – making such a spectacle of yourself right here in front of the whole college. You're said to be brilliant. I must say, you're not acting like it. Take a deep breath and settle down!'

I don't know if it was my sixth-grade-teacher voice or my flowery blouse and absurd hat, but Mahala stopped shouting and dancing around, and stared at me.

'Who are you?'

Well, that wasn't a very polite way to address me, but it was better than the abuse he'd been flinging a moment ago. 'My name is Martin. I am an American now living in England and visiting Cambridge. And please don't launch into a tirade against America and Americans, because I've heard it all before and find it exceedingly tiresome.'

He had opened his mouth. He shut it again. It seemed he wasn't accustomed to being treated like a naughty little boy. I pressed my advantage.

'I don't know about you, but I would like to go inside and continue this conversation out of

179

the sun. Is there any place in the library where we could talk without disturbing other students?'

'I do not care if I disturb anyone!'

'Perhaps not, but I do. Where have they put your rats?'

'In the – how do you know about my rats? Who are you, that you know so much about me?'

'Oh, I know a great deal about a lot of things. We'll go down to the rat hostelry and talk. And you will allow me, please, to take your arm. I do not find stairs at all easy at my age.'

I watched him as I made the remark about stairs, but there was no reaction. Well, maybe it hadn't been Mahala who pushed me at the Fitzwilliam.

I took his arm in a firm grip. He tried to shy away, but I ignored his attempt to be free and just gripped a little harder. 'This is very kind of you,' I said, pretending he had a choice.

We walked into the library and down a half-flight of stairs. Alan and the constable followed, the constable with a slightly stunned look on his face, Alan with a bemused half-smile.

I was bracing myself for my first view of the rats, and it was a good thing. When we entered the storage room where their cages had been put, we were greeted with a chorus of agitated squeaks, so high-pitched as to be painful to the ear.

'They are upset,' said Mahala, somewhat unnecessarily. 'They do not like to be moved, and the females are soon to give birth. It is infamous that they should be moved now.'

'Yes, well, moving isn't pleasant for humans,

either, is it? I'm sure they'll calm down in time. Tell me about them.' I wasn't sure how long my schoolteacher/nanny impersonation was going to work, and I wanted to get as much out of him as I could before he turned defensive and Alan would have to move in with the cop routine.

'They are very fine rats,' said Mahala, his enthusiasm for the moment suppressing his antagonism. 'See how big they are! I have been breeding them for size, but also I am giving them a special diet of my own invention. I will not tell you what it is.'

'Of course not. I probably wouldn't understand anyway, if it involves a lot of supplements.'

'No! It is only special food, food that humans can eat also.' He hesitated. 'My part of Africa, where I live, is very poor. No one has enough to eat. There is little rain. I have combined grains that can thrive in poor soil with little water, to see if this food will make rats grow. And you see! They are enormous! You have said I am brilliant, and now you see that it is true. And they are not only big; they are smarter than the others, too. I can show you—'

'Another time, perhaps. I must say, your efforts to feed the poor are laudable, but just now we would like to know what part of your experiment involves human blood.'

It was a total shock. His face could not turn white, but it went a sort of ashy grey, and he began again to turn his head in a frantic search for a way out.

There was no escape. The constable, a solid

young man, stood in front of the only door to the room. There was no window.

'Easy, son,' said Alan. 'We just want to ask you a few questions.'

'I do not have to talk to you! I do not have to stay here! I know your laws. I do not know who you are, but you have no right to keep me here!'

'As I have said before, I do have that right. My name is Alan Nesbitt and I am a sworn police officer, as is the constable here. However, this is not an official police interrogation, and I'd like to keep it that way. As I also said before, I would prefer a civilized conversation, especially since I suspect your overreaction may not be very good for your rats. They're not usually so noisy, are they?'

'You are upsetting them,' said Mahala, but he had moderated his tone.

'No, sir, I believe *you* are upsetting them. They do not, if I recall my daughter's childhood pets accurately, like human anger and loud voices. I believe there is a conference room upstairs where we might speak in some privacy.'

'I do not wish to speak with you at all.'

'But you're going to, dear,' I said gently, 'and it would be much better for your rats if we went elsewhere.'

He turned on me. 'And who are *you*? Are you some kind of policeman, too? They have women in the police in this country, I know, but you do not look like one.'

Chalk one up to the hat and the blouse. 'No, I'm not with the police. I am Mr Nesbitt's wife, and I am interested in what has been happening in the Hutchins Building. I am also interested in your rats. I believe that they are usually housed two to a cage, but yours are alone. Can you tell me why that is?'

'I have bred them for size, as I have told you. They are too big now for two in a cage. They are also more aggressive than ordinary laboratory rats. They might harm one another if I put two together.'

'Oh, I see. Did you anticipate the aggression when you began your research?' As we talked, Mahala was being gradually eased out the door and up the stairs, the constable in the lead, with Alan bringing up the rear behind Mahala and me.

'It was always possible. Larger individuals of a given species often exhibit aggression, although the opposite can also be true.'

'Ah, yes, the "gentle giant" phenomenon. I've known it in humans. A very kind and gentle handyman who used to do work for me and my first husband, back in Indiana, was immense – well over six feet tall and probably three hundred pounds. Or, let's see, what would that be in stones? Or do you use kilos in your country?'

'Yes, and here in England in the sciences, also. Or simply grams, for most rats. Many of my rats, though, weigh far more than one kilo. My largest one approaches two. Soon, with my special feeding, they will all be over two kilos, and I will have to give them bigger cages. My professor—' He stopped talking and looked around him. We had arrived at the conference room, and Alan was just closing the door.

'No! I do not wish to talk to you.'

183

'Mr Mahala, sit down.' Alan's voice was not loud, but there was steel in it.

Mahala sat.

'That's better. Now I must stress to you that you are not under arrest. You do not have to answer any of my questions, and you may leave when you wish. I will also say, however, that your unwillingness to answer reasonable questions may be regarded as suspicious.'

'I simply do not understand,' I put in, 'why you should be so panicky about a few simple questions. You're happy to talk about your rats, about your work. If you have nothing to hide, you shouldn't mind talking to us.'

'In my country the police are cruel. They beat and torture innocent people. I do not like the police!'

'That's understandable,' said Alan, holding on to his patience, 'but you're in England now, and we're not allowed to do any of those things. Now, Mahala, I want you to tell us anything you know about where Tom Grenfell might be.'

He blinked. 'I do not know. He is not at the college?'

'He is neither at the college nor at home. When did you see him last?'

'I do not know him well. He is a graduate student. He is a botanist. Our paths do not cross.'

'But you know who he is, obviously. When did you see him last?'

'He does not like me. We do not see each other.'

'Mahala.' Alan's steel voice again. 'You work in the same building amongst only – how many

184

students? Twenty? Thirty? I ask again, when did you see him last?'

Mahala looked down at his hands. 'I do not remember.'

This was not an official police interrogation. Alan had said so. I felt free to put my oar in. 'I imagine it was when you were cleaning up the last of the blood in the lab, wasn't it?'

'No! He was not there! He did not see me! I—' He stopped suddenly, but not soon enough.

'So you *were* the one who cleaned up the blood,' said Alan. 'I'd like you to tell us about that, if you will. Whose blood was it, and how did it find its way to the laboratory floor?'

Eighteen

Sullen silence. The constable shifted his feet. The muted sounds of the library came through our door.

'The blood I saw on the floor was human blood, Mahala,' I said quietly. 'If it had been cleaned up in the ordinary way, and a doctor had been called, or an ambulance, there might have been a perfectly simple explanation. Someone had been accidentally injured. Accidents do happen.

'But that blood was dealt with stealthily, and no doctor was called. Something untoward has happened, and you must see that the police need to know what. There was a great deal of blood, much more than could have come from a simple cut or a nosebleed. It is even possible that someone has died. You can make this easier if you tell us what you know, but the matter will be investigated thoroughly, with or without your help. And if it is necessary to place you under arrest, even for a short time, what will happen to your rats?'

Mahala muttered something.

'Could you repeat that, please?' said Alan. 'I didn't quite—'

'It was my blood! It is nobody's business but my own!'

'But, Mahala, listen!' I was shocked and distressed. 'If you lost so much blood, you must

186

see a doctor. That had to have been a serious injury, and it's dangerous—'

'You know nothing about it! You know nothing about me! But I will show you, so you will see how foolish you are, all of you!'

He threw off the light jacket he was wearing. A thick bandage was covering part of his left forearm, the arm I had been grasping so firmly. I shivered at the thought of the pain I must have caused him. Some blood had seeped through the layers of gauze.

With one savage motion, Mahala ripped off the bandage, revealing a cut on his inner arm, just below the elbow. The cut was just over an inch long and was seeping quite a lot of blood.

'But . . . but that tiny cut . . . all that blood . . . and it must be newer than last Wednesday. It's still bleeding a little.'

'It had stopped. You took my arm and started it again.'

I shook my head, utterly confused.

'I have a disease. My blood does not clot properly. It is called haemophilia.'

I had been standing near the door. Now I dropped into the nearest chair. 'Oh, how utterly stupid of me. I was so close. The blood on the rock!'

Alan looked as near to exasperated as I've ever seen him. 'Dorothy, the blood was on the floor, or so you've said. Do you now say it was on a rock?'

'No, no, in the book. And that's why they didn't know when the murder took place.'

'I think,' said the constable, who had been

utterly silent, 'that Mrs Martin is referring to the book *Have His Carcase* by Dorothy L. Sayers. The fact that the victim was a haemophiliac plays a very large role in the plot. Ahem.'

Alan's expression cleared. 'Ah. Understandable. But why, Dorothy, do you call yourself stupid?'

'Because I was thinking of that book only yesterday, and the haemophilia part went right by me. I was thinking that this student prank they were planning wouldn't work at all, really, because whatever blood they planned to use would have clotted almost immediately unless they put something in it – an anticoagulant of some sort. We talked about it, Alan. But yours would have worked, wouldn't it, Mahala? At least, I don't know how long it would stay liquid, but you probably do. Only, surely you wouldn't have wanted them to use your own blood! That could be terribly dangerous for you. You could even die! Here, I don't have any bandages with me, but this might help.' I handed him an unopened packet of tissues from my purse.

Mahala ignored them. His face had once more become a mask. 'How do you know about the foolish thing that the students planned to do?'

Alan shot me a look. OK, I shouldn't have mentioned that at this point. I subsided and let him take over.

'You're not the only student we've talked to, you know. We know a good deal about the activities in the Hutchins Building. And I will ask you once more: when did you last see Tom Grenfell?'

'I do not remember.'

188

'How did you come by that cut on your arm?'

'It was an accident. I mishandled a scalpel.'

'What did you do with the scalpel?'

'I do not remember.'

And that continued to be his answer to all questions, though Alan tried for another fifteen or twenty minutes.

When he had finally given up, he asked Mahala for his address, which he very reluctantly provided. I tried to talk with Mahala and urge him to see a doctor, while Alan stepped out of the room to call Elaine.

When he returned, he spoke sternly to Mahala. 'You may go, but you are to stop at the police station to give them a blood sample. If it matches the blood found in the lab, you are free of suspicion. However, we may still wish to speak with you about Tom Grenfell, so I will ask you to keep the police informed of your whereabouts. Do you understand?'

Mahala muttered something surly and stalked out of the room, and we headed back to our room, the constable going to make a more complete report to Elaine.

'Well, that didn't get us anywhere,' I said crossly, flopping on to the bed to ease my protesting muscles. 'I wish Elaine had let the constable bring him in.'

'There are no grounds for arrest. Mahala is uncooperative and rude, but he has not, to our knowledge, done anything illegal. He explained the blood. He claims he knows nothing about Tom. What would you have Elaine do?'

'You think he was telling the truth about all that?'

'He would know that tests could be run. I don't think he would lie about something so easily proved or disproved. The same with his medical records. He may not have been in this country for a long time, but unless he lied about being a haemophiliac, he will have seen a doctor several times.'

'There was an awful lot of blood on that bandage, for such a small cut,' I conceded, 'and it kept on oozing while we talked. All right, he probably does have haemophilia – I *wish* I'd been able to get him to see a doctor about it – and that probably was his blood on the floor. But he wouldn't tell us how or why or when it got there, and he didn't explain why he was so secretive about it. *And* he was lying about how he got the cut.'

'Certainly he was.'

'And the other thing is I don't believe his story about hating the police. I mean, he probably does, maybe with good reason, but that doesn't explain his absolute panic about being questioned. There's something else going on.'

Alan looked at me quizzically. 'I agree. After years of policing experience, I've learned to spot a liar. But how did you know?'

'Same thing. Years of experience. Mine was with schoolchildren, but a liar is a liar. Their behaviour is much the same. The question is what are we going to do about it?'

Alan sighed. 'Unfortunately, there's nothing we *can* do at this juncture. His story about the blood takes the wind out of our investigative sails. As long as there was the possibility of murder, or at the very least assault, we had a reason to seal the building and so on.'

Tired and annoyed as I was, I had to smile at the 'we'. Alan professes to be well content in his retirement, but the old fire horse can't ignore a bell, even when it's officially summoning some other brigade.

He grinned. 'Very well, *Elaine* had a reason. Now she hasn't one, and I'm sure our helpful constable has told her that by now.'

'But she hasn't shut down yet. We could go over and see if her minions have found out anything interesting.'

Alan sighed again. 'She'll let us know if anything turns up. I hate to admit it, love, but I'm tired.'

I nodded. 'Me, too. Tired and discouraged. We seem to reach this stage every time, don't we? When all the promising leads peter out into dead ends. Did you ever see *The African Queen*?'

'Katharine Hepburn and Humphrey Bogart. Splendid film.'

'One of the best. Then you'll remember the scene near the end when they've been poling and even dragging the boat through a narrow channel, and it finally gets stuck in a morass of weeds. That's the way I feel now.'

'Ah, but they get out. The rain comes and raises the water level, and they get out and win the day.'

It was my turn to sigh. 'Then we'd better pray for rain. Meanwhile, I'm going to take a nap.'

191

'It's nearly dinner time. You won't be able to sleep tonight if you sleep now.'

'Right. I'll chance it.'

I could hardly keep my eyes open long enough to stretch out comfortably and pull the spare blanket over my clothes; I'd taken off only my shoes. I was asleep in minutes, and so was distinctly annoyed when my phone set off its infuriating jangle just when I was sinking into the deep comfort of oblivion.

I was lying on it. With some difficulty I pulled it out of my pocket and glared at it for a moment before stabbing at the stupid icon that meant 'answer'.

'Yes?' I growled.

'Dorothy? Are you all right? You sound as if you've caught cold.'

I cleared my throat and tried to clear my mind. 'Oh, Nigel. No, I'm fine. Just a frog in my throat.'

'Oh, I thought I might have caught you at a bad moment.'

'Wicked child! You're much too observant. As a matter of fact, I'd just settled into a nap, and you woke me up. Let me put the phone down for a minute so I can get to the kettle and make some coffee.'

I ignored the croaks from the phone until I had the kettle full and turned on. 'Now. What were you saying?'

'Only that you'll pay for the nap *and* the coffee when you try to sleep tonight.'

'You sound just like Alan. You both know me too well. What time is it?'

'A little after six, and I have some information

for you, or at least some ideas. Are you awake enough to listen?'

'Now I am. Wide awake, in fact.' I moved the few feet to Alan's bed and poked him. 'Wake up, love. It's Nigel, and he has something for us. Talk loud, Nigel, and Alan and I will both listen.'

'You asked me,' he began, 'to think about the sort of prank a student of the sciences might think worthy of the noble annals of Cambridge, along with the cars dangling from bridges and atop roofs, and so on. Now, those feats were all very well in their day, as was the placing of various objects on the pinnacles of King's. As a matter of fact, had I remained a little longer at King's, some friends and I . . . but no matter. You're concerned with present-day students.'

'I'll get you to tell us someday.'

'Ah, now that I'm an old married man with children, the stories of my youth are buried forever. Well. You must remember, Dorothy and Alan, that technology is firmly in control now, not only of the world, but especially of the minds of the young.'

'And the younger the mind, the greater the absorption,' said Alan.

'Indeed. That is why I asked you, Dorothy, if I might posit the cooperation of students in other scientific fields.'

'You did, and I agreed. But I don't know what you're getting at.'

'I'm thinking of robotics.'

Alan and I looked at each other. Robots. Those strange insect-like creatures in the market. Made, the man had said, by students here at Cambridge.

193

'Hello? Anybody still there? Hello?'

'Yes, Nigel, sorry. It's just that Alan and I saw some robots in the market only this morning, and I don't quite see how they'd tie in with a student prank. Look, we'd better tell you what we know so far.' I briefly sketched what Terence had told us.

'Yes, that would fit, although . . . But here's what I came up with.' Nigel sounded excited. 'I talked to some of the chaps studying robotics here at Sherebury, and they say there's some world-class work going on in the field at two or three of the Cambridge colleges. They've come up with some marketable devices, in fact.'

'Yes, that's what Alan and I saw. They didn't seem very practical to me, and they're terribly expensive.'

'Well, they would be, wouldn't they? The avant-garde, as it were. But suppose those inventors were to get together with the biologists at St Stephen's. I think they could come up with something truly spectacular, perhaps a remote-controlled robot that looked exactly like a lab animal. You mentioned blood. Wouldn't it be a fantastic joke if someone were to stab this creature as it walked across the quadrangle, and it bled – and kept right on going?'

'Like one of the Stepford Wives,' I mused.

'Excuse me?'

'Never mind. A book and movie. Before you were born. Nigel, that's brilliant, and it answers a few of our questions.'

'Only a few?'

'Nigel, you've been a great help,' said Alan,

'but you've perhaps raised as many questions as you've answered. I don't suppose your fertile imagination can explain the disappearance of one of the students? A botanist, by the way.'

Nigel whistled. The sound came down the airwaves in ear-piercing fashion. 'A botanist. Not likely to be directly involved in the planning of the prank, then. No, I haven't the slightest idea. Would you like me to ask in the botany department here?'

'Why not?' But my voice held little hope. Sherebury is a long way from Cambridge, and not only in miles.

'Just one more thing, Nigel, and we'll let you get back to Inga and the children. What would you say is the greatest problem confronting university students these days? That is, what would cause them the greatest distress?'

'Hmm. Not an easy question. If I remember my own days at King's, our greatest worry, leaving out examinations, was how to live our lives the way we wished with a minimum of official interference.'

'I assume that means that some of your activities would not have met with official approval,' said Alan with the hint of a chuckle.

'Most of them, actually. And as you know, I did eventually fall foul of the regulations and was sent down.'

'And a great pity, too,' I said sternly, and then checked myself. This was no time for a lecture on irresponsibility, and in fact it wasn't needed. Nigel's life might have been very different if he'd continued with his studies, but it could hardly be

195

better. Sometimes things do work out for the best.

'So,' I said when we'd ended the call, 'what do you think is causing Mahala's distress?'

'I think Nigel put his finger on it. He's worried about a serious encounter with the authorities. Except in his case, I have the distinct feeling it's not the university regulations he's worried about, but the law.'

'He's certainly afraid of you.'

Alan struck one fist into his other palm. 'Confound it, I wish we – I wish *Elaine* had a good reason to question him officially. I'm quite sure that boy is at the root of whatever's going on in this college, but without at least a hint of evidence, she can't bring him in.'

'No. Andrews would be on her back the minute she tried. Cultural sensitivity, town-and-gown relationships, you name it.'

'And he'd be right, Dorothy. I can't bear the man, but the law is the law. One can't interrogate someone because his manner is offensive, or one doesn't like his looks.'

'Well, Elaine can't. But I can, can't I? I'm not official. I never was. And I established a certain rapport with him for a while today. Suppose I were to help him move his rats back to their own sweet little home, as soon as it's allowed.'

'For one thing, among many others, he would sense your repugnance to the beasts. He may be ill-mannered and all the rest, but he is neither stupid nor unperceptive. How long do you think your celebrated rapport would last, the first time you looked at a rat with loathing?'

Alan had a point. 'I'll just have to be careful

about my reactions. Who knows, I may learn to love the disgusting little creatures.'

'Furthermore,' Alan went on, as if I hadn't spoken, 'this chap is plainly unstable emotionally. Don't forget he may have once pushed you downstairs. You could have been killed, Dorothy!'

'I know. My guardian angel was obviously working overtime. But I don't think he was the one, Alan, I truly don't. He didn't show any reaction at all when I mentioned stairs. Besides, he's fairly conspicuous, with his very dark skin. I know I wasn't paying any particular attention, but I think I would have spotted him if he'd been there.'

'I don't like it, Dorothy.'

The poor man! His well-developed English instinct for getting the women and children out of the way of danger was surfacing again.

'Suppose I were to take someone with me,' I said. 'Someone who wouldn't be a threat to Mahala.'

'For example?'

'I'll bet Jennifer knows someone, or Terence. Some stalwart student – perhaps a hearty type whose brain is not his most prominent feature. If he's obviously a mental lightweight, Mahala would have contempt for him and would dismiss him as any sort of threat. Besides, he could help us carry those miserable rats.'

'You're going to have to stop thinking of them in those terms,' he said with a resigned sigh as he picked up his phone.

Nineteen

Terence was able to come up with just the person we needed. 'His name is Jim Ashby. He plays rugby for St Stephen's, rows for the college, and does a good many other sports as well. If he has ever been seen attending a lecture or studying in the library, the word hasn't reached me. A nice lad, but thick as two planks.'

'How does he manage to stay at the university?'

'He hasn't had to take any examinations yet. How he got in at all is the real question.'

'Can you find him and have him call me or Dorothy?'

'He'll be on the river or the tennis courts. I'll find him, but it may take a little while. He doesn't carry his phone – says it distracts him while he's working. By which he means playing.'

Alan reported to me, and with that I had to be content. Not willingly. I had got over my sleepiness and wanted to get on with it. 'Well, then, let's go over to the Hutchins Building and find out how soon they're going to open it up again. Then we'll know when I can plan to tackle Mahala about helping.'

'We've not got a lot of time before supper. If you want to eat in hall, that is.'

'It won't take long. And then we can work out our plans about eating, depending on what Elaine says.'

But all thoughts of supper vanished when we talked to Elaine. We were approaching the front door of the Hutchins Building when she flew out and ran to us. 'He's alive!' she cried. 'I just talked to him!'

She meant Tom, of course. 'Is he all right? Where has he been? Is he coming home?' Alan and I peppered her with questions, which she waved away.

'That's just it. I don't know! He rang up just now, not on his own phone, but when I answered, he said only a few words before we were cut off. And when I tried calling back, the mobile was out of service. I don't know what to do!' She turned away to try to hide her tears.

I stood there, helpless. I knew from my own experience that when a person is fighting for composure, sympathy is the last thing she wants.

Alan sensibly reacted like a cop. 'What exactly did he say?' His voice was crisp and businesslike.

'Nothing helpful. Only my name, and "I'm OK, but—" and then nothing.'

'Any background noises?'

She shrugged. 'You know what mobiles are. The signal wasn't good. I heard nothing but his voice, and that wasn't clear.'

'Not a strong signal. That could mean he's not in a city or town.'

'Or that the phone's battery was low, or he was near a solid structure, or . . . almost anything.'

'You'll try to trace the phone, of course.'

'I'll try. It's much harder when we're dealing with mobiles. Landlines were traceable to a subscriber and a location. Mobiles . . .' She shrugged again. 'But I'll phone the station and give them the number, and see what they can do. Excuse me.'

'She's no worse off than before,' said Alan. We had let Elaine get a little ahead of us before going into the building. 'In fact, better, because now she knows for sure that he's alive.'

'But it's such tantalizing knowledge! Alive, but where? Alive, but why can't he use his phone? Alive, but why was the call cut off? Alive, but obviously in trouble. She's frantically trying to think how to find him, and there's no better way now than before, but she feels even more helpless.'

Alan said nothing. There was nothing to say.

Nora, who was apparently Elaine's most senior forensic investigator, came to talk to us as we walked into the building. 'We were just about to shut down here when the super got the call. With the blood coming, apparently, from an accident, there's nothing for us to do here. Steve is taking the tape down now and reopening the building.'

'Did you find anything of any interest in the more intensive search?'

She shrugged. 'This and that. Some soft porn in somebody's locker. A little stash of scalpels and syringes, apparently used, but clean.'

Alan's attention sharpened. 'Syringes?'

'Very small ones. No druggie would want them. Some really old comic books about Godzilla, most of them in Japanese.' She shrugged. 'No accounting for taste, I suppose. There was really nothing of any importance.'

'Do all the students have lockers here in the building?'

'I don't know how many students work here,' she said, the patience in her voice undercut by weariness. 'There are ten lockers, all of them in one room on the second floor. There were lab coats in most of them.'

'CCTV footage?' Alan glanced up at the camera over the door.

'First thing we checked, of course. Not working.' Her patience was definitely wearing thin.

We thanked her and let her finish her job. 'That wasn't very interesting,' I complained as we plodded to the dining hall.

'Except for the syringes. I have to believe the woman when she says they're not the sort addicts would use, but dashed if I can work out why anyone else would want used syringes. If they're plastic, they couldn't even be sterilized again.'

'And everybody nowadays uses the throwaways, syringe and needle all in one.' I threw my hands out, disposing of the idea. 'I think we should skip supper. Let's go back to the library to see if we can help Mahala with his rats.'

'To see if *you* can help,' Alan corrected. 'He doesn't like me. And you need to find that stalwart dunce to go along. We'll have time to eat, and we need some rest in any case.'

'But what if Mahala gets away before I can go back there?'

'Darling, he's not going to "get away". You forget the rats – the passion of his life. He'll never be far away from them.'

I wasn't satisfied, but I had to concede the

point. If I didn't take someone with me to meet Mahala, Alan was going to put his foot down and veto the whole project. I sighed and followed him to the hall, where serving was about to end and the pickings were somewhat slim.

The stalwart dunce phoned just as we'd finished eating. He sounded pleasant enough. 'Mr Nesbitt? You don't know me, but a friend said you need help with something?'

'Ah. You must be Mr Ashby.'

'Oh, yes, sorry. Jim Ashby, at your service.'

'It's actually my wife who requires some assistance. Here she is.'

He handed me the phone. We went through the usual my-name-isn't-Nesbitt routine, and then I explained my mission, including only the information I considered necessary.

'Rats?' he said cheerily. 'I'm your man. I love rats. Had a pair when I was a kid. Sweet little things. I'll just need to clean up a bit; been on the courts, you know.'

'Oh, please don't bother,' I said hastily, visions of a fleeing Mahala rushing through my brain.

'No bother. Where is it you need me to go?'

'The library, but truly—'

'Right-o. I'll see you in about twenty minutes. Or thereabouts.'

I gave Alan's phone back to him. 'What's the matter? He can't come?'

'He wants to clean up first. He's been "on the courts", whatever that means. Tennis, I suppose. It's sweet, I suppose, that he doesn't want to show up all hot and sweaty, but every minute wasted is one more chance for Mahala to

202

disappear. And after that frustrating call from Tom, we need to talk to him more than ever.'

'Yes. There's time. I'll walk you over there and vanish as soon as Ashby appears.'

The long twilight of an April evening was beginning to settle over the college as we walked slowly to the library. The beauty and serenity seemed to touch even the noisy students; their voices were softer, their laughter less raucous. I wished the turmoil in my own mind could be similarly quieted, but too many trains of thought were criss-crossing. There was going to be a major train wreck, I thought uneasily. What could a missing student, robotic rats and the blood of a haemophiliac have to do with each other? What kind of pattern could they make that would also accommodate a nearly hysterical student, terrified of the police? My mind conjured up a horrific picture of colliding locomotives, spilling out bleeding rats by the hundreds.

I stumbled. Alan caught my arm and kept me upright. 'Daydreaming, darling?'

'More like day nightmares.' I shook my head to clear it and looked up. We had arrived at the library.

It, too, looked serene and idyllic. The glow of lights within turned our twilit world to a soft blue. One could almost believe in the peaceful world of academe where, as Sayers's Harriet Vane had put it, the restoration of 'a lost iota subscript' was of supreme importance.

But even in Harriet Vane's fictional world, the clamour and confusion and, yes, the crime of the real world came pressing in, intruding on the blessed peace. The serenity of an Oxbridge college was an illusion.

The serenity right here was abruptly shattered by the loud noise of something clattering to the ground, a high-pitched squealing and a male voice screaming words I couldn't understand, but whose profane nature was easily deduced.

'Oh, Lord, he's dropped one of the rats!' I stifled the scream that tried to escape, and looked around for a bench to climb on in case the miserable thing escaped.

Alan took a firm hold of my hand. 'Steady, old girl. You'll be all right. Here, pop into the reading room. No rats there.'

'No. I have to see what's happening. Just don't go anywhere!'

I did feel safer at the top of the stairs leading to the main entrance to the library. I didn't know how fast a rat could move, or how good it was at climbing stairs, but at least from this vantage point I could see more of my surroundings. Not particularly well, though. The day had reached that stage so aptly described in *Macbeth* as 'almost at odds with morning, which is which'. Except in this case it was day fading into night, the light now an indeterminate grey that consigned everything to obscurity, everything except those objects in the small pools of yellow light cast by occasional street lamps.

One such object revealed itself to be a plastic cage, still, as far as I could tell, intact and inhabited. As I watched apprehensively, a man rushed into the light, did something to the cage, picked it up and began to murmur words I couldn't understand. Again, though, I was sure I knew what he was saying.

'Dorothy, I do *not* think this is a good idea,' Alan was saying, when a large figure loped up the steps, two at a time, and skidded to a stop at my side. 'You'll be Mrs Martin. Terence said you'd be wearing a hat. I'm Jim Ashby.'

He was probably the most amazing physical specimen I've ever seen in my life. Alan is a substantial man, but Jim dwarfed him in both height and girth. And he was, incredibly, not even panting after rushing his impressive weight up a longish flight of stairs. Alan took one look, recognized that I was adequately protected and faded into the background.

More anguished profanity sounded from below. Jim frowned. 'Looks like that fellow could use a spot of help. 'Scuse me.' He loped down the stairs as fast as he had climbed them, arriving at the scene of Mahala's distress just as the frantic rat escaped the cage and ran squealing into the shrubbery.

I made my slow and careful way down the stairs, trying to see what was happening, but it was too dark. When I reached the bottom, though, and could see better, there was Jim, gently cradling a huge white rat on one arm, while with the other hand he stroked it, murmuring words of comfort. And Mahala – angry, defensive Mahala – stood and smiled, reaching out eager hands for the animal.

'Thank you, man, thank you! I feared she would be lost, or hurt. She is valuable, you understand.'

'Beautiful, too. Never saw one as big as her.' With what looked like reluctance, Jim handed the rat over to her keeper, who ran his hands anxiously over her plump body. 'Don't think there's much amiss with her. She was running as fast as those little legs would carry her.'

'I thank you again for catching her. I hope that this will not cause her to abort her babies, but I am worried. Stress, and a fall – it is not good.'

Jim whistled. 'I'd say not! Where were you taking her?'

'They are all to go back to their home in the Hutchins Building. They should never have been taken away! This could ruin nearly two years of work – important work!' Mahala was getting excited again.

'Oh, they'll be fine. Rats are pretty tough. But if you have more to move, I could help, if you like. I like rats.'

'I can see that you do. I must move twelve of them, and I would be glad of your help.'

I stepped up, then, trying to look as if I'd just come on the scene. 'Good evening, Mahala. Having a little trouble with your rats?'

He frowned. Jim, who was perhaps not quite as dim as advertised, smiled at me. 'He has to move a dozen of these big beauties across the college grounds, so I said I'd help. I can carry two at a time.'

'Oh, dear. What a pity it has to be done on foot. But listen, I have an idea. Since you're both students, I'll bet the library would let us borrow some book carts. We could probably fit four cages on each, and do it all in one trip.'

'That is a good idea,' said Mahala in tones of astonishment. 'I will ask.'

'Why don't you stay here and tend to Mrs Whiskers here? Jim can get the cart – or carts. Three of them if they'll let you have that many, Jim.'

'Mrs Whiskers?' Mahala looked mystified.

I laughed. 'After a character in an English children's book. An intelligent and capable rat, though a bit of a thief, I'm afraid. Look, I'll go and get the cage for you. It will be easier to get her back into it with another pair of hands helping.'

That meant I would actually have to touch the thing. I had to admit, though, that up close she had enough resemblance to a cat to make me feel a little less repugnance.

I didn't have to test it, though. Jim came back with the carts before I found the cage, so he helped Mahala get Mrs Whiskers back inside. Her water bottle had become dislodged when the cage fell, spilling water all over her bedding, so Mahala simply emptied the soggy stuff out on the grass. 'She can do without for a little time,' he said, and firmly placed the rat in the cage, and closed and latched the door. She didn't seem to like the slippery plastic floor, but she was plainly tired after her adventure and settled down quickly.

Good grief! I was beginning to identify a rat's moods and preferences. Where would this end?

It didn't take long to load the remaining cages on the carts. Jim was the greatest possible help. It was he who tirelessly trotted down the stairs to the room where the rats were temporarily housed and trotted up again, bearing two cages at a time – something like nine pounds of squealing, wiggling rats. Mahala and I situated them securely on the carts, and we worked out a route to the Hutchins Building that involved grass almost all the way. Paths would have been much easier had they been solidly paved, but the gravel pathways, while attractive, weren't friendly to anything with wheels.

We had to be very careful not to jog the cages off the carts, which were just barely big enough to accommodate their loads. So our progress was slow. That was fine with me. I needed all the time I could get with Mahala, while he was in a good mood.

'Where in Africa do you come from, Mahala?' I asked as we carefully wheeled our carts across the smooth lawn.

He named a country I'd heard of, but couldn't place at the moment. I shook my head. 'I'm afraid I don't know where that is, exactly. I'm woefully ignorant of African geography, except for some of the bigger countries. I'm from the state of Indiana, by the way. I don't imagine you've ever heard of it?'

I made it a question, and he shook his head. 'Is it near New York or California?'

'Oh, dear, you're just as bad as me. No, it's quite far from either of those states. Indiana is in what's called the Midwest, the central part of the country. Perhaps you've heard of the city of Chicago?'

He eased his cart over a path that crossed our stretch of grass and then nodded. 'There is a university there, is there not? And a great deal of crime? That is where you live?' He took one end of my cart and helped me lift it to safety on to the grass.

'Several universities, and, sadly, yes, a great deal of crime. But I never did live there. I live in England now, but I was born and raised almost three hundred miles from Chicago, in a quiet little town called Hillsburg. Chicago, though, is the biggest city in the Midwest, and the nearest to my town that most people over here recognize.'

'Was your town rich or poor?'

Uh-oh. This was perilous territory. 'We didn't think we were rich, but looking back on it, I suppose we were.'

Mahala shrugged. 'All Americans are rich.'

'Most of us, probably. But there is great poverty in some areas. America, too, has people who do not have enough to eat, whose children beg on the streets, whose aged relatives must go without medicines because they have no money to buy them.'

'I do not believe you,' he said flatly. 'All Americans are rich. It is well known.'

Time to change the subject. 'Mahala, why did you choose to experiment with rats? I would have thought some animal nearer in nature to humans would have been a more likely choice.'

Again a shrug. 'The higher animals are expensive and take far longer to breed. Rats are cheap. They are also very intelligent and easy to work with. Also, one does not have to begin at the beginning. There is a very large body of previous research with rats, so that the norms are established. You would not know about norms.'

'I do, though. My father and my first husband were both biologists. I'm neither fluent in terminology nor learned in the biological sciences, but I do know the basics.' I took a deep breath and looked back to see how closely Jim was following us. 'I also know quite a lot about people. I taught children for many years in Indiana, and Mahala, I can nearly always tell when someone is lying.'

Twenty

He said nothing, but he stumbled. His cart rocked and one of the cages jogged perilously close to the edge of the top shelf. I stopped and reached over to push it back to safety.

'No! You will not touch my animals! I do not like you. Go away!'

The rats began to squeak.

'You're upsetting them, Mahala. You know they don't like angry voices.'

'You have called me a liar! That is not a good thing to say.' He moved away angrily.

'It's true, though. I'm quite sure you didn't tell the truth about how you got the cut on your arm. Look out – there's a pathway just ahead. Don't jostle your cart! Mrs Whiskers is on it, and you don't want her to fall again.'

'Why would you care? You do not like rats. I can tell.'

'No. I don't care much for rats, as a general rule. But I don't want to see any animal suffer, and when animals are loved, as you love your rats, they become more lovable themselves.'

'You – you have seen that I love my rats? You do not think that is foolish?'

'No, Mahala. I have two cats and a dog, and I love them dearly. Why shouldn't you love your rats?'

'But you and your husband want to arrest me

211

and put me in prison, and then my rats would die, and I—' He stopped talking abruptly, and stopped pushing his cart as well. We were under a street light, and I could see, with astonishment, that tears were coursing down his dark cheeks.

I thought I'd better not notice. This proud, arrogant man would not cry easily, nor would he want anyone to see, much less a woman and a foreigner.

'No, Mahala, we do not want to put you in prison. We just want some answers about what has been happening here at St Stephen's, and we want to find Tom Grenfell. We believe that you might help us.'

He caught hold of my arm. His grip was painful. Behind us, Jim cleared his throat. Mahala paid no attention. 'You do not lie to me? You swear it?' His voice was ragged.

We were in front of the chapel, whose clock chose that moment to chime. 'I swear it, Mahala.' I solemnly made the sign of the cross. 'We want only the truth.'

He dropped my arm. A sob escaped him, instantly covered up with a cough.

'Look, let's get your animals safely back to their home. Jim and I can help you feed them or whatever they might need at this point, and then maybe we could go somewhere and talk.' He needed time to recover his composure. Of course, he might also recover his belligerence, but I thought I had to take that chance.

There was a young man going in the front door as we approached it. He nodded stiffly. Mahala nodded in return. The young man was a student,

212

then, I guessed. It was plain the two knew each other, and equally plain that they were not friends. Well, Terence had said that Mahala had no real friends in the department. How sad for him, I thought for the first time. Thousands of miles from home, and his only friends were rats.

It took a little longer than I had expected to get the rats safely tucked away for the night. For one thing, the Hutchins Building had no elevator, so we had to carry the cages up the stairs. That is, the two young men had to do that. I helped bring them into the building, but I knew all those stairs were beyond me. My titanium knees are pretty cooperative, but several trips up and down several flights of stairs? No. So I waited until all the rats had gone up before I went up myself, partly to see if I could help, partly to make sure Mahala hadn't changed his mind and decided to bolt.

I found him in amiable conversation with Jim. 'She is the best one,' Mahala was saying, pointing out a rat with pride. 'She is strong and smart.'

'The prettiest, too,' said Jim fondly, stroking the little animal with one finger.

To me all the rats looked exactly alike – disgusting. But I didn't dare show Mahala my distaste. 'Where is Mrs Whiskers?' I asked, forcing myself to come farther into the room.

Mahala smiled. Actually smiled. 'Here. I gave her fresh bedding, you see. I would let you hold her, but she has become calm, and it is bad for her and her babies to be excited.'

'Oh, that's all right,' I said hastily. 'Of course you mustn't disturb her. I'm sure she'll be all right once she's had a quiet night's sleep. Oh, and they are quiet, aren't they? No more squeaking.'

'They are happy to be home. We will leave them to rest.'

Well, I couldn't understand, really, how having one's cage on an accustomed shelf in an accustomed room rather than an unfamiliar shelf in an unfamiliar room made much difference, but then I'm not a rat. A matter of light and odours, I supposed.

'Might I come and visit them sometimes?' asked Jim, sounding a little wistful. 'I'm not allowed pets here.'

Mahala snapped off the lights and locked the door. 'Tell me when you would like to come, and I will meet you here. The door is kept locked, you understand.'

'Right. It's important work you're doing. Well . . .' Jim looked at me, a question in his eyes.

'Jim, Mahala and I are going out for a drink. Mahala, would you mind if Jim joined us?'

'I don't drink,' said Jim, and at the same time Mahala said, 'I do not know . . .'

I had to make a quick decision. It looked as if Mahala didn't want anyone else around when he talked to me. Alan would be most upset at the idea of my going anywhere with Mahala, unescorted. But a public place would surely be safe enough; anyway, I was beginning to believe that the poor boy posed no threat, at least not to me. Could anyone who loved animals as he clearly did be a murderer?

That, I realized, was spurious logic at best, just

214

plain nonsense at worst. On the other hand, there was no real evidence that a murder had been committed. The only person from the university community who had been reported missing was Tom Grenfell, and he was alive, or at any rate had been a few hours ago. Mahala had said the blood on the floor was his own.

I made up my mind. Mahala was here, he was in a compliant mood just now, and he probably had some answers to important questions. By the time I had to explain myself to Alan, I'd have information that would placate him.

'Oh, of course, you're in training, aren't you?' I smiled at Jim. 'Go get your sleep, and thank you so much for your help. Oh, and Jim, do me a favour, will you? I forgot to charge my phone. Would you call Alan for me and tell him I'll be a bit late getting back, and not to worry?' I gave him the number and a wink.

I'd told a blatant lie about my phone, which was charged up and ready to go, but I didn't want to talk to Alan myself just now. He'd make demands, and I preferred not to defy him openly. I love my husband, but there are times when I need to make my own decisions. In fact, I thought I'd turn my phone off while I was with Mahala. I shrugged off the pang of conscience that cost me and turned to him. 'Where shall we go? I don't know many pubs around here.'

'I do not, either. I do not like pubs. They are noisy and crowded. There is a quiet place in the next street where we could have coffee.'

'That sounds perfect, if it isn't too far away. I'm a bit tired and achy.' Mahala's only response to that was to slow his pace somewhat, and I was more firmly convinced that he knew nothing about my fall at the Fitzwilliam.

The café he had chosen was small and somewhat shabby, without the trappings of a Starbucks or the other chain coffee houses, but it was clean. We sat down, and I was about to ask Mahala what he would like when he stood and asked me.

Oh, dear. I'd almost made a big mistake. Doubtless Mahala had little money, but his male pride meant he would not allow a woman to pay. 'Just coffee, please. It had better be decaf at this hour of the evening, or I'll never get to sleep.' He sketched a little bow and went to the counter.

When he came back with our coffees, I began the conversation with the typical American questions. 'Coming from West Africa, Mahala, how did you end up at St Stephen's?'

'My country, Burkina Faso – do you know anything about it?'

'Actually, I do. My church in the States once sent a team of people to help dig wells there. I can understand why you are concerned about your people. From what I learned then, your country suffers from terrible poverty.'

'Yes. Poverty, government corruption, illness, poor education – almost no one can read. But we are not a stupid people!'

'Well, plainly you're not stupid. How is it that you speak such good English? I think I heard somewhere that French is the official language in Burkina Faso.'

'I also speak French. I speak my native language, and other native languages. There are many languages in my country. That is one reason education is so difficult to establish, but only one reason.' He sighed. 'There are so many problems, and it seems that each one must be solved before the others can be approached. As for me, I was very fortunate. I am a Christian, and went to a school led by an English priest. That is very unusual. Most of the missionaries are French, but this school was closer to me than any of the others, and it was free, so I could go to it more easily.'

He sipped his coffee. 'It was still not easy, you understand. I worked all day with my father, who had a small farm, with chickens, some sheep and cattle, a few crops. We were very poor, and I was the only son to help my father. I was tired at the end of the day, but I walked to the school and worked hard there, too. The teacher stayed behind until night to teach me. Sometimes I had to sleep there, because it is not always safe to walk the roads at night.'

'Wild animals? Lions?'

His slight smile was bleak. 'There are a few lions, but not many. They have been hunted to death, to give white men trophies to hang on their walls. Those that are left have learned to avoid humans. There are sometimes packs of wild dogs, but the great danger is from people. The military, or gangs of bandits, or terrorists . . .' He spread his hands. 'So I sometimes slept at the school, but I would rise very early, to go back home to tend the animals.

'It was not an easy life, but I was learning much. And then my father was killed by terrorists.' He said it in a matter-of-fact way that chilled my blood. 'I was at school, or they would have killed me, too. My mother and my sisters were working in the fields and ran away, but the terrorists burned down our house and stole all our animals. Nothing was left for us.'

My coffee was cold, but I drank some of it anyway. I couldn't think of anything to say in the face of such stark tragedy.

'I stayed at the school. There was no other place for me to go. The priest, Father Ron, was good to me. I worked for my keep, tending the chickens they kept for food, helping teach the younger ones. Father Ron worked very hard to learn what had become of my family, and was finally told that my mother had found work as a cook in an orphanage in Nigeria. My sisters . . .' Again he spread his hands, and I thought I saw in his eyes what might have become of his sisters. I tried not to think about it.

'And that is my story. Father Ron saw that I was very good in scientific studies. He arranged for me to sit my examinations in Nigeria, and took me to Lagos. I learned later that he paid the examination fee himself. He helped me apply for scholarships and paid, himself, for my transport to England. He has been like a father to me.'

I swallowed. 'He is a white man?'

'Yes. But his heart, I think, is African.'

'Then – forgive me, Mahala, but I must ask – why is it that you seem to hate white people so? The other students . . .'

Again that unamused smile. 'I do not hate them because they are white. I hate them because they are lazy. They have had everything handed to them on a plate, all their lives. They do not know what it means to study with no books, with an empty belly, after a long day of hard work. They do not know what it is to live always in the shadow of terror. They think it is a hard thing to have to write an essay instead of going out to play, on the river or the tennis courts or the football field or the cricket pitch. And they hate me because I think such things are foolish.'

'Then why don't you hate me, too? Anyone can tell by looking at me that I've never suffered any serious privation. I'm well fed, too well fed. I have clothes to keep me warm, and a car to drive and a house to live in. The only frightful personal loss I've ever experienced was the death of my first husband, and that was of natural causes. I've never had to struggle, not really.' I was jeopardizing the fragile relationship I'd built with him, but I really wanted to know why he'd accepted me.

He took his time about replying. 'I do not know,' he said finally. 'Perhaps it is because you are kind. You are like Father Ron. You have shown that you care about me, and about my rats. Even though you are afraid of them.' This time the smile was almost genuine. 'You do not like them, but you helped me with them anyway. That is the sign of a good heart. So I trust you, and I am going to answer your questions.'

Now we'd come to it. I swallowed again. 'Thank you for telling me about your life. It helps me to understand a lot. And forgive me for not . . . well, not being able to overcome my fear of rats. Maybe one day I'll learn better. But right now I need to know all *you* know about what's been happening at St Stephen's. Tom Grenfell is still missing, and I'm sure his mother is worried sick about him. I hope that together you and I may be able to work out what's happened to him.'

'I do not know where he is. I told you that.'

'I know you did, and I believe you. But you do know much more than you've told us about the goings-on among the students in the Hutchins Building.'

To my alarm, he stood, but all he said was, 'I will get us more coffee.'

The first cup had been pretty dire, but my mouth was dry. Maybe if I put enough milk and sugar in it, I could down another. 'Decaf again for me, please.'

When he had brought our coffees and sat down again, I said, 'Now. You didn't tell the truth about how you got that cut on your arm. I'm sorry, by the way, that I made it start bleeding again.'

He looked down at his cup. 'No. I did not want you to know that I had been fighting.'

'I thought it might be something like that. But, Mahala, isn't it dangerous for you to get into a fight? Even a slight blow might be very serious for you – internal bleeding and so on.'

'My disease is a rather mild form of haemophilia. I do not have the bleeding at the joints that afflicts some, but, of course, I bruise very easily. It was much worse when I lived in Africa. There was no access to the medications I need, and several times when I hurt myself on the farm I bled for a long time. That is one reason I never participate in games of any kind. It makes the students here despise me. They think I am a coward, or that I think myself better than they. And I do!' he added fiercely. 'I am smarter than they are. I work harder. I am worthy of respect!'

'No doubt,' I said rather drily, 'though generally the English give more respect to those who don't demand it. You'd have more friends, Mahala, if you didn't show so clearly how you feel about your classmates. However . . . You got into a fight.'

'It was because of my rats. The other students wanted to play a joke – a prank, they called it. Foolishness! At first they intended to take one of the other animals – a guinea pig – and make him appear as if dead, and then make him come alive. They planned to scatter blood around to make people believe he really was dead, and they asked me if I would extract some from one of my rats. The rats are big, you see, and very healthy, and the students said it wouldn't hurt them to lose a small amount of blood.'

'But you said you wouldn't, and that's when the fight started.'

'Not then, not yet. I thought a bit and said I was going to kill a chicken soon. I told them it was for a ritual.'

'But you're a Christian. I don't understand.'

'In Africa, the old religions are often mixed in with Christianity. Father Ron never worried about that. He said God would understand. Here, though, I do not practise the old rituals. The English do not like it. They are afraid of the old religions.'

221

'Why did you tell them that's what you were doing, then?'

Again he avoided my eyes. 'I keep chickens for food, for eggs and meat. I am poor. I did not want them to know that I cannot always go to the supermarket and buy my food, as they can.'

'And then for some reason you couldn't get the chicken, after all.'

'Foxes had taken most of them. There were only two left. I could not spare one.'

'So you brought a cat. I heard that part of the story from Terence, and I have to say I don't like it much. I may be afraid of rats, but I'm very fond of cats, and the idea of killing one appals me.'

He looked at me in astonishment. 'But there was never any talk of killing it! I would have extracted its blood, as they wanted me to do with the rat. It was a big cat, a stray, but strong and healthy. The loss of a little blood would not have hurt it at all. But then . . .'

'Yes. What happened then?'

'The students could not agree about a schedule for their joke. Some thought it should wait until the end of term; some wanted to do it right away. Of course, the blood would have to be extracted very near to the time they wished to use it, because even with an anticoagulant added, it would not stay fresh forever. So I let the cat go. I knew I could catch it again when they were ready, if I chose to do so. I was growing more and more impatient with the foolishness, in any case. It was taking time away from my studies and my rats, and my work is important! It may one day help feed my people, and other peoples all over Africa.'

'So you let the cat go.'

'I took it back to near the house where I live. It is familiar with that area, and there are, I think, people there who feed it. I had no wish to leave it in a place where it would starve. I am not a cruel person, whatever you think!'

'I don't think you're cruel, Mahala. I did, when I thought you were going to kill a cat, but that was before I saw how much you care about your rats, and before you explained about the cat. But you still haven't told me how your arm was injured.'

'There is a student, a first-year. I do not know his name. I do not like him. He has quarrelled with me, tried to tell me I was feeding my rats improperly. He has no idea what I am trying to do! He knows nothing about rats, nothing about zoology, nothing, nothing!'

As his voice rose, people turned to look at us. I touched his hand and brought out my school-teacher voice again. 'Now, Mahala. Calm down. I'm not arguing with you. We'll agree that the boy *is* ignorant and annoying. Go on with your story.'

He was shaking. 'He came to me, this stupid boy. He is one of the leaders of the group planning the foolish joke. He said that they had changed their mind about what they wanted to do, and they would need a great deal of blood, because they were going to use a huge rat. "Ratzilla", they would call it. They would pretend it was one of mine, grown to almost human size,

223

but it would really be a robot. And it would run about over the college grounds, frightening everyone, and one of the students would try to stab it with a knife, and it would spurt blood, lots of blood, but it would not stop.'

Mahala was trying to control his voice, but he was shaking with anger. 'They would make me a laughing stock, me and my rats. They would treat my work like a joke. He said they would need a great deal of blood, and perhaps I should kill the cat, after all, or there might be enough in one of my rats. He had a scalpel in his hand and he waved it about as if ready to kill one of my rats, and I struck out at him, and the scalpel cut my arm, over a vein, and it began to bleed and would not stop, and he was afraid and ran away.'

I sat silent for a few moments, considering what I learned. I was certain it was the truth. It fit with what I already knew, and moreover with Nigel's robotics idea. I could see how it all could have happened. But . . .

'I see,' I said at last. 'Why did you then take the blood to the lab downstairs? At least, I'm assuming this didn't all happen in that lab. You don't work there, do you?'

'Sometimes. Not that day. It was upstairs in my room, with my rats. It upset them, the shouting and the smell of blood.'

'They can smell blood?'

Mahala gave me a pitying look. 'Even humans can smell blood. Rats have a better, a much better sense of smell than humans, even than dogs. They are intelligent, sensitive creatures.'

'I'm learning that. But I still don't understand

why you saved the blood, or at any rate took it downstairs.'

'I bled a great deal before I could put on a bandage and then inject my medication. Fortunately there was a basin at hand. I held it under the cut until I could get the bleeding stopped, so there was only a tiny amount spilt on the floor. I took the basin away to dispose of it properly; there are strict rules about the disposal of blood, especially human blood. But as I carried it downstairs, I was still very angry. I thought I would find a way to turn the joke back on those fatuous students. I would use their own idea against them. I was too angry to think clearly, but I was sure I could find a way to use blood to make them look as foolish and stupid as they are.

'There are anticoagulant chemicals kept in the zoology lab. I thought I would add them to my blood, which does not coagulate well anyway, and see how long it could be kept liquid in a sealed container. Then I would have time to plan my revenge. But I was angry, and somewhat unsteady from the loss of blood, and when I heard someone coming into the building from the rear, it startled me, and I stumbled and spilt the blood out of the basin on to the floor.'

And that, I thought, was literally where I came in. 'Yes, all right. And then after I left, you came back and cleaned up quickly, but something prevented you from doing a thorough job until Friday afternoon.'

'There were people using the lab later that day and all day Thursday. And then on Thursday evening, when it was not scheduled for a class, one of my pregnant rats was showing signs of distress. She is not due to deliver for a week, but I had to stay with her.'

'Of course you did. Well, that explains it all, doesn't it? Except for what has happened to Tom. And why you were so frightened earlier this evening, when Alan and I tried to talk to you.'

His face, which had been candid and friendly until then, closed up. 'I have told you I do not know where Grenfell is. I have told you that I do not like the police. I was not frightened. I was anxious about my rats. And I must go now and tend to them. Goodnight.'

'Thank you for my coffee,' I called to the door as it closed behind him.

Twenty-One

Well, so much for that. I gathered up my purse and jacket, and headed for the door. The café was, I thought, about ready to close for the night. There were only two other customers, and they were finishing their coffee. I fished my phone out of my bag, turned it on, and noted the time. After ten. Heavens, Alan would be frantically wondering where I was. I figured out how to check for messages, and, sure enough, there were three from him.

Oh, dear. I really shouldn't have caused him all that worry. The only thing to do now was to call and ask him to come and get me. He would be really angry if I walked back alone through dark and mostly deserted streets. Cambridge on a weeknight is nothing like as crowded as during the day, and the café was on a side street far from the pubs. I took a deep breath and punched the buttons that let me return Alan's latest call.

'Dorothy! Are you all right?'

'I'm fine. Don't worry. I'm at a café in – wait a minute.' I looked up at the clerk who was counting the money in the till. 'What's the address here? My friend brought me and I wasn't paying attention. Here, could you tell my husband?' I handed her the phone, taking it back after she'd given Alan clear directions about how to get here. 'It's only a couple of minutes from the college;

227

don't bother to drive. I could have walked back, but I thought you'd rather I had an escort. No, Mahala's left. I'll tell you everything when I see you. And I repeat, stop fretting. I'm fine.'

The clerk kindly let me wait inside, though she was ready to lock up. She looked to be all of nineteen or twenty, and I suppose to her I was a doddering old lady with one foot in the grave, and off my rocker as well. Wearing a *hat*, of all things! Definitely not safe to be out on the dark street alone.

When I was a child and strayed away from my parents in a department store, or stayed longer than I was supposed to at the zoo or the skating rink or a party, I was greeted, when I finally rejoined them, first with relief and then with fury. 'Oh, thank heavens you're back, where have you *been*!' pretty much summed it up, the last few words spoken in absolute rage. I'm the same way now when one of our pets is missing for too long. So I knew what to expect from Alan, and he didn't disappoint me. I listened and nodded and murmured understanding and apologies as we walked back to our home-from-home.

'Very well, then, love,' he said as we walked into our room and shut the door behind us. 'I've got that out of my system. Now we sit down and have a civilized drink – I laid in supplies while you were gone – and you can tell me what you think was worth frightening me out of seven years' growth.'

'I think you've done all your growing.' I took off my hat and ran my hands through my short hair. 'And if you start getting shorter in your old

228

age, along with everybody else, I refuse to take the blame. Make mine a stiff one. It's been a trying day.' I piled pillows against the headboard and a couple under my knees and stretched out on the bed with a luxurious sigh.

'Here you are, madam. Now, your story, please.'

I took a long, satisfying pull at my drink. 'Aah! I needed that. Well, for a start, I didn't find out anything at all about Tom's whereabouts. I didn't get around to asking about that until the end of my little chat with Mahala, and I do mean the end. The question shut off communications as if I'd flipped a switch. "I don't know, I have to go see my rats, goodbye."'

'Which means he *does* know something.'

'Knows or suspects, and whatever it is, it scares him to death. He denied that, too. Being scared, I mean. Just said again that he didn't like the police. Alan, he's an amazingly courageous person. It would take something really dreadful to frighten him. Listen to what he's been through in his young life.' I tried to summarize, but the story still brought tears to my eyes. 'I can easily see why he'd hate people like us, who know nothing about suffering on that scale.'

Alan nodded. 'Gangs of bandits, the army, terrorists who killed his father and destroyed his home – yes. That could teach him to hate. It could also teach him violence.'

'But then there was the other influence in his life – the priest who was kind, who taught him to value his own abilities, who helped him on the way to Cambridge and the achievement of his heart's desire – helping his own people. He

229

has some admirable qualities, Alan, truly. But there's something more going on in his life, something he hasn't told us about, and I don't have a single idea what it might be.'

'Hmm.' Alan put his glass down on the bedside table and tented his hands in his familiar lecturing pose. 'Let's think about it. He's frightened, and most particularly frightened of the police. That implies that he's involved in something illegal.'

'Ye-es,' I said reluctantly. 'But what?'

'He's poor. He told you so. He keeps chickens in order to eat. I suspect that was why he decided not to kill one for the prank. It was probably his food for the next week.'

'So you think he has stolen something in order to stay solvent?'

'Has stolen or is stealing. The chance of being convicted of a single crime is worrisome, but would not, I think, cause the kind of panic we witnessed. I believe his activity is ongoing.'

'But what could he steal that would provide him any significant amount of money? Students don't keep valuable jewellery in their rooms, or great wads of cash. Electronics are worth something, I suppose, but if lots of thefts had been happening, Elaine would know about them, and she hasn't mentioned anything of the kind.'

'No. But there is something else that brings in a lot of money, and is highly illegal.'

'Drugs. But Alan, think! If Mahala were dealing in drugs, he'd have some signs of prosperity. Maybe not fancy rings and chains and that sort of thing, like American street gangs, but a nice place to live, or at least money to buy food so he didn't have to keep chickens. Elaine can look into his lifestyle, of course, but to me it doesn't look like that of a dealer. And he certainly isn't a user. Even I can spot the signs, and *you* would have picked up on it in a minute.'

'Maybe he's sending money home to Burkina Faso.'

'To whom? He has no family there anymore. I suppose he could send some to his mother in Nigeria, but she's working and may not need it. He didn't say much about his sisters, but from the way he didn't say it, he plainly thinks they are either dead or forced into prostitution. Father Ron wouldn't take the money if he had any idea it was drug money. And he'd know, Alan. He knows Mahala hasn't any way to make honest money – not yet, until he gets his degree.'

'You've come around to his side, haven't you, love? It was bound to happen sooner or later. You are a great collector of strays.'

'I feel sorry for underdogs,' I said defensively. 'That's the English in me coming out.'

'All right. Touché. You will, I trust, not forget that an unfortunate background, dire poverty, unpopularity, all the rest, do not necessarily make a person trustworthy. Often quite the reverse, in fact.'

'Point taken. Neither does a love for animals. We're told Hitler loved his dog. But, Alan, you have to admit I'm often right about people, and something about Mahala tells me he's not a criminal at heart. Yes, he's rude and arrogant and defensive and difficult, and he has a quick temper, but I admire what he's trying to do, against fearsome odds. And I'm always impressed by intelligence, which that young man has in abundance. I know he's up to something. But whatever it is, I'll bet it's for a good reason.'

In which opinion, as it turned out, I was both right and disastrously wrong.

We talked for another hour or so, going round in circles and, as one might expect, getting nowhere. I slept badly, waking now and then from disturbing dreams, none of which I could remember in the morning. I woke late, with the headache I deserved after all the bourbon I'd put away, and no idea what to do next.

Alan had slept late, too, unusually for him, and was just getting out of the shower when I staggered out of bed. He filled the kettle and turned it on. I took my turn in the bathroom. Neither of us said anything coherent until we'd had a few sips of coffee. Then I muttered, 'We're stuck, aren't we?'

Alan shrugged and grunted.

My phone rang, making me jump. 'I've got to change that ringtone!' I pawed through my purse and finally found the dratted thing just as the clamour stopped. The number displayed was unfamiliar, but it probably wasn't a telemarketer. Too early in the day, and the phone number was too new for anybody much to have it. I poked the appropriate spots and got an immediate response.

'Dorothy? Thank God! I tried to call Alan and got no answer.' It was Elaine, and she sounded almost hysterical.

'Elaine, what *is* it?'

232

She was talking over my words. 'Can you come here right away? Both of you?'

'Yes, but where are you? And what's happened?'

'The police station. I got – oh, I have to go.' She rang off.

I probably looked as confused as I felt. 'That was Elaine,' I told Alan. 'She's beside herself, not making a lot of sense. She wants us at the police station ASAP. I think something awful's happened. Oh, Alan, maybe they've found Tom . . .' I couldn't complete the thought.

'No point in speculating, darling. The quicker you get dressed the quicker we can get there.'

I threw on the first clothes that came to hand, added a sweater that didn't match, and we were off.

Alan was quite right, of course. Speculation was futile. That didn't keep me from dreaming up one horrible scenario after another as we drove to the station. We hotfooted it to Elaine's office, to find her in the midst of a meeting, firing rapid orders to her subordinates. Alan made sure she saw that we were there and then stood out of the way as men and women hurried away, presumably to do her bidding.

She stood looking blankly at us.

'You asked us to come,' said Alan gently.

She shook herself. 'Yes. This just came in the post.'

She held out a box, about six inches long by a couple of inches wide, the sort with a hinged lid that they used to use for fancy pen-and-pencil sets. Alan opened it, took one look, and closed the box again, swearing quietly.

He never swears. 'What?' I asked urgently, reaching for the box.

He handed it back to Elaine. 'Was there a note? Any other communication?'

'A text. To my personal mobile, not here to the station.'

'A ransom demand?'

'Not exactly. It simply said "STOP LOOKING".'

'Alan. Elaine. *What* is going on? What's in the box?'

Alan turned to me, his face bleak. 'The box contains a human finger, Dorothy.'

Twenty-Two

I was overcome with such a rush of nausea and disgust and fear and sympathy for Elaine that I didn't hear Alan's next few words. When I could pay attention again, Elaine was saying, 'I don't know. There's nothing distinctive about it. A little finger, probably left hand, certainly from a young person. They'll take it away and print it, and try to match it with prints in his room, but if they don't find a match, it needn't mean anything one way or another.' Her voice, her whole being, was under severe control. I wanted to give her a hug, offer sympathy and reassurance, but I knew that was the last thing she wanted or needed just then.

She went on. 'The investigation is under way. I don't know why I called you here. My people are doing all that can be done. I'm sorry to have bothered you.'

'I understand,' said Alan in a strictly-business voice. 'We'll leave you to it. You'll let us know?'

She nodded. Alan steered me out the door.

'Alan, that poor woman!' I said as soon as we were out of earshot.

'Yes. She'll be going through hell just now.'

'I wonder if she's told his parents yet.'

'Probably. It's the first thing I would have done, in similar circumstances. One of the damnable chores that go with the job, like notifying the next of kin of a murder victim.'

235

'Do you think it means Tom has been killed?'

Alan shook his head impatiently. 'Speculating again, Dorothy. They don't even know for sure that the finger is his. Fingerprinting it may decide that.'

'But, as Elaine said, if there isn't a match, it could just mean that he never touched anything in his room with that particular finger. Your left little finger isn't one of the ones you use a lot.'

'No.' We moved on out of the building to our car.

'Is it speculating to wonder what the note means?' I asked as I belted myself in.

Alan permitted himself a tiny smile. 'No, that comes under the heading of deduction. One has to make guesses of that sort.'

'Well, then?'

'The obvious inference is that it means either "stop looking for Tom" or "stop investigating the St Stephen's mysteries".'

'Or both.'

'Indeed.' Alan braked sharply to avoid a cyclist who had appeared out of a blind drive, and I was silent while he negotiated the Cambridge morning traffic.

He parked the car in the multistorey garage he'd found not too far from St Stephen's, and we sat there for a minute or two, not sure where to go or what to do. There seemed to be nothing we *could* do to help, and yet inaction was just not possible.

'Breakfast?' asked Alan finally.

I shuddered. 'I couldn't possibly eat anything. I wouldn't mind a cup of decent coffee, though. It might help my headache.'

'Right.' We headed for the market.

It was another gorgeous day. The market thronged with tourists browsing for presents from Cambridge, students pursuing bargains in T-shirts and snacks, housewives shopping for supper. The scene was colourful, noisy and full of life. It seemed all wrong, when somewhere Tom Grenfell was in terrible trouble, or dead.

'Life goes on, love.'

'I know. It's heartless.'

'Or hopeful. No matter what happens, the ordinary business of life keeps marching along, providing a counterweight to doom and gloom.'

'I suppose.' I wasn't convinced, but I was a little comforted.

We found the little café where Elaine and I had become acquainted, and ordered coffee. The smell of baked goodies was overwhelming. My stomach rumbled, but I thought of a severed finger and had no desire to eat.

We didn't talk. I was content to let the sounds of Cambridge swirl around me while caffeine ratcheted my brain up to full speed. Alan had that faraway look that meant he, too, was thinking furiously.

When we'd finished our coffee, he stood. 'Mahala?' he said. It wasn't really a question.

I nodded. 'Elaine's probably already sent someone to talk to him, though. He's our only lead.'

'Even so, she won't mind having us ask a few questions ourselves. He might talk to you, when he wouldn't to anyone else.'

I shrugged and made my way through the maze of tables and chairs to the door.

'Right. Will he be at home or working at the Hutchins Building?'

'Oh, working, definiely. He's a workaholic. Anyway, he has no friends except those miserable rats. He'll be with them.'

But he wasn't. We went into the building and made our way up to the rat dormitory. A young woman was tending them, replacing water bottles, giving them fresh food and bedding.

'No, I haven't seen Mahala. He's always here. It's very odd. Three of the females are due to have their babies any day now; he should be here.' She sounded surprised, but not terribly interested. Well, of course, she didn't like Mahala. Nobody did.

Alan handed her a card. 'Phone me if he turns up, please. It's very important.'

She glanced at the card, one of his 'civilian' ones, and pocketed it. 'You could try the zoology lab downstairs. He works there sometimes, though not usually at this time of day.'

'Will you be here looking after the rats?'

'No fear! I can't stand rats. I mostly feed the guinea pigs, but they sent me here because *somebody* needed to do it.' Her resentment sounded loud and clear. I doubted very much if she'd pass Alan's message along to Mahala.

We did a quick scan of the building, knocking on locked doors and interrupting students at work. We created a fair amount of irritation, but we didn't find Mahala.

Alan had Mahala's address – the right one this time, we hoped – but he had to ask the porter how to get there. It seemed the boy lived on the very edge of town.

Once we got away from the city centre, driving was easier, and Alan had no trouble finding the address. It was a seedy house in a seedy neighbourhood, but it did at least look inhabited. 'I'm coming with you,' I said firmly as Alan unbuckled his seat belt.

'Of course. You have a rapport with him.'

The door was answered by a very large young black man with a scowl on his face. He said nothing, just stood filling the doorway.

'Good morning,' I said brightly. 'I'm a friend of Mahala's. Is he at home?'

'No.'

The man started to close the door.

'Wait! I really need to talk to him. Where can I find him?'

'Don't know.' The door was closing further.

'Just a moment, sir.' Alan's voice had become very official. 'It is important that we find him as soon as possible. Do you have any idea where he might be? Or would it be possible to look in his room? He might have left a diary that would give us a place to start.'

'This is my house. I do not know you. I do not know where he is, nor do I care.'

This time the door closed firmly, and we heard the snick of a lock.

'So Mahala's missing, too. Alan, this is getting really frightening!'

But Alan had pulled out his phone and was speaking into it in an undertone. 'Yes, we'll stay here until your people come. Yes. I don't think so, but certainly not cooperative. Yes.' He ended the call.

'Elaine?'

Alan nodded. 'She's sending someone immediately. I don't have the authority to detain this chap and require him to answer some questions. She does.'

'But will she? I know I'd like to see him questioned by someone in authority, but he's done nothing wrong, really – not that we know of. She didn't detain Mahala. What's the difference?'

'The difference, though I hate to remind you, is a severed finger. The stakes are higher now. And until her people get here, we want to make sure this chap doesn't disappear, too. Do you have your little notebook in your bag?'

I almost always carry a small spiral-bound pad with me. I rummaged, found it and pulled it out. 'Do you want me to make a note about something?'

'No, if you're willing to sacrifice it, I thought it would make an effective wedge.'

He lifted his eyebrows and I nodded. He folded the thing in half, bending the spiral coil out of all usefulness, and wedged it under the front door. 'There. That'll do to secure this one while we walk around the house to see if there's another door.'

'Brilliant!'

'Also illegal. Fire code. One may not obstruct an exit. However, it's only for a minute or two.'

The conversation had been conducted in a near whisper, and our progress around the house was as quiet as we could manage. I had little doubt that Mahala's unpleasant housemate was watching every move we made, and I was extremely glad to have my stalwart husband by my side.

The back door gave on into a little porch or shed which was cluttered with discarded furniture and broken gardening implements, rags and old newspapers, and other detritus. 'No way out there,' I said.

'Not without earth-moving equipment,' Alan agreed.

There was a small, shabby little hut at the back of the property, with a wire netting fence around it. 'The chickens?'

Alan nodded. 'I'll just check.' He poked his head in the door. 'Nesting boxes, no chickens. The fox must have got the rest. No Mahala, either.'

I shook my head in frustration. We moved to a place where we could watch the front door without being in full view of the windows and waited for the police to arrive. The occupant made no attempt to leave, or none that we could see. 'That wedge wouldn't hold very long if he really wanted to get out,' I said. 'He's huge, and powerful, I should think.'

'No, but it would take him a moment or two, and I hope I'd be able to hold the door.'

'With my help.'

'No, my dear, definitely *not* with your help. You've already been injured in the course of this frustrating investigation. I'm not going to allow you to be pitted against that Incredible Hulk in there.'

Well, we'd see about that, I thought. But there was no point in arguing.

We didn't have long to wait. Two police cars pulled up a few minutes later and uniformed officers piled out of one. From the other came two plain-clothes men and Elaine. She looked more formidable than any of the others.

'Still there?' she queried us.

Alan said, 'Yes.' I knew better than to say anything at all. This was no time for me to stick my oar in.

Elaine signalled to one of the men, who looked to be Asian and was nearly bursting out of his uniform. Though nothing like as big as a Sumo wrestler, there was a distinct resemblance. Yes, he could deal with Mr Hostile in there.

And so he did, but not entirely easily. The officer removed the wedge from the door and pounded on it. When Mahala's housemate opened the door and saw the uniformed officer, he responded with a furious shout and tried to slam the door. The officer's foot was in the way. The man gave the officer a shove. He didn't move an inch, but that shove gave Elaine all the excuse she needed to take him into custody.

My admiration for the English police, always high, went up a notch or two that morning. With very little more fuss or noise, the man was escorted to one of the police cars, helped inside with courteous firmness, and it took off. No siren, no commotion. I was sure that the neighbours had watched the whole thing with avid interest, but there could be no accusations of police brutality.

Elaine stayed behind for a moment. 'Well done, both of you.' She sounded strained and exhausted, but in full command of herself. 'There was a huge jam at the Chesterton Road roundabout – a

242

car smash – or we'd have been here before you.' She turned to me. 'Dorothy, you're convinced, then, that Mahala is involved in Tom's disappearance?'

She was, I noted, not yet referring to an abduction – or worse. 'I don't know how much he's involved. I'm certain that he knows a great deal more than he's saying. When you do find him, he may not talk. He doesn't like the police.'

'Yes, he's demonstrated that, hasn't he? I have that Nigerian constable I mentioned on tap to talk to him. He's not a detective, but he's sharp, and, with some coaching, I think he might get more out of that little pain in the neck than anyone else at the station. I must go and see if I can't speed up a search warrant for this house.'

I didn't ask if there'd been any further word from or about Tom. She would have said.

We were in the car heading back to our room when I rebelled. 'Alan, we need a new point of view. A new way of looking at this. I know I keep saying that, but events keep turning corners, and we keep getting lost trying to follow them. We're not going to get anywhere just sitting around in our room stewing. And it's a beautiful day. Where could we go to get away from all this?' I made a sweeping gesture that included St Stephen's and the university and the city of Cambridge and our whole problem. 'There must be parks or something. I need some fresh air and serenity.'

'I don't know the area well, love. Let's park the car and find a TI office.'

The Tourist Information services in Great

Britain are wonderful. I discovered them when Frank and I first visited England, and we learned to rely on them. They can tell you how to find the church or museum or stately home you're looking for. They can point out the nearest pub or the shop where you can buy a walking stick. They will not only tell you about hotels and B and Bs, but they'll call and book you a room. And I've never encountered any personnel too rushed to be courteous and helpful.

The Cambridge one was, of course, in the Market Square. 'Yes, of course,' was the reply when we asked about quiet places for refreshment of the spirit. 'There are any number of nature reserves in the fens.'

'Are there woods anywhere?' I have a thing about woods; I find them restorative.

'There are, certainly. But if you were planning to walk, I'm afraid you'd find most of them rather damp at this time of year.'

'Rather damp' in Brit speak can mean anything from slightly moist to you need hipboots.

'Actually,' said Alan, 'I think we're just looking for a place of peace and quiet. We'd be happy just to sit and look at an interesting landscape.'

'Then I'd suggest one of the fen reserves. The fens are always damp, of course, but there are boardwalks, and bird-watching shelters which ought to be perfect for you.'

She showed Alan a map, and after some conversation, he chose one that seemed relatively easy to reach and obtained detailed directions for how to get there. 'Your satnav may well not work in

244

that area,' she said, 'but you should do splendidly with the map and your notes.'

Alan smiled. 'We haven't invested in satnav yet, so the directions are invaluable. I assume there's a village nearby where we can get some sort of lunch.'

'Well, no. This is a very isolated part of the fen, with nothing one could call a village. There is one farm, not a very busy place these days, but Mrs Bradford does sell eggs. She might be able to give you tea, at least. I've a brochure somewhere . . . ah, here it is. I seem to have only one left. There's been quite a little run on them lately; I'll need to ask her for more. Now, from the reserve, you'll want to . . .' She marked the map, and Alan added to his notes.

'Thank you so very much,' he said when she had finished. 'You've been a great help.'

Neither Alan nor I have relished the idea of a disembodied voice telling us when and where to turn, nor do we entirely trust the technology. After we had driven for nearly an hour, however, turning this way and that, finding ourselves in barnyards and lanes that petered out to nothing, I began to think more kindly of the 'lady in the dashboard'. I was also ravenously hungry.

'Alan, let's give up on the nature reserve,' I said. 'If I don't get some food inside me soon, my head is going to split.'

'Sorry, darling. These fen roads are maddening. At least we haven't ended up in a ditch, like Lord Peter. And it isn't winter, and we're near a house.'

'Then that must be the farm the tourist lady

245

was talking about. She said there was only the one hereabouts. Let's try it.'

It was an attractive house, solid and comfortable-looking, a house that had probably stood for at least two hundred years, and would stand for two hundred more. A few trees softened the flat surrounding landscape. It would be a pleasant place to live.

I thought about its remote location as Alan got out to open the gate. Suppose I had kidnapped someone and wanted to stash him somewhere while I did whatever it was I needed to do. Never mind that for the moment. There would be worse places than a remote farm. I wondered how far we actually were from Cambridge as the crow flew. I wondered how any villains could possibly know about remote farms, and remembered the brochure in the Tourist Information office. 'Quite a little run on them lately.' Hmm.

'I'll just see if anyone is at home,' said Alan, getting out of the car. He was back in less than a minute. 'We're in luck, darling. Mrs Bradford – that's her name – is just preparing lunch and has invited us to share it with her.'

'But we can't barge in like that on a total stranger!'

'She's a widow, and somewhat lonely, I think. I'm quite sure the invitation is sincere.'

My stomach rumbled; my head sustained an especially vicious jab.

'Well . . . but I'm not dressed to go visiting.'

Alan just opened the door and held out his hand.

Twenty-Three

One look at Mrs Bradford and I knew Alan was quite right. She was a comfortable sort of woman in her fifties, dressed in an old skirt and sweater and wearing a flowery coverall. The house was full of savoury odours. We were greeted, also, by a large dog of indeterminate breed, who came up and put his nose under each of our hands in turn. 'You won't mind Rufus. He adores people, and we seldom have visitors. Oh, someone gets lost now and again, like you, and people come to buy my eggs, but they don't usually stay but a moment. Now, sit down and let me bring you some tea. Dinner won't be half a tick.'

The room was lovely. Exposed beams, rough-hewn and aged to a lovely colour, went perfectly with the rag rugs on the wide oaken boards of the floor. The furniture was chintz-covered and squashy, the sort that's heavenly to sit in and nearly impossible to get out of. Bowls of spring flowers sat on the brick hearth to one side of a small fire, and photographs hung on every wall and sat on every surface.

I felt the tension draining away as the excellent tea eased my headache.

Lunch – 'dinner' to the countrywoman – was a marvellously homey hodgepodge of bangers and mash, 'mushy' peas (which I usually can't stand, but these were well-buttered and well-seasoned and seemed to go well with the sausage) and home-made pickles, with a treacle tart for dessert that melted in the mouth. There was lots of tea to wash everything down, and when I got up from the table to help with the dishes, I felt very much better.

Mrs Bradford was scandalized by my offer to help. 'No, no, sit down. You're a guest! I'll just rinse these and stack them. It won't take me two ticks.'

'We can't just eat and run,' I said in an undertone to Alan as we repaired to the front room in front of the fire. 'And anyway I've had an idea.'

'Shh.' He put his finger to his lips as our hostess bustled into the room.

'Well, now,' she said, 'that's that. I never have been one to wash up after every meal. Silly waste of time, not to mention water and soap, when there's just one person. It was another story, back in the day. Oh, the meals I used to cook! Used up every dish and every pot in the house. But then there were plenty to help in the kitchen afterwards.'

'You have a big family, Mrs Bradford?' Alan gestured at the pictures.

'Seven children, eighteen grandchildren,' she said with a broad smile.

'You don't look anything like old enough to have eighteen grandchildren,' I said truthfully.

'Bless you, dear, I was married at seventeen. Two of the grands are married, so there'll be some greats coming along before you know it.' Her smile dimmed a bit. 'None of them live nearby, though. The boys all went into the

248

services and moved away. One's in Papua New Guinea, one in Kuala Lumpur, two in Australia. The girls married English boys, but they all live in London or thereabouts.'

'Oh, dear, so you don't see much of your grandchildren,' I said.

'Not so much now that they're all nearly grown. The two oldest – the married ones I told you about – they live in Canada, but the others are still with their parents. Of course, for most of them, that means the other side of the world. The ones in England visited often when they were younger, when my husband was alive.' She allowed a tiny sigh to escape, but then smiled again. 'But I mustn't grumble. You can't live in the past, can you? Now, I know you were headed somewhere when you got lost, and you don't want to spend all afternoon listening to me nattering on. Can I give you directions to wherever you were trying to find?'

'We were just looking for a peaceful place,' I said, 'but I must say I find it hard to imagine a more peaceful place than this.'

'That it is. Too peaceful, sometimes. If it weren't for the animals, I don't know how I'd fill the time.'

'Animals?' I'd seen only Rufus, who lay stretched out in front of the fire in deep sleep, his paws twitching now and then as he chased rabbits in his dreams. 'You have other pets, then?'

'Bless you, no, not pets, except for the barn cats, that're more than half wild. This is still a working farm, you know, though not like it was when Bert was alive. But there's still a cow to be milked, and of course the chickens, and three horses. They're not mine, the horses. I board them, and I have help with them, but it still makes a fair amount of work. Thank the Lord. I couldn't do with sitting on my hands. Would you like to see around the farm?'

That, in fact, was exactly what I wanted to do. My idea about a remote farm was niggling in my head. In truth, I had no idea what I might be looking for, but a leisurely tour of the farm buildings might turn up something. Now, I'm terrified of cows and horses, and I dislike chickens anywhere except in the supermarket, and I loathe farm smells. But I was prepared to suffer a little, if only it might help find Tom.

Alan looked at me. 'I'd love to see the farm,' I said firmly.

Mrs Bradford glanced at my feet. 'Oh, good. You've got sensible trainers on. Would you like to borrow some wellies, though?'

I tried not to think about what I might be walking through in the stables and the barnyard. Oh, well, my sneakers were washable. 'No, I'm sure these'll be fine.'

'Just watch your step. Bessie's out to pasture, of course, but my stable lad only mucks out the stalls in the mornings, and as he's had to go and buy some new tack, the horses haven't been out yet for their exercise.'

Oh, dear. Alan and I struggled out of our chairs and I took his arm. If I should slip in anything in the stable, I wanted to make sure I didn't fall in it.

The stable building was beautiful, a lovely brick

structure in a sort of Victorian Gothic style, with arched windows and doorways, and actually quite clean. Each stall had its own Dutch-style door, painted glistening white. The top halves of the doors were open, and the horses peered at us curiously as we walked past.

'Fine animals,' said Alan, who, as far as I knew, had as little acquaintance with horseflesh as I did. He'd been born and raised in a small seaside town in Cornwall, where the predominant animals were fish. But I had to agree that the horses were beautiful, as horses go. Each was a lovely colour of brown (I don't know the proper terms for horse colouration), and two had white blazes on their faces. They looked well cared for. Their manes and tails were nicely trimmed and combed, and their coats were glossy. And that is the sum total of my knowledge of horses. We explored the stable, though I steered well clear of the stalls, not finding the rear view of a horse as attractive as the front. We were even taken up to the hayloft – the ladder wasn't too bad – and shown the tack room.

As we left the stable to take a look at the cow barn, Alan asked casually, 'Does your stable lad sometimes sleep here?'

'Only when a mare is about to drop a foal, and that hasn't been for a year or two. I look after calving myself. Why do you ask?'

'Oh, I thought I saw signs of occupation in the hay.'

I gave him a sharp look, but he went on blandly, 'Probably just the barn cats making a lovely nest for themselves. Now, you say you have only one cow now?'

'Yes, there used to be a small herd, and we sold milk and butter, and sometimes even made cheese. Now Bessie's the only one, and her milk is for me and the barn cats. This used to be the dairy, you see.' And she pottered happily about, showing us the rest of her farm buildings, which were as spotless as one could expect the homes of animals to be. I hoped to spot the cats, but they stayed out of sight. Nor did I notice anything out of order, though I kept a sharp eye out.

We got away at last, Alan having been given careful directions to a bird sanctuary not far away. I spoke as soon as we were out of the farmyard. 'What was that all about? Someone sleeping in the hay?'

'Someone has certainly been sleeping there, and recently. I played it down because I didn't want that nice woman to be frightened about tramps or gypsies, but the signs were unmistakable.'

My thoughts went, of course, to the one person we knew was missing and might be sleeping rough. 'You know, I've been thinking.' I passed along my idea.

'I had thought about him coming here if he was on the run,' said Alan, 'but surely he would have gone to the house instead of bedding down in the stable. There are worse beds than hay, certainly, but nothing quite matches mattress and pillows and real blankets. But if he was a captive . . .'

That needed some thought. We found the bird sanctuary and sat there silent for a few minutes, letting the peace of the place seep into our souls.

Birds were everywhere; their cries filled the air. I recognized only a few. We were looking at a marsh on the edge of a wood, so there were both water birds and the more familiar English robins (so much smaller and fatter than ours) and nuthatches, along with probably a dozen others I didn't know. Now and then Alan pointed an interesting bird out to me, but by the time I adjusted the field glasses provided in the shelter, it had, of course, flown away.

I put the glasses down. The jumble in my mind had cleared, and my brain was functioning again. 'Alan,' I said, 'why has Elaine been involving herself so personally in all this? Surely that's not standard procedure. In her position, wouldn't she delegate?'

'You know, I've been wondering about that, too. Yes, she is acting very much outside the bounds of standard protocol. Of course, in her position, she can make that kind of decision, but her boss will surely show his displeasure in time.'

'Chief Constable Andrews? I see him as more interested in posturing and seeking headlines than in policing.'

'Oh, he's well known as a blowhard, but in order to maintain his image he has to make a show of supervision from time to time, and I will be very surprised if he doesn't make this morning's raid on Mahala's house an excuse for discipline.'

'But they didn't do anything illegal, or even harsh. They handled that hostile housemate of his with the proverbial kid gloves, even after he assaulted that man-mountain.'

'Still. White officers—'

'And Asian, don't forget.'

'*And* Asian, but mostly white, hauling a black man off to the station—'

'They had plenty of reason! He wasn't cooperating, they needed his information, they need to find Mahala, who may be responsible for at least one criminal act—'

'Yes, dear. You don't have to convince *me*. But it could be made to look like a racist action, and you can be sure Andrews will put that spin on it.'

'But why? Elaine is a thoroughly competent police officer. She's risen through the ranks by hard work. Those under her command plainly enjoy working for her. Why would that idiot of a chief constable want to discredit her?'

'Yes, that's the question, isn't it? You may have hit on it. She's competent and well liked.'

'And he is neither. Just plain jealousy, you think?'

'It could well be.'

But somehow that didn't feel right to me. Not enough to explain his attitude. 'You know, I think there's more to it than that. Some sort of personal grudge.'

'For example?'

But I couldn't come up with anything, and neither could Alan. I mentally shoved aside that problem and went back to Tom and Mahala, for I was sure they were connected.

'What's Mahala's ruling passion in life?' I asked after a while.

'His rats.'

'They're just a means to an end. What he really cares about – I think maybe *all* he cares about – is helping his people back in Africa. He's a dedicated man.'

'Dedicated people can be dangerous.'

'Indeed. And Mahala, in his way, is dangerous. He's single-minded, entirely focussed on that one aim. Look at how he got into a fight with someone who might have made his rats, his project, look ridiculous. Just what would he do to make sure he succeeds in his goal to bring more food to his starving country? Would he kill?'

There was no answer to that question, but we had at last faced it. I was inclined to think not. I had grown fond of Mahala in a way, the sort of way one might befriend a snarling dog that looked hungry. Feed it, but be very cautious.

'Why would he kill Tom Grenfell?' asked Alan. 'Did he pose a threat to Mahala's project? Or to his rats? Or was there some sort of personal conflict?'

'He says not. He says he scarcely knew him. Drat! Why are we using the past tense? Scarcely *knows* him. Tom himself said, or implied, that he knew little about the plans for the prank, and that would further imply that he didn't know Mahala, except in passing. And I don't know how things work here, but back home, at my university, the graduate students and the undergrads hardly lived on the same planet. They didn't mix at all.'

'Terence Faherty knows Mahala better, but he said that no one knows him well. He's a lone wolf, making enemies rather than friends.'

'Well, not enemies, exactly,' I objected. 'People who don't like you aren't your enemies. They just ignore you. The opposite of love isn't hate but indifference.'

'You're right, of course. So we're positing that Mahala barely knows who Tom is and doesn't much care.'

'He would care, though, if Tom somehow got in the way of the rat project and Mahala's ultimate goal.'

And that brought us round full circle to where we had begun. What had Tom seen or done on that day when he disappeared?

'Alan,' I said, 'we need to go back to Mrs Bradford's stable. Or suggest that Elaine send somebody. Just on the off chance that Tom *was* there and might have left something behind.'

'It's a very long shot, Dorothy. I don't know that Elaine has personnel enough for that, at this stage.'

'Well, then let's go ourselves. We could tell Mrs Bradford that I dropped something and need to look for it.'

'Very well.' Alan wasn't enthusiastic. 'I don't know how we'll persuade her not to help us search, but I suppose it's better than doing nothing.'

Which was what we'd been doing a lot of, it seemed.

We had a piece of luck. Mrs Bradford had gone into Newmarket, the nearest town, to do some shopping, we were told by her 'stable lad', who was working with a bridle in the tack room and was sixty if he was a day.

'My wife and I visited here earlier, and she somehow lost a bracelet. Not valuable, but she'd like to find it if she can. Would it be all right if we look around?'

'Oh, yes, Elsie told me all about your visit. Quite an event for her, it was. She almost never sees anyone but me, and after all these years we've pretty well run out of new things to say to each other. An American lady, *and* with a hat, eating her sausages – that'll keep her going for weeks. I expect she's telling the people at the post office all about it right this minute.'

I didn't even try to explain that I've lived here for years and am now a British subject. The accent puts me firmly in my place every time. 'So do you mind if I look for it? I think I might have dropped it in the hayloft. The catch was loose.'

He made a 'be my guest' gesture and went back to the bridle. Alan boosted me up the ladder to the hayloft.

We hadn't moved very far away from the ladder in our quick visit earlier, and, somewhat worried about possible mice and rats, I hadn't noticed anything but hay. Alan was more observant. He pointed to a corner I hadn't noticed at all. There was certainly an indentation in the hay.

Clinging to his arm, I walked with him across the uneven floor, sneezing as dust from the hay we waded through rose up around us.

'Now what?' I whispered.

'Don't whisper. It carries.' His voice was very low, just audible, but without the sibilance of a whisper. 'First we look without touching. Then we can poke about. And don't be too worried about making noise. We're supposed to be looking for a bracelet, remember.'

'I never wear bracelets.'

'I know. It was all I could think of. If it were an earring, you'd have the matching one.'

'Sometimes, my dear, you are really quite bright.'

He made a face and turned to gaze intently at the corner nest.

'All right,' he said after a couple of minutes. 'There's nothing obvious. Now we start to poke.'

'I don't have anything to poke with,' I objected. 'Just my fingers.'

'A pity neither of us carries a walking stick. Never mind. Fingers will have to do. It's just nice clean hay.'

It was scratchy, though. I was pretty sure I was going to end up with a rash on my hands, and I've always tried to take good care of my hands, which used to be rather pretty. Oh, well. I'm too old to have much vanity left, and certainly my hands now are arthritic and liver-spotted. *Get on with the job, Dorothy.*

It was Alan who found it. 'Stand back a little, love,' he said in rather an odd voice, very quiet but somehow intense.

I obediently stood back while he carefully brushed aside some hay, revealing a black trash bag. It wasn't one of the huge ones, and it seemed to be empty, lying crumpled and dusty.

'Good surface for fingerprints,' he said quietly. 'Let me have your cardigan for a moment, if I may.' Wrapping his hand in my sweater, he gently patted the bag all over.

'Ah.' He stopped patting. 'Something here. It would have to be at the very bottom.'

I found the little flashlight in my purse. 'If you can hold the bag open, I think I can look in and see what it is, unless you want to dump it out.'

'Better to leave it where it is, just in case.'

It took some doing to open the bag without leaving fingerprints, but we managed it. And there, down in the corner, apparently glued to the bottom of the bag, was a vial that looked like the sort used for injectable drugs. The rubber seal had been punctured, and the vial had leaked, which was why it stuck to the bag. The label was still readable, though.

Alan and I looked at each other. 'Ampicillin?' I whispered.

Twenty-Four

Alan buried the bag back in the hay. We poked around a little more, but found nothing to indicate who had used the hay as a comfortable nest, perhaps – certainly – as a hiding place. I didn't need to be told that we had to leave everything as nearly as possible as we had found it. Elaine and her troops were going to have to look at this.

'Find it, did you?' asked the man as we came down from the loft. 'Name's Arthur, by the way. Everyone calls me Art.'

'Alan and Dorothy.' Alan extended a hand. 'No, we didn't.'

'I'm thinking maybe I lost it somewhere else. It's really lightweight, and I think it would have just stayed on top of the hay if it had come off up there.'

'I'll keep an eye open,' Art promised.

'Oh, don't bother. As Alan said, it really has no value, except sentimental.'

He looked surprised. 'But we wouldn't want one of the horses eating it, would we? Wouldn't be good for them at all.'

We solemnly agreed that it wouldn't, got directions back to the main road to Cambridge, and waved goodbye.

'And what,' I said once we were back in the car, 'does that vial mean? Was Tom there or not?

And if he was, what was he doing with ampicillin?'

'And not just one vial of it by the looks of it, either, or why would he have been carrying a whole bin liner?'

'Unless – unless the bag really was a trash bag. I mean, used to throw things away. The vial was nearly empty, after all. Maybe Tom, or somebody, used it and threw it away.'

'That kind of vial isn't used by anyone except medical personnel. Ampicillin is given by injection only in case of a serious infection. And the vial would not be carelessly tossed in a bin liner and the bag then carefully buried under a pile of hay in a stranger's stable.'

'Oh. You're right. Well, then. Maybe Art was doctoring one of the horses. I know vets do sometimes let people on farms look after the large animals, and ampicillin is used for animals. Remember when Emmy's ear got infected? She had to have a shot, and then we had to try to give her pills forever.'

'Art would be a possibility, but there's the same objection. He wouldn't bury the vial under the hay. He'd throw it out properly. And if he had something to do with that bag, would he have let us go up into the loft without the slightest hesitation?'

'Oh,' I said again. 'Alan, are we ever going to come across anything that makes sense?'

'Only if we can find the main thread in this whole tangle. Somewhere there's a beginning to it all, and if we can just find it, we can start to find our way to the heart.'

'Like the original "clew" that led to the heart of the labyrinth.'

'Exactly. We've been pawing our way into the ball of yarn and only making a bigger mess, like a cat with a toy.' He pounded the steering wheel in frustration. 'And at this point I wish I could untangle these roads. I think I've got us lost again.'

'No, you haven't. See, way over there are the pinnacles of King's. Lucky this is such flat land. Anything that sticks up shows for miles. So you know the direction to go, if you can just find the roads to take you there.'

'Easier said than done,' he muttered.

I shut up. Alan almost never gets into a snit, but when he does, it's wiser to keep still. Anyway, I was worrying at a thought, trying to chase it and pin it down. It was something Alan had said, something about . . . no, it wouldn't come. I finally let it go and concentrated on the spring landscape, hoping that the usual trick of thinking about something else would work.

We were coming into Cambridge, and Alan had at last got his bearings and relaxed, when it came to me. 'The beginning!' I said.

Alan's hand on the wheel twitched a bit. He corrected his course. 'I thought you'd gone to sleep. You've been quiet for a long time.'

'And I usually chatter all the time. I know. But I've been thinking, trying to remember what you said that struck a chord. The beginning, Alan!'

'I don't know what you mean.'

'We have to go back to the beginning. Somehow

the thread we need, so we can untangle the mess, stretches back into the past. It's like *Gaudy Night*! That's why I've been thinking about that book so much, only I didn't know it. The key to everything that was going on in that book was an event in the past, and once that was unearthed, everything became clear. I'm convinced it's the same here. We have to go back to the past.'

He looked up at the Guildhall. 'There's a good deal of past in Cambridge,' he said with admirable restraint. 'Well over a thousand years. Which bit were you planning to explore?'

I ignored him. 'We know most of Mahala's past; he told me. But the other two people most involved are Tom and Elaine. We know almost nothing about them. We need to find out. There's something there, I'm sure of it.'

'Well, we can't ask Tom about himself.'

'No. But we can ask Elaine. She'll choose what she wants us to know, of course, if there's anything really odd in his background. But you're good at figuring out where the gaps are in people's stories. And then, from what she tells us, we can start to explore *her* past. Somewhere something will converge.'

He took some convincing. 'Dorothy, have you listened to yourself? Do you realize what you're proposing to do? You want to go to a very senior police officer and, in effect, tell her she's conducting an important investigation in the wrong way, and you have a better suggestion. And then you're going to sit down and interrogate her. It's not on, darling.'

'Not if you put in those terms, no. But suppose

we invite her out to dinner. I doubt she's had a proper meal lately. We'll tell her we need an evening away from all the troubles and ask her to suggest a quiet restaurant where they have excellent food, and then ask her to join us. It would be better if I could cook her a meal at home. Sitting in front of a fire in a cosy room is the very best place to relax and talk. But failing that, something in the nature of a really nice inn would do.'

'And you think you can talk her into dropping everything and coming with us.'

'My dear man, we're not asking her to come with us to the far corners of the earth. You know as well as I do – as well as she does – that she doesn't have to be personally present for the investigation to continue. She has a mobile, if there's some sort of startling development. Her people will probably get along better, in fact, when she isn't hovering.'

'You're not going to tell her that!'

'No, I'm going to let her tell me. She's not a stupid woman. Leave it to me, dear. I'll entice her. You just wait and see.'

I was tired. It had been a very long and trying day, and I was longing for a nap. But we had to report to Elaine what we had found in the stable, and we – *I* – had to persuade her to go out to dinner with us. So instead of stopping at our rooms, we went straight to the police station.

The guardian of the car park knew us by now and made no objection when Alan pulled in. 'We'll be half a tick,' he said, and we both went inside.

Our timing was good. Elaine, looking tired and drained, was coming down the stairs as we started up them.

'No progress, I'm sorry to say,' she said. 'That sweet little man who shares Mahala's house has not uttered one word, not even his name. We've had to let him go, though what I'd like to do . . .' She made a neck-wringing gesture. 'He's trouble.'

'Andrews?' asked Alan sympathetically.

'Andrews. You can imagine what he said.'

'I can, unfortunately.'

'Look, Elaine, you've had a horrible day, and ours hasn't been a lot better. We've come across one thing, though, that you may want to follow up. Alan, tell her where that farm is.'

He told her, as best he could, and handed her the brochure he'd been given at the Tourist Information office. 'There was something odd hidden in the hayloft, a bin liner with a used ampoule of ampicillin stuck to the bottom. Dorothy thinks it might be a lead to Tom. Quite honestly, I find the connection tenuous, at best, but we thought you should know about it, just in case.'

'Yes, all right, I should check it out. Any possibility, however slight . . .'

'I'll try to tell your people the best way to get there,' said Alan. 'It's very isolated.'

'I may know it. I'll drive them.'

I laid my hand on her arm. 'Elaine. Alan and I have decided what we need is a really good meal in a place where we could relax, and we'd like you to come with us. You can't keep going forever at this level of tension. If you can suggest a place, we'll change into something decent and join you there. How about it?'

She shook her head. 'It sounds like heaven, but I need to follow up what you've given me.'

Alan said, 'You know, when I was a superintendent, my CC wouldn't allow me to work past my span of usefulness. He preached a frequent homily to the effect that fatigue led to mistakes, and in our business we can't afford mistakes. I'd be willing to bet that you can't think clearly anymore.'

She sighed. 'You're right about that. But—'

'And you've probably reached the point of forgetting which of your people you've asked to do what.'

'Well—'

'I'm not your boss, Elaine, but if I were, I should order you to turn the investigation over to your very capable team. Spend the evening with friends, good food and a modicum of alcohol, and then get a night's sleep. Things will feel better in the morning. I do know what I'm talking about.'

'Of course you do. "Been there, done that", as they say. All right, I give up. But would you be terribly disappointed if we didn't go out? There's an excellent Indian takeaway quite close to my house, if you like Indian food. It's just that I'm not sure I'm up to a real restaurant. We could be very comfortable at my place.'

'That sounds perfect!' I cried. 'Then we wouldn't have to change, either – if you don't mind, that is.'

'And you wouldn't even have to drive,' said

Alan. 'Frankly, I doubt you're alert enough right now to drive safely. Come with us and you can show us the way.'

'Brilliant! I'll just tell them I'm going home, and then we can be off.'

We didn't talk about the case at all while Alan drove us. I commented on the amazingly beautiful weather, not perhaps a very original topic, but soothing. We talked about Indian food and called ahead for it, and when Alan went in to get it and we waited in the car, Elaine actually fell asleep for a few minutes.

She slept neatly, her head leaning back against the headrest. Her mouth stayed shut; no snoring. She looked very young, in fact. The worry smoothed out of her face; her hands lay relaxed in her lap.

I felt very sorry for her. She was going to have to face it all again soon enough.

She roused immediately when Alan got in the car, and I made some comment.

'Oh, I learned the art of the catnap long ago,' she said. 'It's amazing how refreshing it can be. Did you find that, Alan, when you were on active duty?'

'I was never very good at it. I don't let go easily. Even when I managed to sleep in my bed for a reasonable amount of time in the middle of a case, the details kept running through my head. That could be useful, though. Sometimes I'd wake with a fresh idea. Is this your house? Where shall I park?'

Elaine's house was a semi-detached in a pleasant

267

neighbourhood, not large but neat and well kept, with a pocket garden where roses would bloom in summer. Inside, it was a home for a woman who valued her comforts but didn't have a lot of time for fancy trimmings. There was one main room downstairs, serving as living and eating space, and a small kitchen behind it. I saw lots of books but few ornaments, only a pair of pictures on the mantel. 'Tom?' I asked.

'Yes, at age two, and then later with his first bicycle.'

'I thought they had a look of him, but it's hard to tell now, with that beard.'

'Lord, yes, the first time I saw it I swear I didn't know him. Look, sit down and pour yourself a drink while I get some plates and light the fire.'

'I can deal with the fire,' said Alan, 'if you'll allow me.'

'If you will. It only wants a match set to it.'

'What would you like to drink, Elaine?' I asked as I dealt with Alan's and my needs.

'Macallan, please. Neat.'

That was, I knew, a very expensive whisky indeed. I poured some for Alan as well, and a very small tot for me, as Elaine apparently didn't stock bourbon.

In a very few minutes our meal was on the table, sending out heavenly aromas, and the fire was going nicely. We sat down. Elaine took a healthy swig of her drink and gave a huge sigh. 'Oh, how I needed that! Though I shouldn't be taking the time even for dinner, much less a drink.'

'Remember I'm acting *in loco superiori*, or whatever the proper phrase might be. You're under orders to relax and refresh. Cheers.' Alan raised his glass and we followed suit.

Alan and I weren't really hungry, but everything smelled wonderful, so for a few minutes we dealt with our curries and biryanis and naan and chutneys, our conversation limited to 'could I have another naan, please' and 'my word, this is good' and the like.

After a while Elaine said, 'Oh, I forgot beer. I usually have lager with Indian. Anyone want some?'

I was finding that my scotch went very nicely with curry, and, apparently, Alan was, too. 'It is akin to blasphemy, however, to drink this remarkable whisky with anything so strongly flavoured as curry,' he said, looking at his empty glass with something like reverence.

Elaine got up and brought the bottle to the table. 'I will not allow shibboleths to prevent my enjoying my food and drink in any combination I like. I drink white wine with beef if I want, and red with fish.'

'Whatever turns you on,' I said, pouring myself another small tot that I wasn't sure I needed. But it was really marvellous stuff, even to a bourbon lover.

When we had eaten all we could, and a little more, I helped Elaine clear up the plates, and then we sat down in front of the fire with decaf coffee, except for Alan, who opted for the fully leaded stuff, as he had to drive later.

I mentally girded my loins, took another look

at the photos of Tom, and said, 'He was a really adorable little boy, wasn't he?'

She smiled fondly. 'He looks quite a lot like my sister, actually. And he was so well behaved, always. Oh, he got into the usual amount of trouble, as all boys do, but it was just scrapes – stealing apples, falling out of trees – normal boy high spirits. He was a good student, too. He's always wanted to know about things, everything . . .' Her voice trailed off. She put her coffee down; her hand was shaking.

'He's going to be all right, Elaine. I'm sure of that. And I'm sure we'll find him soon. I hope it isn't painful for you to talk about him, but if Alan and I know more about him, we might be able to come up with some idea of what might have happened.'

'Yes. I can see that.' She paused to get herself under control. 'What would you like to know?'

'Just tell us about him. He's your favourite nephew, I take it.'

'My only nephew. I have only the one sister, and she was never able to have . . . another child. I suppose she rather spoiled him. Well, she and I together. I admit I've always doted on him, and as Ruth's husband died when Tom was just a baby, he had what amounted to two mothers.'

'For an only child.' I smiled. 'Yes, that could easily have been disastrous for him, but he seems to have turned out all right. From what I can tell, he's got his head screwed on straight.'

'Where did he go to school, Elaine?' asked Alan.

'Ruth would have sent him to the

270

comprehensive here, but I thought he'd be better off away from his female-ridden existence, so I persuaded her to send him to Perse.'

Even I had heard of the Perse School. 'Good grief, isn't that terribly expensive? I thought it was really exclusive.'

'It wasn't quite so steep then, and, of course, I helped with the cost. Really, I think it was good for him. They had excellent masters in the sciences, and that's how he was able to win the scholarship to St Stephen's.'

'Is he interested in sports? He's obviously in excellent physical shape.'

'Oh, yes, he's always played rugby. Such a dangerous game, I've always thought, and he got his share of broken bones when he was in school. By the time he came up, though, he'd learned enough that he earned his blue without too many injuries. I don't think he plays much now – he's far too busy – but I know he keeps in condition.'

'Was his father athletic?'

An odd expression crossed her face. 'Not really. Ruth's husband was a nice enough man, but he hadn't much energy for anything. Not even living. As I say, he died young.'

'Heart attack?' I asked. I was probing, poking here and there as I had in the hayloft, in hopes of finding something.

'Pneumonia. He caught a bad cold and it went to flu and then to pneumonia. That was over twenty years ago, and they hadn't some of the drugs then that are effective now. He just drifted away.'

271

'And how old is Tom now?'

'Twenty-three next month.'

'So he's been without a father most of his life. What a pity. Still, it doesn't seem to have hurt him much.'

Elaine shook her head and buried her face in her cup, but not before I saw her tears.

I waited. There was something more to come, I was sure.

'If only,' she whispered. 'If only that were true.'

If only *what* were true? 'I'm sorry, Elaine. I'm lost.'

Alan stood and brought the bottle of whisky, and poured a little into her empty coffee cup. She raised her head and nodded her thanks.

'You said he'd been without a father all these years. I wish that were true.'

I frowned. 'But you said—'

'I said that Ruth's husband died when Tom was a baby. He was not Tom's father. Nor is Ruth his mother.'

'He was adopted?' I was confused.

It was Alan who got it. 'Tom is your son, isn't he, Elaine?'

Twenty-Five

Elaine sipped her whisky and then put the cup aside with a thump. 'No more. I need to be alert tomorrow. Yes, Alan, Tom is my son. He doesn't know that, and I don't intend to tell him.'

'Medical records,' I murmured, half to myself.

'I have no interesting medical conditions, nothing he need ever worry about.'

'But what about his father? Is there anything about him that Tom should know?'

Elaine sighed. 'He already knows more than he cares to.'

She looked at her coffee cup. Alan picked up the bottle of Macallan. She shook her head. There was a long pause. 'I suppose,' she said slowly, 'I'd better tell you the whole story, now that you've guessed part of it.'

'Only if you want to.' I felt guilty. I'd wanted to explore this woman's past, but now it was turning out to be a pretty painful exercise.

'It would be a relief to tell somebody. I've kept it bottled up all these years, and they do say that's not good for a person.

'I was just thirty and had been working here in Cambridge for a few years. I'd been concentrating so hard on my job, studying about police work when I wasn't on duty, that I hadn't much time for a personal life. And thirty is a dangerous age for a woman.'

'It is,' I agreed. 'Especially for an unmarried woman. You begin to think people are looking at you oddly, wondering why you haven't found a man, which is obviously the life goal of any woman. And you begin to look at yourself, wondering the same thing. Am I pursuing the wrong goals? Is marriage and family really what counts in life? Oh, I was married in my early twenties, myself, but I saw so much of that sort of uncertainty in friends, fellow teachers.'

'Yes, and I had reached a stage in my career where I could sit back and take stock, stop running quite so hard. So, of course . . .'

'You fell in love.'

She gave a grim little laugh. 'And "fell" is the right word. Right off a cliff. There was no thought involved, no logic, no weighing of which course to take. He was a solicitor in Huntingdon whom I met over a police matter. He was very nice-looking and well mannered, and he told me he thought I was beautiful. Nobody had ever told me that before – nor since, I might add. I was lost after the first warm glance.'

We waited.

'And it was all a sham. Oh, there was an idyllic couple of months. We spent almost every minute together. He took me to little out-of-the-way inns. We went for long walks in the fenlands. I thought it was all so romantic.

'And then I found out why he never took me to local restaurants or fancy hotels. It was when I told him I was pregnant, and wasn't it lovely, and we could get married quietly and be together the rest of our lives.

274

'He was married. To the daughter of a bishop. She was the one with the money.' She said it with cool detachment, as if it had happened to someone else.

'Oh, no! The miserable, cheating . . .'

'"Bastard" is the word you're looking for, I think. Alan, would you mind getting me some water? I daren't drink any more whisky, and I'm parched.'

'What did he think you were supposed to do – just vanish off the face of the earth with his child?'

'He didn't care what I did, but he wanted the child to vanish. He graciously said he would pay for a private abortion. He was furious when I refused.'

'Oh, what a sweetheart! So what did you do?'

'In most circumstances, a woman wouldn't have had a problem. There wasn't a lot of stigma attached to an unwed pregnancy by then, not like a couple of decades earlier. But as a member of the police, I had to be a lot more careful. I was having a hard enough time gaining acceptance in the force as a woman. As a pregnant woman – well, I ask you.'

'Andrews wasn't chief constable then, was he?'

'No, thank God. He'd have found some excuse to have me sacked. No, it was old Fenton – did you know him, Alan?'

'Bill Fenton? Yes, for my sins. I can't say I cared for him a great deal.'

'He was an idiot,' said Elaine, 'and the most ineffectual man ever to grace that office, but his incompetence worked in my favour, as did my

275

general shape. I've never been a sylph, and I favour comfortable clothes, so it was easy to hide the pregnancy till well into the sixth month. I don't think anyone knew, except my doctor, of course. She was most cooperative. She invented an illness for me that required complete rest for three months, preferably at a seaside nursing home, and Fenton, the old fool, believed every word. Actually, I went to stay with my sister, who lived in Gerrard's Cross then.

'Ruth and her husband wanted children so badly, but she had never been able to conceive. My baby seemed to them like a gift from God. He was born at a local hospital, and as soon as I was well enough to go home, I finalized the arrangements for his legal adoption and came back to work.'

'That must have been a hard time for you.' Childless myself, and not by choice, I was near tears at the thought of this nice woman having to leave her brand-new son.

'It was. I wanted that little boy so much it was a physical pain. But at least I could visit him whenever I had time off, and it wasn't too long before her husband got a job near Cambridge and they moved here. Then it was almost as good as having him with me.'

'Almost, but not quite,' said Alan quietly. 'I remember when mine were small. One never knows when the exciting moments will happen – the first word, the first step, the funny incidents, the near tragedies. I missed most of them, working the uncertain hours of a policeman. You would have, too, if he'd been with you.'

'Yes, I made myself believe that. And Ruth was so good about letting me be a part of his life. After a while I almost adjusted to the situation. Ruth's husband died, and the three of us grew even closer. His being at school in Cambridge meant I could see him often, even in term time.

'So things went along that way. We were quite happy, actually. Ruth was doing a splendid job with Tom; he was thriving. I was rising in the ranks and spending every penny I could spare on his education and so on, and never grudging a penny of it.

'But then when he was nearly fifteen, his name and picture got into the newspapers in connection with an academic award he'd won at school, and his father saw it, made the connection and wrote me a letter.'

'What had he been doing all this time?'

'I didn't know and didn't care. He'd changed firms after our pathetic little affair, afraid I'd pester him for child support. I couldn't find him to sign the adoption papers, but as it was obvious he wanted nothing to do with his son, I didn't worry about that. I was delighted to see the back of him.'

'I should say so! He sounds like a real sleaze.'

'All that and then some. And that letter . . .' She clenched her hands on the arm of the chair and then noticed what she was doing and deliberately relaxed them. 'It seemed he'd been involved with a good many other women through the years, and his wife found out.'

'The bishop's daughter.'

'Right. There was a divorce; I imagine she and

her father took a dim view of his philandering. I did mention, didn't I, that she was the one with the money. The divorce was messy enough that his law firm decided they no longer needed his services. That left the sleaze with very little. So he wrote to me and told me he thought it was time he played a part in his son's life.'

'He really wanted money, I imagine,' said Alan. 'His kind always does.'

'And he thought I'd pay him to stay away from Tom. He was right, too. Tom had been told he was adopted, but he'd never shown any real curiosity about his birth parents, and Ruth never told him. As far as he was concerned, Ruth was his mother, and he'd pretty much forgotten her husband. His name was Tom, too – young Tom was named after him.'

'So you paid up?' Alan was frowning. 'I know that, as a police officer, you know it's always a bad idea to pay blackmail. As a parent, I do understand. But I also know how much the police are paid, and I'd not have thought it was enough to keep a child in a very expensive school *and* pay blackmail.'

'You're right, of course. The school provides some assistance for parents who need it, and Ruth obviously did. She and her husband never had a great deal of money – he owned a garden centre and got along reasonably well, but there was never anything left over. When he died, Ruth went back to the sort of clerical job she'd had before they married, but it paid rather badly. They had owned the house, so she didn't have a mortgage to worry about, or she couldn't have coped.

I helped her out from time to time when I could, but you got it in one when you said I could ill afford another demand on my resources. And yet I couldn't have the sleaze interfering in Tom's life.'

'What did you do?' I asked. 'I mean, it's none of my business, but I can't imagine how you dealt with it all.'

'You won't believe it, either of you, but I was fool enough to believe him when he said if I gave him five thousand pounds, he'd go away and never trouble me again.'

Alan shook his head. 'A blackmailer always comes back to the well.'

'I knew that, but I made myself believe that this case was different. So I sold everything I possessed that was of any value. I had a little jewellery from my grandmother, a painting or two, a few rare books. It didn't add up to as much as he wanted, but I was able to squeeze the rest out by trimming my expenses.'

'Did Ruth know about any of this?'

'Not then; I didn't want to worry her. I should have known he'd come back. It was almost two years later, just long enough that I'd begun to feel it might be all right.'

'Of course he did. Another letter?' Alan's voice was full of sympathy.

'No. This time he came to the police station.'

Twenty-Six

Neither of us could find anything to say. After a long silence, I got out of my chair. 'Elaine, I think we all need some tea. Do you mind if I make a pot?'

'That's a good idea. Let me.'

I would have protested, but it was her kitchen, after all, and she'd probably be better with something to do. I went with her and we worked together in silence. I was wondering how this woman had been able to function at all with all the pressure she'd faced over the years from her terribly demanding job and the chaos of her private life.

It's wonderful how the humble ordinariness of a pot of tea can dispel drama. Whoever called it 'the cup that cheers but does not inebriate' hit the nail on the head. What could be more normal than sitting around a fire with tea? Elaine had found some chocolate biscuits, too, and although I didn't need another morsel of food, I wanted the comfort of chocolate.

When we were settled with the tea things in front of us, Alan said, 'You know, Elaine, you needn't tell us any more if it's too hard for you. Painful stories can always wait.'

'This one can't,' she said firmly. 'If my ramblings lead you to any inkling of where Tom might be, the pain doesn't matter.'

'Very well.' Alan nodded. 'So the man came to the police station.'

'He turned up at a horrible time. He would! I was a DCI then and had just finished a frightful case – a child murder. You'll remember it, I expect. The baby stolen from the supermarket?'

I felt a chill go through me. I remembered it myself; it wasn't all that many years ago. The mother had turned her back for a moment, and when she turned around the child was gone from her shopping trolley. After a frantic search lasting almost a week, the police had discovered the little girl in the hands of a demented, childless woman. Although the police had used the utmost tact and their most skilled negotiators, the woman went to pieces and killed both the baby and herself.

'Yes, I remember,' said Alan quietly. 'The worst sort there can be. You would have felt wretched.'

'It was, I think, the worst time in my life. And then George showed up. By special intervention of all the devils in hell, I was downstairs in the lobby at the time. *And* Andrews was there.'

'Oh, *dear*! Did he suspect something?' I asked.

'Of course. He hasn't worked it out – not so far – but he knows I have a secret, and he hates it.'

'So that's why he's out to get you. Alan and I were sure there was some reason.'

'That's one of the reasons.'

'At any rate,' said Alan, calling us gently back to order, 'Tom's father showed up. You knew him straight away? After all that time?'

'Oh, yes. He hadn't changed. Some men age very well, particularly the irresponsible ones. No worries, you see.' She poured herself a little more tea. 'He was better-looking than ever, with just a bit of grey at the temples to give him that distinguished look. He smiled, that crocodile smile of his that once enchanted me, and acted surprised to see me. Oh, there's no point in going into the whole thing. He did it very well: pretended he was there to report a minor theft and asked me out to lunch in a way I could hardly refuse in front of everyone, and then when we were well away from the station, he told me he needed more money. I told him I didn't have any, which was quite true, and said I'd apply for a restraining order if he tried to see Tom.

'It was a bluff, and he called it. He said that Tom was now an adult, that he, George, had done nothing whatever to make any authority think he was dangerous to the boy, and anyway I wouldn't want to admit that he was my son.' Her hands were clenched again; again she relaxed them.

'I was out of options. I told him that I would readily admit to being Tom's mother, but not now. He was finishing his A levels, and I said I *personally* would see George dead before allowing him to interfere with the boy's educational goals. That *wasn't* a bluff. I would have done it, even if it cost me my own life. I think George didn't quite expect that. At any rate he said he'd stay away from the boy until he had finished his exams, or until I came up with the money. Then he disappeared again, and I haven't had an easy moment since.'

'What happened?' asked Alan.

'He kept his word and left Tom alone until the

282

exams were over and done with. Tom passed brilliantly, I might add. Then one day the sleaze phoned me to say he still needed money. I told him – well, I told him quite a number of things, but I couldn't pay up, and so . . . he found Tom and told him he was his father.'

'And that you were his mother?' I chimed in.

'No. I don't know why not. Doubtless he has some devious reason of his own.'

'And how did Tom react?' I poured myself another cup of tea, which by now was lukewarm.

'At first he was pleased. The sleaze took him out for treats, football games, that sort of thing. Of course, Tom told his mother and me all about it. It's a glorious time in a young man's life, when he's finished school and hasn't yet got into the rigors of university. He enjoyed being taken about by a pleasant father.

'But then things changed, just before he matriculated at St Stephen's.'

'He did his undergraduate work there, too?'

Elaine nodded. 'Yes, he's always loved the place. I prefer the older colleges, their history and traditions. But St Stephen's has always been noted for the sciences, and science has always been Tom's passion.'

'So something changed,' I prompted.

'Yes, he stopped being so open with Ruth and me, told us less of what he was doing, just . . . closed up, somehow. Ruth thought it was simply that he was growing up, needing to cut the apron strings, but I worried, so one day I invited him out for a slap-up lunch and got it out of him. He

283

didn't want to tell me at first, because of me being in the police, but I am rather good at encouraging people to talk, so in the end he opened up.'

'He had become involved in something illegal,' said Alan with a sigh.

'Not quite, but nightmarishly close. The sleaze had taken him to a party, and Tom, who is both intelligent and observant, realized that the place was heaving with drugs. He didn't tell me where the party was, or what kinds of drugs were involved, but from what he did say, I gathered it was all sorts, from cannabis on up to crack cocaine and worse. He wanted nothing to do with it. As I say, he isn't stupid. But he was devastated at seeing that side of his father.'

'The loss of innocence.' I shook my head.

'Yes, but more than that. He'd never known a father, and when he first met the sleaze, he thought he was terrific. The unmasking was a terrible shock. After that he saw much less of the sleaze, made excuses when he came around, that sort of thing. But he couldn't always avoid contact, and it was making him miserable, and there wasn't a thing I could do about it!'

'But, Elaine, why is his father so anxious to stay in contact with Tom?' I asked. 'It isn't as if he is a good father, in any sense, and it doesn't sound as if he really cares about him. I don't understand.'

'I think it's simply to torture me. I've stopped playing his game. Not willingly. I would have continued to pay his blackmail, but I couldn't at the time. Now that I have a better income, I could pay, and I would if I thought it would make an end to it all. But he won't answer my phone calls, and I don't know where he is. He just shows up out of the blue when it strikes his fancy. He wants to keep this up as long as he knows it's driving me frantic.'

'So the question is,' said Alan, 'do you think Tom has been kidnapped by his father?'

'Of course, that's the obvious explanation. But why, then, has there been no ransom demand? And what the *bloody* hell is the meaning of that finger and the obscure note?'

The teapot was empty and the fire had burned itself out, and all of us were exhausted. Emotion can be far more tiring than physical labour, and we'd lived through an eternity of it in a few hours.

And there were still no answers. Alan asked if Elaine needed help getting her car back, but she said she'd phone a driver in the morning, so we said goodnight and went back to our room at St Stephen's. I fell into bed and slept as if drugged, and if I dreamed, I remembered nothing in the morning.

I awoke disoriented and out of sorts, with a slight headache. For a moment I couldn't remember why I felt almost ill, and then Elaine's story washed over me. I turned over and buried my head in the pillow, willing sleep to return.

It wouldn't, of course. Once my mind had started to work, it refused to shut down again, so I got up, went to the bathroom and then turned on the kettle. While I waited for it to boil, I dressed sketchily and peered out the window.

It was raining, the slow, steady sort of rain that can go on all day.

Wonderful. Just what I needed to complete my depression. I debated going back to bed, but I was dressed, and it seemed too much trouble. I made coffee, nibbled one of the rather dry biscuits the college provided for its guests and waited for Alan to wake up.

I was finishing my coffee when he got up, murmured something that might have been 'good morning' and went to shower. I made a second cup of coffee when I heard the water stop.

We were both coherent by that time. He looked at the coffee I'd put by his bed and grimaced. 'I don't think I can face instant this morning, love. Shall we go and see what the college has on offer?'

'Just let me get my shoes on.' We put on wet-weather gear, found our umbrellas and walked as fast as we could to the dining hall.

I wasn't very hungry. Elaine's tale about her son's nasty father had taken away most of my appetite. Even the sausages didn't tempt me. I knew I needed something, though, and a packet of cornflakes with yogurt filled the empty spaces without making great demands on my rather iffy digestive system.

'I wish we could take a nice long walk,' I said fretfully as I struggled back into my raincoat. 'I need to do some serious thinking, and I do that best when walking.'

'Maybe the rain will taper off,' said Alan without much hope. 'Meanwhile, we could visit the chapel. If nothing's going on in there, it would be a good, quiet place to think and talk.'

Well, it wasn't an ideal solution, but it was certainly better than the other option – sitting in our room, which grew claustrophobic after a while. Anyway, the chapel was closer. We could use it as a stopover to catch our breath and dry off a bit, if nothing else.

The chapel was deserted. We chose a pew at the back, tucked away in a corner, and knelt for a moment. I offered a fervent prayer for Elaine and Tom and the whole complicated situation, and then sat back and tried to compose my jumbled thoughts into some sort of order.

'Dorothy,' said Alan after a little time, 'what struck you most about last night's revelations? We went there to learn Elaine's story, hoping that it might give us a clue to Tom's whereabouts and the rest of the mess. Did you pick up on anything in particular?'

'I think only the terrible waste of it all. Elaine could have had a fulfilling life with her brilliant son and probably, later, with a good man who would have understood the situation and sympathized. Instead, Horrible George destroys her trust of men in general, leaves her to act as surrogate mother, blackmails her until he has bled her dry, lets their son be brought up fatherless, and then steps in to torment both of them. It's a dreadful story.'

'Yes, it's all of that, and, of course, I feel the same. I'd like to have five minutes alone with George. But what caught my attention was one word: drugs.'

287

'Well, you're a policeman. Of course you noticed . . . Oh!'

'Exactly. George tried to introduce Tom to the drugs scene. I would bet a thousand pounds that his goal was to push him into addiction and then force him to deal. That's the usual pattern.'

I started to say what I thought of George, and then remembered where I was and modified my language. 'That is diabolical!'

'Yes, well, we've already worked out that George is not an admirable person. From what Elaine has said, he would do such a thing without turning a hair. We wondered why he was still pursuing Tom. That could be the reason.'

'And . . . oh, Lord! Alan, let's get out of here. I can't even think what I want to think in an odour of sanctity.'

It was still raining. We stood under the portico and looked out a little helplessly. Everywhere there were puddles, dimpled with raindrops. Students splashed past, the hoods of their waterproofs pulled up over their heads, plastic covers on their backpacks.

'Let's go to the car,' said Alan.

'And go where? This is a walking town. We'd have to park and walk to get anywhere at all.'

'Not so. There's an indoor car park attached to one of the big shopping centres, if I can find it in the one-way system. I know malls are not your favourite places, but it will be dry and well lit, with plenty of space to walk, and chairs if you want to sit.'

I grumbled a bit, but there weren't many choices. Stay where we were, where my thoughts felt constrained, or go to our room, or get soaking wet walking to some congenial café, or go to a mall. The mall won.

It was crowded and noisy. Everyone who wanted to shop had made the same choice. We walked for a few minutes, dodging people and parcels and prams, and finally, in desperation, went into an expensive-looking coffee place. Alan ordered lattes for both of us.

'Now. To continue.' Alan tented his fingers, and I knew he was about to expound. 'Given that our villain tried once to ensnare our victim, and is still stalking him, what conclusion can we draw?'

I blinked at his narrative style, but realized he was being deliberately obscure to foil any eavesdroppers. 'I suppose the sleaze hasn't attained his goal, but is still trying.'

'I agree. Oh, thank you.' This to the waiter who brought our coffee. Alan went on. 'Now, laying that aside for a moment, let's remember what we found yesterday.'

'Oh, gosh, was it only yesterday? It seems like a century ago. But it wasn't – um – that is, it was perfectly legitimate.'

'That sort of thing can be very valuable, too, given certain circumstances.'

'Such as,' I said very quietly indeed, 'a developing country.'

'Exactly.'

So. Mahala, from a developing country, could have good reason to steal medicinal drugs to send back to his people. I would have to find out – or Elaine would – what kind of security measures were in place in the Hutchins Building. Certainly any drugs that might be abused would be locked up with a tight control system, but I wasn't sure there would be any drugs like that. Maybe minute doses of morphine or some other painkiller, in case one of the animals had to be subjected to a painful procedure. Maybe small quantities of whatever drugs they used for the euthanasia of old or sick animals. I didn't know enough about the set-up to be intelligent about it. 'But, Alan. If the sleaze was trying to ensnare our victim into – what you said – then we would be talking about – oh, I can't talk this way!' I lowered my voice to its absolute limit of audibility. 'There would have to be illegal drugs in the picture, surely.'

'Probably, if Tom were to be used as dealer. But what if it were Mahala stealing antibiotics and then being – shall we say – *persuaded* to turn them over to black-market dealers? And what if Tom found out about it?'

'Oh, good Lord! He would go straight to his aunt, wouldn't he? But he hasn't, so that means . . .'

'That means he has been prevented from doing so. Somehow. He hasn't been heard from for two days.'

'And nobody's seen Mahala, as far as we know, since Monday.'

'G has both of them.' Alan made it a statement.

'He or some of his henchmen. Or else . . .'

Neither of us wanted even to think about the other possibility.

Twenty-Seven

We got out of there and found a quiet place where we could phone Elaine. Alan, met with some obstructiveness, became very cold and commanding indeed. 'This is Chief Constable Alan Nesbitt, calling on official business, and I must speak to Superintendent Barker at once. If she is out of the station, patch me through to her mobile.'

'It isn't that, sir,' I heard the agitated voice at the other end say. 'She's in conference with Chief Constable Andrews.'

Alan hardened his voice still further. 'If she were in conference with the Queen, I would still need to speak with her. Immediately! Put me through.'

'Poor kid,' I mouthed at Alan. 'He's scared to death. Damned if he does and damned if he doesn't.'

'Yes? Who is it? I told you not to put calls through.' It was Andrews, sounding extremely irritated.

'Andrews, this is Nesbitt. I'm sure I'm very sorry to interrupt, but it is necessary for me to speak to Elaine Barker. An emergency has come up, and I need her immediately.'

'But we – I—'

'At once, please.' Technically, Andrews outranked Alan, who as a retiree had no real rank at all. But Alan was of a forceful disposition, and Andrews, like all bullies, wilted at real authority. I heard him grumbling as he handed the phone to Elaine.

'Elaine. Alan. Get out of that idiot's office – make some excuse – and then call me back as soon as you can speak freely. It's extremely important.'

'Got it.' She hung up and we walked to our car while we waited for her return call. It came in less than a minute. 'What is it? Andrews'll have my guts for garters.'

'I hope he finds them uncomfortable. Elaine, Dorothy and I think we've worked out a scenario. Speculative, but probable. If true, it means extreme danger for both Tom and Mahala. They must both be found as soon as humanly possible. It involves a highly illegal operation that must be stopped. I can't tell you what to do, but if this were my jurisdiction, I'd escalate the manhunt to your limit, and concentrate on Mrs Bradford's farm. Dorothy and I are headed your way; we can explain when we get there.'

'Right. Where are you? I'll send an escort.' The worried, uncertain Elaine of last night was gone; the decisive commander was back.

By the time Alan pulled out of the car park, a police car was waiting for us, blue light flashing. Alan blinked his headlights, the driver nodded, and we were off, siren sounding, on a hair-raising drive through Cambridge traffic made worse than ever by the rain.

I breathed again once we stopped in the station

car park. A uniformed officer met us as we stepped out. 'I'll park your car for you, sir, madam. You're to go straight up.'

Alan was good at a quick synopsis, an art I've never mastered. In a few words he summarized our deductions for Elaine. 'As you can see, we have no solid proof, but that vial of ampicillin we found is certainly suggestive, added to the rest of the very vague information we have. We believe that Mahala and/or Tom spent some time in that hayloft, and that he or they have been taken away and may be in very grave danger. If they are in the hands of drug dealers . . .' He didn't need to finish the sentence.

'Every man and woman I could spare is working the search. It won't be easy.'

'No. The area is vast and includes so many places where they could possibly be.'

'Yes. I've already sent them to the obvious places – Tom's rooms in college, Mahala's house, George's home. We'll include the Bradford farm. I'll also send teams to known drug dealers and the places they frequent – rave clubs, abandoned houses – you know the sort of thing as well as I do.'

'You've pulled his housemate in again?' I asked.

'Of course. This time I've charged him with obstruction of justice and threatened him with everything I could think of. He'll talk or I'll know the reason why.'

'I presume that was why your chief was on your case just now.' I shook my head. 'Of all the sorry excuses for a public servant!'

She dismissed him. 'I'm past worrying about him. He can try to sack me if he wants. It would cost him a great deal of trouble, and even if he succeeded in the end, I'd not greatly care. My only concern just now is finding my son.' Her desk phone rang. Her knuckles were white as she picked it up. 'Barker.' Her face lost colour as she listened.

She hung up the phone and sat down abruptly. 'Mahala is here.'

'Here? At the station? But he's scared to death of the police!'

There was a knock at the door, and Mahala walked in, more or less held up by Jim Ashby.

Mahala looked terrible. His clothes were wet and falling off of him. His face was puffy, his lip was bleeding and one eye was swollen nearly shut. I saw on one shoulder, where his shirt had been ripped away, what looked sickeningly like a series of cigarette burns. I stood and pushed my chair towards him, and he fell into it.

We all turned towards Jim, who was also wet and somewhat dishevelled. 'I found him,' he said simply. 'I was rowing. The rain made it hard to see where I was going, and when it let up a bit, I had drifted close to a boathouse. I don't think anyone uses it anymore; it's pretty far north of the colleges. But there were three men in it, and it looked as though they were knocking someone about. I couldn't have that, so I pulled the boat in to the shore, and when I saw it was Mahala who was getting the rough end of the scrap, I'm afraid I lost my temper. I broke one of the oars. St Stephen's won't be happy about that. They're not cheap.'

'You saved my life,' said Mahala. It came out garbled, what with pain and a split lip, but the gratitude was clear.

Elaine had picked up the phone and uttered some crisp orders. Now she said, 'Mahala, I've ordered an ambulance to take you to hospital. You need to be treated immediately. But I'm afraid I'll have to send a constable with you, if you think you can answer some questions. We need to know all you can tell us about these yobs, as soon as possible. Can you talk a little, do you think?'

'I will tell you what I know. They meant to kill me. They are bad men, and they are looking for your nephew.'

Elaine turned to Jim and asked sharply, 'How badly did you injure them? I gather you did injure them, if you broke an oar.'

'Yes, ma'am. Between the oar and my fists, none of them will be feeling chipper for a few days.'

'Can they walk?'

'I reckon – when they wake up.'

'Right. Tell me where they can be found.'

He did so, and before he had finished there was another tap on the door. The ambulance men were there with a stretcher, accompanied by a uniformed policeman. His skin was very dark, and I thought he was perhaps the Nigerian constable Elaine had told us about.

'Right then, Richard, I want you to take a report from Mahala about the men who did this to him, but don't push it. He's very badly hurt and needs treatment and rest. As soon as you have at least

a few details, report back to me. Off you go.'
More phoning, then she turned to Jim. 'I'd like
you to stay for a moment if you will. I need a
bit more information about your encounter. And
thank you for bringing Mahala to me. What is
your name, by the way?'

Introductions over, Jim sat down to tell his
story, but there wasn't a lot to tell. He had been
rowing, he'd seen the three men punching
someone, had seen it was Mahala, and had run
to the rescue. 'A fair fight is one thing,' he said,
'but three against one is quite another. I think
Mahala is right. Those lads were trying to kill
him. And they had burned him – did you see?'

'I did. That says to me that they were trying
to extract some information from him. Did you
hear them ask any questions?'

'No, mostly they were just swearing at him.
He said, though, when we were coming here, that
they wanted to make him tell them where your
nephew was, and he kept saying he didn't know,
but they didn't believe him.'

Elaine sagged a bit at that, but she said only,
'Can you describe them?'

He scratched his head. 'Can't say I noticed
much about them except what they were doing.
They weren't very big, and they didn't know how
to fight. I didn't have much trouble with them.'

Elaine almost smiled. 'I'll wager you didn't.
Their clothes?'

Jim shrugged. 'Jeans and tees. What everyone
wears.'

She gave it up. 'All right, if they're still unconscious and where you left them, we'll find them

easily enough. Jim, I'm most grateful to you. If you'd like a change of clothing before you leave, I'm sure—'

'Thank you, ma'am, but I'd just get wet again. I left a taxi waiting, so I'd better get home.'

'Right.' Elaine pulled a wad of notes out of her handbag. 'Here, that's for the taxi. Give the desk sergeant your phone number before you leave.'

'Well,' she said when he had left, 'that's one missing person accounted for. But if he persisted, while he was being beaten nearly to death, in claiming he didn't know Tom's whereabouts, I think it's safe to assume he doesn't.'

'No,' said Alan. 'But if goons are looking for him, that means they don't know where he is, either. Which is a hopeful sign, don't you think?'

'I daren't let myself hope.'

'Of course you don't,' I said. 'But I've had an idea just now, because of what Alan said. If the bad guys don't know where Tom is, and Mahala doesn't know, that could mean that he really was taken by those awful people, but somehow managed to escape. I think he was in that stable and buried that trash bag for some reason, and got away. And that means your people could maybe track him from there. I mean, it's a thought. I know there's nothing you could call evidence, but—'

'It's a thought worth pursuing. I'll have to draft you into the service.' Again she picked up the phone and issued orders.

'Now, as much as I want to go out and look myself, I need to stay here and wait for reports. Mahala may give us some clues. My search teams may find something useful. They also serve who only stand and wait, but my God, it's hard!'

'I always used to keep a bottle of brandy in my desk for emergencies,' said Alan thoughtfully.

She actually smiled. 'And this is an emergency if ever there was one.' She opened a drawer. 'Anyone else?'

We shook our heads. She poured a small tot into her coffee cup and gulped it down. 'Right. Now, if Andrews comes charging in, he can smell my breath and add tippling to my long list of offences.'

'And bad luck to him,' I said. 'Alan, do we need to stay here in this woman's way while she tries to organize everything?'

'We do not. Elaine, you'll call us the minute you hear anything?'

She nodded. 'I won't get embarrassing, but you know . . . well, there'll be a better time for thanks.'

We waved and left.

'Mrs Bradford's farm?' Alan asked as we got into the car. It wasn't really a question. I just nodded.

'Where else?'

'If I can find it,' he said under his breath. I didn't utter a word as he followed roads that curved and became narrow lanes. We did, indeed, find ourselves once at a dead end, and once nearly in a marsh, but Alan recovered, turned around and began to drive with more confidence.

Meanwhile, we both kept an eye out for any sign of Tom Grenfell. I was irrationally sure that he would be around here somewhere. He'd been in that stable; of that I was positive. All right, laugh at women's intuition, but now and then it comes through. Tom had been there. He'd been taken away or had somehow managed to escape. Would he have headed for St Stephen's, or simply tried to stay out of sight until he could find help?

I had no idea what sort of police presence there might be in tiny fenland villages. In the days of Christie and Sayers and the rest, there would have been one constable with a bicycle, living with his family in a house, the front room of which served as the police station. Probably, the bicycle had now been replaced by a car, but I knew for a fact that there were places in the Scottish Hebrides where the police house was still a reality. So if Tom had gone looking for a police station, would he, a product of the twenty-first century, have recognized one if he saw it? He would, I reasoned, have been travelling by night, and the fens on a moonless night were probably as black as the pit. Even if there had been a moon – and I couldn't remember – moonlight creates deceptive shadows. And the recent hours of rain would have been made life even more miserable for the poor guy.

If I was right. If he was on the run and not lying imprisoned somewhere. Or – I made myself admit it – or dead.

I was so lost in my thoughts that I was extremely startled when Alan brought the car to an abrupt stop. I looked around. There was no house, no farm, no fields in sight. Only the fen, miserably desolate in the rain.

'What? Why did you stop?'

'I thought I saw something in the road. I'm just going to have a look.' He was out of the car before I could ask any questions, and back very quickly. He was holding a bundle of something in his hands, something long and thin and slimy with mud.

'Eww! Is that a dead snake?'

'No.' Alan reached in the side pocket of the door for the rag he always kept there. 'I'm not an expert on anything to do with the horse world, but I'd say this was once a rein. A very nice one, braided leather. It's been cut to bits, or rather hacked.' He wiped off as much mud as he could and showed me the repellent objects.

There were several pieces, varying in length from about three feet to only a few inches.

I looked at Alan. 'The stable "lad" – what was his name?'

'Arthur. Art.'

'He had gone into town to buy some new tack.'

'And when we first met him, he was working with a bridle. As I say, I'm not an expert, but he could well have been attaching new reins.'

'And you think this could be the old one.'

Alan nodded. 'It's a wild leap of the imagination, but why would someone cut apart a perfectly good rein and then leave it in the road? It's hard to tell, as badly as it's been treated, but wouldn't you say this long bit looks as though it's been tied in a knot? See how it's twisted, here . . . and here.'

'And look! One end of this one is cut cleanly, but the other end looks as though it's been sawed through, or even torn. It's a mess.'

Alan was silent, staring into the rain. At last he spoke, very quietly. 'I have brought a captive to a stable in a very lonely part of the fens. It is necessary to keep him there until someone can tell me what I am to do with him. I've put a plastic bag over his head, but loosely. I don't want him to suffocate, but he mustn't see me or the others with me, assuming there are others. I haven't made very good plans, because this has all happened too fast. I look around for something to use to tie him up and find a lovely long rein. I carry a good sharp knife. I cut the reins into appropriate lengths for hands and feet. Just before my companions and I leave, I take the plastic bag off the victim.'

'And has he been sedated all this time? How have they kept him under control?'

'What about that knife? That could be very persuasive.'

I shuddered. 'And especially since he couldn't see. He would never know quite where they were, how close the knife was. I'd certainly cooperate if someone threatened me that way.'

'We're making this all up, don't forget.'

'No, Alan, not quite. I admit we don't have solid evidence for all of it, but there's the reins, and the plastic bag with the ampicillin. I wonder why they left that behind.'

'A sudden noise? Mrs Bradford coming out to take one last look at the horses, perhaps, or even just one of the horses stamping or snorting. You know, I'm getting a picture of these villains as a distinctly amateurish lot. They take Tom there without so much as duct tape to secure him.'

'You're starting to believe your story, aren't you? And so am I. Partly because of the plastic bag. I'm sure Tom hid that so he'd have some kind of proof of his story, when he got to where he was able to tell someone. And I can finish your story for you, too – or almost.' I settled into a storytelling mood.

'The bad guys have just left. They took that awful bag off, thank God. I was afraid they were going to use it to kill me, and it was awful not to be able to see. I still can't see much. It's so dark that for a while I wonder if I'm in a cave. But there's the smell of horses, which is reassuring. I was in the country when they caught up with me. I must still be in the country. Maybe – I can smell hay, too – maybe in a stable.

'They've tied me up, but not very expertly.' Here I dropped back into my normal voice. 'I don't know how he got loose. There must have been something rough that he could rub against. Anyway, he managed to get his hands free, and then doing his feet would be easy. Slow, in the dark, but easy. He buries the bag. I wonder if he knew what was in it.'

Alan shrugged. 'Don't know. Does it matter, at this point?'

'Probably not. Anyway, he's free, and he leaves the stable. I don't know why he took his bonds with him, though. And when did all this happen?'

'As to when,' Alan said, 'it had to be before they took Mahala. They would have come back and found Tom gone, and then sought out Mahala to make him tell them where Tom was. And the pieces of rein – I don't have an answer for that.

Perhaps he took them so they wouldn't know how he freed himself.'

'Would they care? He was gone; that's all they would notice. Anyway, he did take the bonds. But why did he drop them? It would be a stupid thing to do, telling the villains where he was, or at any rate where he'd been.'

Alan made an impatient gesture. 'There's a lot we don't know. One thing we do know, or think we know, is that Tom was here, right here on this road, not long ago.'

'Unless we've been spinning fairy tales.'

Alan put the car in gear. 'If we have, we'll find nothing. But those fairy tales sound reasonable to me, and we have no better ideas. I'm going to find a place by the road to leave the car, and then you and I are going to start searching.'

'*After* you phone Elaine to tell her what we've found. If we're going to go for a walk in the rain, *in* a marsh, I want somebody else sharing the misery.'

Twenty-Eight

I look back, now, on that wretched slog through the fens as one of the most unpleasant hours of a long lifetime. Alan was with me, which was the only thing that made it bearable or even possible. I stumbled countless times when the apparently solid ground under me turned into a mud hole. Once I stepped into something that felt very much like quicksand, and only Alan's strong arm kept me from absolute panic. We were both wet through in a matter of minutes, and when a cold wind sprang up, our misery was complete.

Elaine was happy to send other searchers to join us, but since Alan couldn't be very definite about our location, they took their time about getting there, and I was beginning to feel abandoned and, worse, useless.

The last straw was when I caught my foot on some diabolical invisible root. I screamed and went down. Alan managed to keep me from falling on my face, but I landed on some of the bruises that were just beginning to heal, and I hurt a lot.

'Alan, this is insane. I'm covered in mud, I'm catching cold, and we could do this for hours and never—'

'Hush!' He held up a commanding hand. 'I thought – yes, there it is again.' Dropping my hand, he strode off, leaving me dripping wet and furious.

Then I heard it, too, and, forgetting my distress, I set off after him.

Two days later, quite a little crowd of us were assembled in front of Elaine's fire. Tom, newly released from the hospital where he had been treated for exposure and various minor injuries, was the star of the show. He, Alan, Mahala, Jim Ashby, Elaine and I sat drinking various warming and soothing beverages, and exchanging stories. Elaine had invited the Everidges, father and daughter, and Terence, but they'd begged off, having other obligations, and asked to be told the whole story later.

'We might never have found him if it hadn't been for Dorothy's fall,' said Alan. 'Yes, thank you.' He held out his glass for another tot of whisky. 'She screamed, and then shouted, and Tom heard it and thought he knew that voice. He was well hidden in his little burrow, and not about to come out until he was sure he wouldn't run into the villains.'

I sneezed. 'It's somewhat humiliating to be identified by a scream, but I'm really happy it turned out as it did.'

'Me, too,' Tom croaked. His cold had settled in his throat. 'I was pretty cold and hungry by that time, but too scared to show myself.'

'Fill us in on the details,' I requested. 'I think we've figured out the broad outline, but we're probably wrong about a lot of the little stuff.'

'It started – what's today?'

'Friday.'

'And, Aunt Elaine, when did I meet you and Dr Everidge in the lab?'

'Sunday afternoon.'

'Only five days ago! Feels like forever. Right. I met you. I went up to my lab to get my notes about the prank. While I was there, I happened to look out of my window, and I saw Mahala leaving the building with a bin liner stuffed full of something. I thought that was a bit off, so I decided to see where he was going.'

'And it never occurred to you,' said Elaine, 'to phone and tell us you were leaving the building.'

'I *am* sorry about that, truly! But I never meant to be gone for more than a few minutes. If Mahala was taking the bag to a rubbish bin somewhere, that was OK, if a little odd. I didn't think he'd go far with it; it looked heavy.'

'This is all my fault,' mourned Mahala. He shifted in his chair, and I could see that not all his discomfort was caused by his recent injuries. 'I began by stealing small things, things for my people. But then they saw what I was doing, and said they would tell the police if I did not steal things for them.'

'Things like drugs?' asked Alan at the same time as I asked, 'Who are "they", Mahala?'

He answered both of us at once. 'I do not know, still I do not know, who they are. Not students, I believe. They are not intelligent, and they are bad people. They wanted me to get morphine and the like for them, but when I told them we had no such drugs at the college, they agreed to take medical drugs.'

I gave Alan an 'Aha!' look.

'We know a fair amount about them now,' said Elaine. 'They're petty crooks, addicts, of course, in the pay and under the control of . . . of your father, Tom, I'm sorry to say. And, Mahala, you're to stop beating yourself up. You pinched nothing that mattered, at least to start. Dr Everidge has told us that he'd have given you the Petri dishes and syringes and that lot if he'd known you wanted them for your people. Of course, the ampicillin is another story, but we can sort that out later. It's not your fault that the sleaze learned what you were doing and decided you could be useful in his nasty little schemes. But I'm still not quite sure how Tom got snared.'

'Sheer stupidity,' said Tom. 'I followed Mahala because I thought he might be up to something shady – sorry, Mahala – but it didn't even occur to me to watch my back. I saw him hand the bag to someone in a van, and I moved nearer to see better – and that's the last I remember until I woke up in the back of the van with a frightful headache.' His hand moved to the back of his head. 'There's still a nasty lump there. And my mobile was gone, and so were the driver and his friend. They weren't very bright lads, you know. They hadn't tied me up or anything, and one of them had left his mobile on the front seat. I was just reaching for it when I heard them coming back from wherever they'd been, so I lay back and pretended I was still out of business.'

'Where was the van parked?' asked Alan.

'In the fens somewhere. I got a quick look out of the window, and there was nothing but weed

307

and water, and a farm quite a long way away. I don't know what the men were doing out of the car; there wasn't a pub or anything else in sight.'

'Probably leaving the bag of goodies at the farm,' said Elaine. 'We think it was used for a drop. Ideal situation. But go on, Tom.'

'Well, they came back and we drove around for a bit. I was still pretending to be unconscious, so they felt free to talk. They were trying to decide what to do with me. They phoned their boss. I didn't know who he was then, but I worked it out later. He must have been hopping mad, because I could hear him shouting on the other end of the line. Anyway, the two fools decided they'd better keep me alive for a while, so they found a pub. They knew I was awake by then, so one of them stayed in the car while the other fetched a sandwich and a bottle of beer for me. I think the beer must have been drugged, because I fell asleep and slept right through to the next day.'

'And that's when you tried to phone me.'

'Yes, well, I was pretty well fed up by that time. They'd gone off again, and this time I managed to get hold of the phone and make the call, but they came back before I could tell you anything.'

'And then,' I said, 'they decided to put you away for safekeeping until their boss told them what to do with you. And they hit upon a farm in the most deserted part of the fen.'

'They knew the place. You're right, Aunt Elaine – they'd hidden their loot there before. But how did you know I'd been there?'

'You forget that Alan was a detective once,' I said with a smile.

'And Dorothy is a detective without portfolio,' said Elaine, and raised her glass to me.

Tom's account of his escape tallied with our scenario pretty closely, except for one small detail. 'They were livid with me before they left, because one of them cut off his little finger when he was cutting up that strap they tied around me.' Elaine made a little exclamation. 'I didn't see it happen,' Tom went on, 'but I heard plenty! I thought I'd breathed my last breath then, I can tell you, but then they went away and I managed to get that cursed bag off my head, and you know the rest.'

'Why did you take the straps with you?' I was still curious about that one. 'And why did you bury the bag in the straw?'

'I'm not sure. You'll understand I wasn't thinking too clearly. I think I just wanted to get rid of the bag in case someone wanted to use it on me again, and I may have had some vague idea the straps would be of use. I lost them while I was on the run, though.'

'And what a good thing, because they led us to you.' I smiled at Tom. 'And, Jim, your courageous rescue of Mahala led Elaine to the goons, and they in turn to the villain behind it all. So,' I raised my glass, 'here's to Tom's safe return, and the capture of several nasty people.'

'Who might well have got away with it,' said Alan, 'if my wife hadn't refused to forget about a pool of blood on the floor.'

'Which, in the end, had nothing to do with the

309

case.' I coughed and took a swig of whisky to ease my scratchy throat.

'But it was because you snooped into it,' said Elaine, 'that someone decided you might stumble across something important, and shoved you down the stairs, which made me start to take the matter seriously, and led eventually to all the rest. Who pushed her, Mahala, do you know?'

'One of the gang.' The word sounded odd in Mahala's precise, clipped English. 'I do not know who. I did not know about that, Mrs Martin, I swear it to you. It is not the action of a good person, to push a lady down the stairs. I would have tried to stop it if I had known.'

'Don't worry, Mahala,' I said. 'I know you're not a violent person. You love animals; that makes you OK in my book.' He looked puzzled. 'Sorry, I mean, I have a high regard for you. And speaking of animals, have you been able to check on your rats?'

'I must go back to them as soon as Superintendent Barker will allow me. I have telephoned the student who was minding them, and she says they are fine, but she does not like them. I must check for myself.'

He was back almost to his normal single-minded self, and I marvelled at the resiliency of the young.

'And also speaking of animals,' Elaine said to me, 'you were concerned about a missing guinea pig?'

'Oh, I suppose I was. I'd almost forgotten.'

'Her minder took her home. She is now the proud mother of quadruplets. Mother and babies doing well.'

'Good.' I sneezed again.

'Take her home, Alan,' said Elaine. 'She's going to have a terrible cold, and terrible memories of Cambridge.'

'A cold, yes. And a few memories I'd rather not have, but also some new friends. On balance, I think all's well that ends well. Except, I suppose, the students will forget about their elaborate prank, with all that's gone wrong.'

Mahala scowled, but everyone else in the room looked surprised.

'Oh, I shouldn't think so,' said Alan. 'Why ever should they?'

Twenty-Nine

Alan and I sat in the choir at King's, Elaine and Tom next to us. Our bodies were in that beautiful place, our eyes delighting in the magnificent fan-vaulted ceiling and the afternoon sun streaming through the lovely stained glass, but our spirits were soaring with the voices of the choir, lifting us out of time and place to regions of pure joy.

The music ended. One of the choral scholars got up to read the lesson, finishing with 'Thanks be to God'.

I took Alan's hand, looked at Elaine and Tom, and whispered an echoing 'Thanks be to God'.